REQUIRES IMPROVEMENT

Paul Jenkins

Cath,

Thank you for your support!

PJ

ISBN 978-1-5262-0214-7

Cover Design © Adam Rowlinson, 2016

Interior illustrations © Jennie Sergeant 2016

Printed and Bound by Book Printing UK, Remus House,
Coltsfoot Drive, Woodston, Peterborough, PE2 9BF

www.thedramastudio.wordpress.com

__THANK YOU__

This project was funded through Kickstarter crowdfunding, with supporters pledging to support the project online. Aside from those who supported the book through pre-ordering a copy, many helped contribute to the startup costs of the first print run. Could I particularly thank the people below, and all those others who have contributed to the project along the way.

Sandra Apps
Adrian Bass
Martin Chepner
Dee Compton
Julie Eatwell
Stephen Goodlad
Jason Heatley
Dan Jeffries
Philip Jenkins
Mary Kerr
Debbie Lovering
Amy Martin
Simon Murch
Stuart McQueen
Peter Nash
Lynne Newbrook
Richard Parker
Patricia Spencer
Simon Valentine-Marsh
Beckie Voller
Kevin Walsh

Lee Ball
Heidi Carter
Laura Chepner
Robert Cooley
Pete Fillery
Noel Gulliver
Andrea Hemmett
Carol Jenkins
Kelly Jenkins-Hoare
Rachel Kirkpatrick
Mark Lovering
Mike Martin
Andrew McCluskey
Paula McQueen
Neil Newbrook
Conner Panaro
Iain Peacock
Tracey Spencer
Anna Valentine-Marsh
Elizabeth Vile

Could I also take the opportunity to thank Adam Rowlinson for the excellent cover design, Jennie Sergeant for the interior illustrations and Christine Gillies for her editing skills. What a team! Thank you!

For Lisa, Christopher & Thomas

I couldn't have done it without you.

Dedicated to the memory of Doris Nash,

who never missed a show.

AUTUMN TERM

Chapter One

Slip, Sliding, Away

From up here, you could see right across the island. There wasn't a cloud in the sky, which, with the sun burning so brightly in the midday sky, had turned a china blue. The mountains in the distance, the green trees to the north, the sandy beaches sprawling across the coast - the whole island was oozing with tranquility. Even taking into consideration that he was standing in the biggest tourist attraction in town, there was no doubt in his mind that he was within touching distance of Paradise.

He couldn't have been more miserable.

As he turned to see the passenger planes slowly turning into their landing runs, bringing hordes more sun-seekers for their yearly intake of vitamin D, he considered the possibility of a quick leap over the fence and an 80-foot drop to end it all. It was a procedure that would take him 10 seconds tops, but would mean an almost inexhaustible amount of hassle for everyone else. He'd never really considered suicide as an option before. Things had never really got that bad; but now, after everything that had happened this week, he was beginning to do the calculations on how much everyone would care and for how long.

The sun-seekers up here on the platform with him would, of course, be devastated, and it would cause a minor boom in the European psychiatry industry as there were near to a hundred people about – and of those at least forty were kids who looked under 10. He felt guilty about that, but their travel insurance would cover the costs of the therapy and they'd always have a holiday story to tell their grandkids.

His work colleagues? Well, they would probably have some sort of service. There might be one or two who would grieve for a bit but, at best, he was an outsider at work. Certainly not one of the in crowd. Maybe he'd get an award dedicated to him at the presentation evening. Thinking about work gave him about 950 other reactions to consider but he couldn't be held responsible for all of them in this instance. It was August. He was supposed to be off duty.

Mum? Well, news of her only son's tragic yet overtly dramatic death may well send her spiralling off the wagon again but that was going to happen whether he skipped off this mortal coil or not. No point in beating around the bush at this point.

And so we get down to brass tacks.

Katie.

Katie was a difficult one to answer. Had they rowed a lot recently? Would she blame herself? Probably not; and, anyway, she knew enough about Jim's demons to put two and two together. He was sure that there was something within her that always knew that this was some sort of destiny and, in time, she would probably accept his reasons for taking the plunge and opting for the afterlife. (If there was one of course. Did he have time to debate that up here? Probably not. That one would have to be left to chance.)

Of course Katie would be devastated. She was his wife, after all, and they had planned a life together. It had kitchen designs in it and everything. The problem with the best-laid plans of mice and men is that cheese and horrendous errors of judgement happen, meaning that life becomes an inescapable pile of dog doo. Katie would get it. It would take her a while but she'd understand.

And then one day, she'd explain it to the baby. Somehow.

What the hell would she say to their as yet unborn child? Was Daddy a hero or a villain in this bizarre storyline? He'd tried to be the good guy all his life, but life wasn't exactly a keen rewarder. In fact, life had been solidly taking the piss out of Jim for quite a while now. He was exhausted, utterly aimless and had been nursing the same dull headache for the last....well, as long as he could remember. Everywhere he went was a wrong turn and, quite frankly, he was sick to death of his very existence making him feeling dizzy. Three steps and a quick leap and it would be over...

"You gonna move pal?"

Last night a Scouser saved my life.

Jim stopped his hypnotic and essentially suicidal stare into the middle distance, realising that the queue had moved up two flights and that he was holding everyone up. His Englishness kicked in and he apologised profusely, before deftly skipping up the metal staircase to the launching platform for the 'Barracuda'. Once settled back in his place, he took a quick glance behind at where he had considered ending it all. There was no way of getting back down there now, and this part of the ride was caged in from all sides. A spectacular - if somewhat gruesome - exit from life was going to have to wait for another day.

When it came to Jim's turn to slide, he sat patiently at the entrance to the tube as jets of cold water pumped down around his legs and feet. Usually, he would have felt the chill down his spine (he hated being in cold water at the best of times) but today it was just gushing around him, lapping over his legs like he was in a jacuzzi. Sirens were going off all around, presumably as an added effect to the 'terror' that he was about to experience. Or, more precisely it was his cue to shuffle off his bum and get down the slide. Luckily, he had his impatient friend, Super Scouse, behind to help gee him along.

"Jesus mate, will you just get a feckin' move on, we're all waiting here"

Super Scouse to the rescue once again.

Jim looked up at the teenage Spanish lifeguard who, it appears, had been gesticulating at him profusely for some time. He shuffled forward and began his descent into the 'belly of fear itself'. Or a plastic tube. It very much depends on whether you believe what the poster at the foot of the slide is telling you or not. As it turned out, the poster wasn't far from the truth, as the whole ride seemed to Jim like one a slow motion journey through everything he wanted to forget about. Each twist and turn providing a new terrible reminder of everything that had gone before.

A slow beginning. No A*'s, 1 A, 3 B's, 5 C's, 6 D's, 3 E's, an F and a U. Left. Left again. 9 passes, 11 fails. A sharp drop. 45% A*-C. An impossible chicane. Girls underachieving with only two getting pass grades. More turns. The whole cohort down at least one target grade, most of them down two. A annoying bump that hurt his bum. Only one Asian heritage child out of the six in the cohort getting a top grade.

This ride was definitely the belly of fear itself and, as is customary with these attractions, the finale was the most almighty crash that could possibly be thrown at Jim.

A leap into the air and a ten-foot drop.

Kayleigh had got an E.

Splash.

He paddled a few feet forward and stood up straight in the splash pool, hearing the sounds of familiar cheers for Super Scouse who had, by now, landed with great aplomb and a huge wail of triumph in the water behind him. SS headed straight over to his family to relay tales of his feats of daring - not of saving a man's life today, but of the miraculous way he tamed the 'great Barracuda'. His accidental hero status didn't even occur to him - the irritation of Jim's tardiness on the stairs just a passing memory. Jim considered going over to explain his importance in the grand scheme of things, but they were heading off for ice cream already. There didn't appear to be time.

"Excuse me. Sir? Sir! You need to come out of the pool. Now!"

The lifeguard was right. Jim couldn't stand there like a lemon all day. Looks like the world wasn't about to let him fall into a dreamless sleep at all. It was an effort to haul his body back onto the conveyor belt and move himself along like everyone else, but off he went.

13

He trudged slowly back to where Katie had set up camp on the sun beds, finding her immersed in a particularly tricky sudoku. According to the title in the newspaper, this was the killer sudoku. More lethal statistics. That was all he needed right now. At least these ones showed some promise of being fathom-outable. Katie didn't even raise her head from the paper as he approached.

"Good ride?"

"Meh."

"Well that one's the biggest in the park. If you didn't get any kind of thrill from that one then it really was 35 Euros down the drain, wasn't it?"

"I'm sorry. I was trying. I am trying...The stairs...I didn't want to..."

And finally, after three days of manning up, looking on the bright side and not letting the buggers get you down, he broke. Silent tears came pouring out of his eyes as if someone had turned on a tap. Sweet, cleansing tears that made him retch and feel comfort almost simultaneously. He couldn't think or plan his way out of this one - he knew that now - but the tears that stung his eyes and tickled his cheeks would be the first step in healing this god-awful situation.

Crying in silence and the intensity of Katie's concentration meant that she didn't at first notice Jim's sudden (but entirely expected) breakdown. It was only when that awkward five in the top right fitted nicely into its space that she took a moment to glance over to the man she so desperately wanted to cheer the hell up. He clearly hadn't, but at least this was an emotional response, something she hadn't seen in him for close to three days now. She immediately dropped her paper and sat up to hold him.

He cried solidly for nearly three minutes, the odd member of the public stopping briefly to mouth the words "Are you ok?" in various European languages. Katie responded with a thankful smile and a short nod that reassured them that she had this and they could go back to their day of wave pools and water slides. By the time Jim had run out of tears, and his body had stopped heaving, she had repeated this process three times, each time getting more adept at catching the look of the public early to send them on their merry way.

"I haven't got any tissues on me. You want to use the towel?"

He nodded and wiped his face on the hideous electric pink beach towel that his mother had bought for him last Christmas. Katie hated that towel, partly because it didn't match anything that else they had in their cupboards at all back at home, but mostly because of its associations with Sandra generally. The last thing she needed right now was for Jim to have a reminder of just how crappy his so-called upbringing by his mother was. Using it as a snot rag did seem a useful job for the god-awful thing, though, so she let him continue.

"So come on. How bad is it?"

It had been 72 hours since he'd found out the results online and he'd been dodging the question up to now, responding with nonchalant shrugs and some flippant remarks about exam boards being worse than estate agents. Or something similar. She'd

15

guessed that it hadn't gone according to plan - they'd had the inevitable 'post-results sulk week' every year since he'd begun teaching, but this was something different. He'd never cried before (well, not in front of her anyway) so Katie felt it about time that he fessed up and filled her in on the details.
"It's not worth going into..."

That was the last attempt at a deflection that he was going to get away with.

"You bloody well are going into it! You've spent the last three days of our holiday walking around like a zombie, and not a particularly entertaining one at that. Now either you give me some details so that I can start to help a bit or..."

"You can't help. No one can."

Probably true. She knew nothing about education or exam results. But she hated being interrupted in full flow, so ploughed on regardless.

"Either you give some details of what has happened with the exam results now, or I phone them myself and find out. Then you'll look like a complete tool when you have to explain why your wife was phoning up asking for information you could have told her yourself."

Jim went straight on the defensive.

"They won't tell you anything."

"They're a matter of public record. They have to tell me."

She gave him a look that quite clearly was telling him "Don't push me".

"Not yet they don't. They're still only unconfirmed results until all the appeals are in. Then they'll publish them properly."
"And are you likely to have many appeals?"

Clever. She'd got him talking about it, despite himself. He knew she should have joined the police force instead of working in an office. Yes, the world of leisure centre vending machine providers would lose one of its most efficient and hard working administrators, but CID would soon be catching villains left, right and centre. Shergar would have been found if he had gone missing on Katie's watch, that's for sure. She left no stone unturned when she was onto something.

"Come, on, just tell me. I'm not spending the last two days here with you moping about and ruining the rest of this holiday. It's supposed to be a break for the both of us."

He thought back to how he was feeling on the stairwell of the Barracuda. Should he tell her about his brief fling with the idea of ending it all when he was up on the parapet? He looked at her closely. Despite all his trudging about, claiming that the end was indeed nigh, she was still beaming at him with the same infectious smile that made him fall head over heels in love with her in the first place. He looked at her face and then at the bump she had been slowly growing on behalf of them both for last five and a half months. Talk of ending it all could wait for a bit.

Jim then proceeded to spill the beans on the whole results debacle. Every rotten statistic that he'd seen, every target grade missed, every 'I have no idea why she got that'... Katie listened as best she could, knowing close to nothing about most of these children, the course they were on or how the administration for the GCSE Drama exam worked. Jim gradually became more animated as the conversation went on, but it was only when he got to discussing Kayleigh's result that things started to come to a head and the real issue started to become apparent.

Katie had heard a lot about Kayleigh over the last year in comparison to the other students in Jim's care who he tended not to want to talk about much, so she also knew how important it was to Jim, from both a professional and personal point of view, that she did well. He'd put more hours into working with Kayleigh than anyone else, and had moved mountains to get her through the course. Alongside the other wondrous things that teenagers had to cope with, Kayleigh also had Down Syndrome, so it was fair to say that emotions around her exam result would obviously be running fairly high.

Over the eighteen months or so of studying, they had worked on every tiny detail of her performance, from helping her to articulate difficult words (Kayleigh and Jonathan Ross were clearly at the back of the vocal cord queue when they were dishing out R's to articulate with) to controlling her sometimes overtly heavy body movements. Kayleigh had once described herself in a self-evaluation session as walking about like a dinosaur. Jim pointed out that even the bloke in the big purple Barney suit had probably got a GCSE in Drama at some point. Teaching Kayleigh had been a huge amount of hard work, but a hell of a lot of fun too.

"I just can't believe they've bumped her all the way down to an E..."

Jim shook his head in disbelief for what was possibly the tenth time in a minute. He would have to watch it or the 'shake of disbelief' could quickly become a nervous tic.

"She was nailed on for a C grade. I told her she was going to get a C, Katie. She's going to be devastated."

It was true. Somewhere, over three hundred miles away, was a young girl walking around with a mope almost as big as Jim's, her mother trying to get her to focus on the outstanding grade she had got in her English exam and not the disappointing one she had got for Drama. Trying to get a teenager to understand context is, it turns out, quite a difficult task to do. She would, in time, realise just how well she had managed to do in her relative position and that, even though she had 'failed' her Drama course, many of the friends she had made completing it would be with her for life.

Katie listened to Jim's painful monologue about how worthless he was and how he'd failed them all and how he couldn't go back, nodding where necessary, but believing none of it. She loved him just that little bit more with every second that he droned on about how bad it all was. She hoped that, when their wee bundle of joy did arrive in November, he showed even half as much care as he did for the ones who were foisted upon him at school.

Their son (despite her telling Jim otherwise, Katie HAD sneaked a look at the ultrasound and there were definite signs of maleness on the picture) was going to be a very lucky little boy if Daddy continued in this vein. Rational thought very rarely came into it with our Jim. How people were feeling was always at the top of his agenda.

With every word, Jim felt the weight shifting slowly from his shoulders and, by the end of it all, he even managed an attempt at a joke. It wasn't funny, or ultimately worth mentioning again, but the intent was there to bring a bit of mirth into the day. Katie took that as a sign that he was at least bumping along the bottom instead of falling further down.

By the time he had finished going over the minutiae of who got what, and how it was so unbelievable and why, the sun had moved so far in the sky that the tree that Katie was using a shade was now utterly useless and they found themselves bathed in scorching thirty two degree heat - not a particularly wise move for someone in Katie's condition.

"I'm going to get a lolly. They're selling those rocket jobbies that used to be around when we were kids. You coming to get one with me or are you going back up to do that big ride again? The park's only open for another hour so it'll probably be your last chance."

Jim looked up at the super structure of tubes, scaffolding and staircases behind him, hearing the screams of joy as people entered the 'belly of fear itself'. Jim pondered his dark thoughts of less than an hour ago, imagining how things would be now if he'd taken the wrong type of plunge. He looked at Katie and realised at the very least that he didn't have to deal with all this on his own now.

"I'll come and get a lolly with you. Turns out the ride's not as scary as the poster says anyway."

He knew that the results would still be bad tomorrow and that he couldn't get in a time machine and fix it but, for now, he was going with a beautiful woman to get some frozen food colouring on a wooden stick.

Being life-threateningly depressed was going to have to wait for another time. Well, about a week at least. Until the new term started.

Chapter Two

A Fresh Start

Stressed, late, and definitely not in the mood for this. With the hangover of summer still clouding him, Jim was doing his very best to keep his chin up and quash the butterflies having a dogfight inside his stomach. He was failing abysmally.

As he pulled into the car park of Lancashire Academy's shiny new building, Jim could see clearly that someone without a brain was doing their level best to wind him up. HIS parking space had been taken. His perfectly placed, recently resurfaced, and right-next-to-the-door-to-the-Drama-studio space had been snaffled up by some newbie driving a tatty-looking estate car. Jim was far from impressed. Alright, it didn't have a big sign explaining his claim to the space. Or his initials painted nicely on the tarmac like the head or the deputies. But everyone - EVERYONE - knew it belonged to Jim. Words, most of them grumpy, would have to be exchanged when he got into the building. Was this some sort of message about the results? Had we really reached the point that performance-related parking spaces had become a reality?

Jim didn't recognise the Peugeot that had rocked up and plonked itself slap bang in the middle of his territory, nor could he work out at that time why anyone would put an "I ♥Aussie rules" sticker in their back window, but this would at least give him a lead when it came to tracking down the bastard who had nicked his spot. It was fair to say that Jim really wasn't going to be the most tolerant of people this morning.

He manoeuvred the car onto the verge, knowing full well that he would get clobbered by Niall, the school caretaker, later on. But, right now, he had to get in the building before he got a roasting from the new head for being late on the very first day back. As he opened the car door, he took out a newly planted tree shrub, thereby putting the icing on the cake of his dodgy morning. Now he was going to have to locate a trowel as well as dealing with being late to a god-awful In Service Training day (or INSET, as they were more seethingly known amongst his peers).

All he wanted to do was get in, get whatever form he needed from Gareth, the exams officer about how he could appeal Kayleigh's stupid exam result, and get himself a cup of coffee. Nothing else mattered. Parking spaces, low lying shrubs and Australians were not a part of the short-term plan.

It should be made clear at this point that James Alexander Tovey was, for the majority of his life, an extremely amiable man, despite all the evidence to date being to the contrary. Jim frequently found himself getting frustrated at the on-going series of mini challenges that life tends to throw in all our directions (it is the same for all of us isn't it?) but it wasn't common for him to be particularly cantankerous or be sullen about them for long. So far, this little bout of grumpiness had lasted for two weeks solid, ever since the GCSE results were published, causing more than a couple of tiny red flags to be hoisted with Katie at home.

At twenty-nine years old, Jim had overcome more than his fair share in life, despite what could only be described as a 'challenging' start. It was the sort of early life that was usually reserved for TV dramas, or documentaries about ASBO kids who make their way onto the regional news. Losing his father in a bike accident when he was only ten, and caring for a mother who was unable to do so herself through his formative years, could have made Jim another one of life's tragic but inevitable statistics. But something within him had guided him to an altogether more positive place.

That something, of course, was his love of theatre.

He had more or less dropped out of school at 15 to support his Mum at home as she went through her rehab. It was only later that, when Jim had reached 17 that the decision to take catch-up evening classes at the local college to bring himself up to speed with what he had missed in class was taken. This was something that, thankfully, had not taken very much effort on his part, having been a fairly bright button until all the rubbish started pouring itself into his life. Learning seemed to come easily to Jim and, at the first time of asking, he aced the very exams that his school friends had sweated and struggled over just the year before.

It was during his time at college that Jim had first drifted into drama - something that he was sure had been a hand-me-down trait from his father, who Jim knew to have been a bit of a wannabe performer during the short time they'd had together. Vague memories of his dad dressing up in outrageous outfits, impromptu ukulele sessions, and his mother sitting in the living room armchair beaming with joy had spurred him on to learn the craft of stage performance himself.

He took a BTEC in Performing Arts that gave him more than a decent grounding in acting, a passable singing voice and movement skills befitting of any Am-Dram chorus line. He didn't quite fit in with the perma-grin kids around him however.

He was a year older than them, after all, (and his life experience so far had given him an edge on stage that they could never truly replicate) but he loved the camaraderie involved in putting on a show. He was Kenickie. He was the Duke of Cumberland. He was Mr Bumble. Being able to inhabit all these other characters was a big boost for him. It meant that (for a short time at least) he didn't have to be James Tovey.

He performed by day, worked takeaway shifts to bring in the pennies, and used his down time to get (and later keep) his mother on the straight and narrow. By the time Jim had reached the age of twenty, and was ready to pack himself off to study stagecraft at university, his Mum had been solidly off the booze for nearly three years. He didn't stray too far from the nest, only travelling to Manchester from the family home in Preston, but it was enough for Jim and his mum to make a statement that their lives were ready to be lived apart for the first time ever.

Jim trained to be a teacher, and mum Sandra set herself up online selling cheap toiletries that she got imported from Taiwan. Jim met a nice girl called Katie, who he would marry within a year of finishing his course, and mum became a mover and shaker within the stay-at-home internet community. Okay, so she wasn't leaving the house very often - her anxiety wasn't ready to deal with that one just yet - but it ensured that she kept communicating with people, which was the one thing she had stopped doing when Jim's dad had died. Jim knew it wasn't a headline-grabbing life, but it was a million miles away from the car crash that was written in the script for the two of them just a decade before.

There were bumps and scrapes along the way. That much was true. Sandra fell of the wagon at least twice, most notably when

Jim was going through big changes in his life that would potentially make him drift further away. A week before their wedding, Katie came home to find that Sandra (who was staying with them to 'help' before the nuptials) came accompanied by two full bottles of cheap Aldi gin. If nothing else, it showed to Jim that Katie was truly devoted to him and that the baggage that came along with becoming his spouse was not going to bother her. The week before the wedding was spent juggling another bout of cold turkey along with fittings, hair appointments and putting in place a small network of trusted 'spotters' that could keep an eye on Sandra during the wedding breakfast and reception.

Katie worked her way up from Office Junior to Office Manager (it was a small office) and Jim climbed the greasy pole of secondary school teaching. Now in his fifth year, Jim's career had gone into overdrive. Training to be a Drama teacher in the noughties most definitely had its advantages. He had been given grants and subsidies for studying at a time when teacher shortages were causing real issues in the system. Plus, as a shortage subject (Drama in his first placement school had been based within the English department), he had been given the time and space to develop theatrical performance within the school, pretty much on his own.

In only his second year, his department became stand-alone and he was promoted to being the 'Head' of Drama, a title which Katie admitted turned her on just a little and made Jim feel that he was walking on his very own cloud every time he was introduced at a meeting. Jim Tovey, master dramatist, producer of the magical, and the go-to man for razzmatazz, had well and truly arrived.

This morning, however, he had arrived in a foul, desperate and grumpy flap.

Alongside the horrors of finding out the worst exam results in the history of all time whilst on your holidays, there were other factors contributing to this feeling of being totally and utterly pissed off at the world. Even without the joys of facing his colleagues for the first time since the results were published, a tiring weekend of visiting your mother as she talked incessantly about the price of bulk-buy shampoo, a wife that was obsessively preparing the nest for the imminent arrival of the first child, and a horrendous jam caused by a burst water main at the end of his street, had all, in their own way, contributed to Jim's tardiness and appalling mood on this first Monday morning in September. The parking space scandal was just the icing on a very poorly-baked cake.

It didn't get much better when he got round to the front doors and tried to enter.

Swipe. Beep. Click.

Nothing. He tried again.

Swipe. Beep. Clunk.

No parting of the ways, no swishing of the doors that on normal days made him feel like a Jedi. No entry.

The last 'clunk' in fact had not sounded at all healthy and there was a definite sound of 'machinery doing something it really shouldn't' as he stood helplessly in the entrance hall. He made a pathetic wave to the crowds that were starting to emerge from the staff room, and managed to grab the attention of a young-looking girl who happened to be passing.

"Are you ok?"

This was not the time to shout the response, "What a stupid bloody question" through the door, and probably wouldn't be the best way to introduce himself to what was clearly a new member of staff. But he did make a mental note. It was a stupid bloody question.

"My pass isn't working. Can you get the door open for me?"

"I'm sorry. I'm new!"

"I hadn't noticed", he thought.

"Behind the desk there. There's a green key that you need to turn..."

"A green one?"

"Yes, over there....No towards the right... No... Right.. Yes.. No.. YOUR right.. Stage right.. Look.... Over this way..."

Seriously, was this part of the INSET? Was he getting filmed here, taking part in some bizarre 'can you direct a stranger with seemingly no spatial awareness' task? Was the new head going to pop out and mark him on his ability to stay calm when faced with someone who literally couldn't turn a key without clear directions?

'It's next to where the phone is. No, not that way. Over a bit. Back towards...'

This was going to get nasty. He could tell.

Beep. Swish.

Smiles all round. Hurrah! Jim was in.

"Thank you. You must be one of the new recruits."

It still amazed Jim how quickly he could move from Defcon 5, where he was ready to inflict serious pain on another human being, to his more chilled out, friendly self that he was showing right now. Either he'd learned over the years to be very tolerant of others, or he was a psychopath. His recent worries over his mental state would (unlike his car) have to be parked safely for now, as he was about to meet...

"Steph."

'Steph' was now his new friend and clearly needed some guidance on the way that the morning was to run. Either that, or she had attachment issues, as she hadn't made her way back to the massed crowds milling about in the staff room area.

"Nice to meet you, Steph. I'm Jim, Head of Drama. New teacher?"

"Support assistant. I'm going to be working with a year 8 lad in a wheelchair?"

"Ben?"

"That's him. I haven't had chance to meet him yet, though."

"Oh, if you're working with Ben, you'll be fine. He's great. Well, he is when he's not in a complete mood. Good kid. Set 2."

"Well you know much more than me. I only had my interview yesterday. I haven't got a clue what I'm doing."
"All the SEN stuff will be in Debbie's office. Over there."

Jim pointed out the Special Educational Needs office to the newbie as they moved inevitably towards the assembly hall, where the crowds were massing. Jim should really have chosen to be a tour rep instead of a Drama teacher. He was a natural at this 'making people feel at ease and showing them about' lark.

"Thanks. Do you mind if I sit next to you when we get into the hall? I haven't met anyone else yet."

"Sure. As long as you don't mind me snoring. I tend to nod off during INSET training."

Steph hadn't quite made a judgement on Jim yet, and let out a nervous giggle as she tried to work out if he was being serious or not about taking a nap during the proceedings. She liked the fact that he sounded vaguely rebellious, though, so followed him into the assembly hall, making a note to herself to check out the Drama department properly when she got the tour of the building that she had been promised earlier.

By now, Jim himself had forgotten all about his rough start to the morning - the burst water main, the parking issues, the uprooted shrub, the gameshow-like challenge to actually get into the building. He knew that, at heart, they were a series of unfortunate events and that there was no point in getting het up about them. Niall would reset his entrance pass, the council would fix the road and, somehow or another, he'd find himself a trowel and do his bit to tackle climate change with the annoying tree shrub. He was chilled. Mostly.

So, why couldn't he shake off this Kayleigh thing? It was only one of about twenty questionable results but, for some reason, that seemed to be the only thing that he could focus on as they made their way into the assembly hall together. He spotted Gareth from exams across the other side of the room. Gareth spotted him, too, and gave him a friendly smile and a nod that simply said, "Yeah I know. Come and see me later."

All would be okay. It had been an admin error somewhere in the system. They would appeal the results and they would all be sorted. Kayleigh would have her C grade and everyone would shuffle quietly along doing what they do best. Teaching the kids to be awesome.

He sat down in the seat next to Steph and waited for the training session to get going, as it was due to start in a few short minutes. At the same time, from the back of the hall, there was a loud guffaw from the PE staff as they shared a joke with what appeared to be one of their new colleagues. Jim observed the new guy. He was mid-twenties, dark-haired and had his face coated in what was some extensively designed stubble. Under his arm was a folder with a large sticker: "I ♥ Aussie rules."

"I'll be right back", said Jim to Steph, as he moved quickly back up to Defcon 3.

31

To: JIM TOVEY <j.tovey@lancsacademy.inspire.com>

From: GARETH LAWSON <g.lawson@lancsacademy.inspire.com>

Time: Today at 8:17am

Subject: Drama results

Hi Jim,

Thanks for the list you left in my tray last night. 21 kids is quite a lot for a remark!

We can do it but, having checked with your board, it means that we have to resubmit the whole cohort for that practical unit (I think you mentioned it was DRM03?).

For the number of kids you had it comes £630 for the remark, which is only refundable if, when they re-examine it, they decide to mark the kids up significantly. (ie up at least one grade boundary)

I'll tell you up front, I'm not hopeful - most of these kids are at least 4 marks off getting a C so you'd probably end up losing more than you gain. Plus they'll possibly even choose to mark the ones you've got on the list as being okay now down further.

If I were you I'd leave it, but of course it's your budget. I'll leave it with you but I need to know by end of play tomorrow if you want me to go ahead and appeal.

Well done for Fiddler on the Roof by the way - didn't catch you at the end of last term - my kids thought it was great. Ginny's started at a dance class now. Says she wants to be on the stage!

All the best

Gareth

P.S I'd run all this by whoever your new line manager is first as well. Mick said at SLT on Friday night he was going to have a switch around - info should be out with you and all the other Heads of Dept soon.

Chapter Three

You've Got Mail

Fitzgerald... Fitzgerald. P.E department... F... F...

F. Sorted.

Moss... That's the woman from R.E that spoke on the training morning on the first day about the bullying policy... Moss... M... M... L. M. N. O...

M.

This was a slow, tedious process and one that Steph was absolutely certain was not in her job description. She was a support assistant, not a delivery girl. If she'd wanted a job in the post office, she'd have applied for one. Okay, so the kid she was employed to support hadn't even come in to school yet (Ben wasn't back from holiday when term started last Wednesday, and he had physiotherapy at the hospital until at least lunchtime today) but Steph was certain that getting her to sort the post was some sort of crappy initiation task.

Plus, these in-trays were laid out in a ridiculous way. It was like doing a challenge on that old TV programme that her dad had made her watch on that game show channel. What was it? The Krippin factor, or something? A whole bunch of 80s bods trying to figure out impossible puzzles for no reason. There wasn't even a proper prize. She'd have been useless at it - she couldn't even work out where the post went.

Admittedly, Debbie (who managed all the support assistants) had been right. This was possibly the best way to learn all the staff names. Most of the post had the department names on as well as the person it was addressed to, so she was learning pretty quickly which name belonged to whom. It still didn't help her with the faces, but that was surely going to come over time. Right now, she was going to have to wade through and get to know everybody's character based on the amount of pointless junk mail they had received. From watching many of them grumpily clear out their trays on the first couple of mornings, most of what she was currently delivering was going to head straight for the recycling anyway.

Back to the grindstone… Moss....

"Anything for Drama?"

Steph quickly realised she that she had been daydreaming, but recognised the voice straightaway as one of the very few that had taken the time out of their day to speak to her. It was that Drama teacher who had got stuck at the front door and who she'd sat with in the training. Well, that was until he had gone storming off to have a row with that nice looking Australian bloke in the tracksuit that she assumed worked in P.E. She hoped he'd calmed down a bit now, as he seemed none too pleased on that first morning.

He was dressed more like a Drama teacher now, in a black polo shirt and black chinos as opposed to the scruffy looking T-shirt and jeans he had turned up with on the training day. He still stuck out like a sore thumb from the rest of the staff, but at least now it looked like he'd made an effort. As someone who always dressed to impress, Steph never really got why people ever left the house looking anything other than immaculate. On that first day, she had spent hours getting ready for her new job. This bloke arrived looking like he had got straight out of bed and put on the first clothes that he could find on the floor. (Which, if truth be told, he had).

Realising that she was leaving him waiting, she had a quick flick through the pile.

"There's nothing addressed to Drama in here", she said, confidently, trying desperately to sound competent in her new job. "There might be something for you personally though. What was your surname again? Sorry, I'm still trying to learn everyone."

"Tovey. Jim Tovey"

He hadn't intended it to sound quite so Bond-like but he was getting a bit of a cold and it came out as ever-so-slightly gruff and ever-so-slightly stupid. Steph let out a tiny giggle. The combination of seeing a bloke in what appeared to be his early-thirties, dressed entirely in black, acting like some sort of Daniel Craig wannabe somehow overrode her 'This bloke might be quite important so don't take the piss out of him' instinct. Luckily, he smiled as well.

"Licenced to teach Drama."

He gave her a wink, recovering from the obvious embarrassment of accidentally sounding like a prize plum.

She had a quick glance through the hundredweight of envelopes again, but came back to him with nothing new. By the way he reacted, it appeared that this was welcome news. Only the stuff that was in his tray from the previous summer term was left now. She watched him reach up and pull down a mound of papers - at least fifty letters and circulars, which she was sure must have been important to somebody.

"Were you away at the end of last term?"

Steph was trying not to highlight his apparent lack of ability when it came to paperwork, and decided to publically give him the benefit of the doubt. He was self-deprecating enough to rebuff her charity straight away, however, citing an altogether different reason for the administrative backlog.

"We have our school show in the last week of summer term. Everything stops in that week. I barely get a chance to sit down, let alone go through this lot. You've probably seen the photos on the board in reception."

"Oh yeah. What was it? Blazing Fiddles or something?"

"Fiddler on the Roof. It's a musical"

"Oh. Right."

Steph tried desperately to sound interested, but just wasn't. Singing and dancing had never really been her thing. Other than the stuff on that was on X Factor or Strictly, obviously. They were proper singers and dancers, weren't they? Not these ones that got all dressed up in olden-days costumes and sang all that opera stuff. She'd never really understood why people would be halfway through saying things to each other then suddenly burst into song when talking would have done them just as well. Nobody sang in Corrie, after all, and that was real life.

She went back to looking for the mysterious Moss amongst the giant grid of wooden in-trays before her. There must have been about a hundred and fifty of them. The teachers had a section, the cleaners had a section. There even was a special section for the Senior Leadership Team, who she was quickly starting to find out were just referred to as venomously by the rest of the staff as simply SLT. Three letters that generally were spat out rather than said. The bosses clearly weren't popular.

"You piece of shit..."

Bond from the Drama department was clearly agitated about something, and Steph turned sharply to check that he wasn't speaking about her.

"Sorry, didn't mean to swear. I wasn't aiming that at you..."

The quick apology reassured her temporarily, though she was now intrigued as to what it was that could have caused his outburst. On his part, having being told just ten minutes before by Gareth that an appeal for any of last year's Drama candidates was fine but it would cost him £600 out of his Drama budget, he realised that he may be coming across as just as tad... well... mad. On her part, Steph made no bones about being a nosey person wanting to find out what was going on, maintaining that you never found out anything in life unless you were brave enough to ask for it. So she asked. A minute later, she wished she hadn't.

He started by reading her the hand-written note, which had been photocopied (what kind of person did that instead of sending an email?) in full, and in an exceptionally pompous voice.

Jim,

As you know, Dylan from my Chemistry group, 10SC1, has been taking part in your school production of Fiddler on the Roof. Unfortunately, this has been exceptionally detrimental to his work in Science. He was asked last week to produce a piece of homework, which he failed to hand in. This is the second time that this has happened in three weeks, so it is becoming a worrying pattern. On both occasions, he has blamed his lack of extension work on having to learn lines for your play. While it's nice that the children at Lancashire Academy have got a hobby, you should really be thinking about the detrimental effect it has on their actual academic studies. I just thought I'd highlight to you the effect that working on your extra-curricular plays has on the academic achievement of even the nicest and hardworking of Year 10 boys. I hope he'll be able to catch up next year.

Tim Sweeney, Chemistry.

CC Janet Murphy, Assistant Head

"Dylan. Is that the kid in the photos with the fake beard?"

Steph was still playing catch-up, both with 'who the hell are all these people?' and 'what the hell happens in the fiddle play?'. By the look on Jim's face right now (which was somewhere nestled between disbelief and rage), she wasn't going to get an answer to either of those questions. Usually, when you know that a volcano is about to blow, you run but, in this circumstance, it seemed a tad over-reactive. She was going to have to stand there while the top of this one blew.

"What a bastard!   What an absolute bastard!   Sorry for my language. But what a cock! Do you know who he is? He's that Science teacher who came in at the end of last term to cover Julie Morris when she was off on her maternity. He's not even a permanent member of bloody staff! Who the hell does he think he is? I didn't wander into his poxy science club - not that I think they even HAVE a Science club - and tell him how much the kids should really be working on my subject, did I? No. But, because he teaches a 'proper' subject like Science, he thinks he can lord it up over the rest of us and tell us how we're all just wasting our time 'playing about'. Who the hell does he think he is?!"

Contrary to what she originally suspected about the volcano being terrifying, Steph found herself snorting with laughter. She knew it was wrong. This guy was clearly upset about how he'd been treated by the bloke from Science, and laughing at him was most definitely the wrong thing to do in any given circumstance. But it was the arms. The arms were everywhere, flopping about like an octopus on speed. That, combined with the funny faces (and believe you me, they were hilarious), made the involuntary spasms of laughter almost inevitable. She tried to keep it in. She really did.

Jim stopped and looked at the effect that his tantrum was having on his audience. It took him just a matter of moments before he also found himself creased in two, realising just what a camp old ham he was being about the whole thing. You're being a diva, Mr Tovey. You need to take a step back. He put the note in his back pocket and tried to compose himself a little.

"Sorry. Unprofessional of me. Shouldn't really be rubbishing other members of staff, even ones who aren't here anymore."

Steph could be supportive when she needed to be. Ranting and arm-flailing aside, what the science bod had said was a bit out of order. Even she could see that.

"It's not right though is it? I mean, the kids do Drama. It's like a proper subject, too. It's still one of their GCSE's isn't it?"

That's the best defence you're likely to get Mr Tovey. I'd take it and run.

Drama is like a proper subject too.

"I'd better get back to this post or I'll never finish. You got any idea where Moss is?"

Jim smiled. Steph's uninitiated status was confirmed.

"Angela Moss is in R.E"

"Yeah, I thought that, but she's not with the rest of the humanities teachers. There's only Peter Moss but he's in History"

"That's because Angela's also an assistant head. She's in the SLT section over here."

This was winding Steph up something chronic.

"No, I looked there. There are lots of trays in that bit but no Moss."

41

"That's because Angela's only 4 foot 8. Hers is right down the bottom, there. See, it's an easy system to fathom. You'll learn."

And with that, James Bond meets Danny La Rue flounced out of the staff room. Within minutes he would be at his desk, writing a pointless response to the now ex-member of staff. In the absence of the man himself, he would have to address it to Janet Murphy. She was responsible for the induction of new teachers and, particularly, for line-managing those who were on short-term cover contracts.

He hadn't had much contact with Janet before – after all, she was in Modern Foreign Languages and there wasn't much crossover with Drama - but Jim thought it important that she saw what a narrow-minded twonk they had sent her from the agency so that she didn't end up employing him again. Plus, the conniving little so-and-so had copied her in on the note so Jim was now obliged to make his defence.

All the computers in the workroom were being used by NQT's (none of which he recognised, he'd have to make a point of introducing himself to them later) so he also hand-wrote it on the back of the original note. At least this way he could get it down on paper while it was all still fresh in his head.

Dear Janet,

Today, I received this letter (I found it amongst a pile of old papers - not sure how it got there) from the guy who was covering Science last term for Julie Morris. I couldn't believe it when I read it at first, but I thought it best to hand it over to you so that you are aware of it in case the agency try to send him over to us again. Hardly a team player, is he?

42

If you get the chance to give any feedback to the agency, you might want to make them aware that cast lists were sent out months before the production, with teachers being made fully aware of the time demands on the kids during the last two weeks of term. I sent that cast list out several times by email - and, of course, announced it in briefings - so he definitely knew about the show.

I would have thought that this would have been an opportunity for a member of the team to praise and congratulate one of the students for his involvement, not moan to a colleague about how many Science homeworks they had missed.

I have never allowed a student to use Drama as an excuse for a lack of work. However, most members of staff are tolerant during the production period, especially of kids like Dylan who take on the lead roles.

I will check with Dylan (and Julie Morris, who is now back teaching him Chemistry) as soon as possible to make sure that he is not behind and, if necessary, assist him if he is struggling (which I find hard to believe, from what I remember of his last interim report results).

Most of all, I think that it's sad that a member of staff from another department (even a temporary one) couldn't find the time to come and support Dylan in the show yet found the need to carp from the sidelines. Maybe not the kind of person we need at LA in the future, eh?

Hope you have a good week.

Jim Tovey, Drama.

Sorted.

That should be the last Jim would hear of that.

43

Chapter Four

Delivery for the Man in Black

Man, this year 8 class had been hard work.

Was his lesson plan becoming tired? Unlikely, as it was the fourth time he had taught this session this week. His introduction to Romeo and Juliet had been a staple 'go-to' lesson for years. Introducing gang warfare to pre-teens, using staring contests, silent role-play and a kicking Rage Against the Machine soundtrack, was a sure-fire winner. Kids usually came out from this session buzzing, enthused about Shakespeare, ready to tackle the bard's greatest love story with gusto and aplomb.

Indeed, the other three sessions this week had required Jim spending a good five minutes building in some 'chill time' at the end of the lesson to calm the kids back down again, so that they were in some sort of vague mindset for tackling whichever 'sit down and bloody well listen' subject they had next on their timetable.

This lot just sat slumped in their chairs. Motionless, bored, despondent. If they were a gas they would have been inert.

None of the planned activities had been successful. None of his jokes had worked. And they were HILARIOUS. One of the bottom set Year 8s had actually fallen off a chair with the amount of mirth created by Jim in his lesson yesterday. The girls from the day before had delayed his lesson by a full ten minutes with their giggling and snorting fits that had even the most timid and nervous kids rolling in the aisles.

With this lot - complete silence. Maybe it was because this lesson was the first one of the day and not the afternoon sessions that the others had been. Maybe it was because they were playing catch up, being a full two weeks behind the rest of their year group, due to their first Drama lessons being cancelled for a whole-year assembly with the head in week one, and then assessment tests the following week. Or maybe it was just that, statistically, he had a full complement of people who were 'just not that into it, sir'.

Cut to the plenary, Tovey. You need to stick on the video with explosions that makes Shakespeare look cool. You've lost this one.

"So. Before we have a look at this YouTube clip of the Baz Luhrman version of the play, what do we know now about the two families that we didn't know before we started?"

Somewhere in the building, the sound of a toilet flushing could be heard. It was that quiet.

"Anyone? Ben?"

Ben gave Jim the eyes. The eyes reserved for teachers who singled out people for no good reason. The eyes that said, "Why have you picked on me?"

The reasoning was simple, not that Ben had figured it out yet. In later years the penny would drop but in the mind of a twelve-year-old boy, such awareness of his place in the grander scheme of life was well beyond his reach.

He had been picked on because, out of the fourteen kids currently present for this first Drama lesson of the new term, Ben was the only one who Jim was able to marry up both by name on the paper and face in the room. These thirteen others, these disciples of dullness, had been so non-descript for the previous thirty-five minutes that he could not single out one of them for targeted questioning.

None of them had been taught Drama by Jim in Year 7, having missed out due to a 'fantastic opportunity' for them to do an extra session of Maths each week. This experimental numeracy programme was been hailed as the future for teaching mixed-ability mathematics, and the academy trust had organised for all the schools in the chain to be bussed out once a week to a premier league football stadium. This would, apparently, greatly increase their chances of becoming the next big thing in arithmetic or geometry or something. The fact that they were losing something as inconsequential as Drama was, quite frankly, a bonus and saved a headache for all, giving Jim some much-needed time to do the administration for the school show. For two sessions a fortnight, Jim had gained extra frees, while the kids in question had taken part in a programme with an education company which (a) had gone into receivership during the summer and (b) was, it turns out, rubbish at teaching Maths. The result was a group of kids who had no idea of expectations placed on them in a Drama lesson, and Jim completely unable to pick any of these kids out of a line-up.

How, therefore, did Jim know Ben's name above all the others? Well, that one was simple. Ben was the one in the wheelchair.

He was fairly distinctive. Ben had memos written about him, whole staff meetings convened in his absence, and amendments to the structure of the very building they were standing in carried out over the summer months preceding his arrival at Lancashire Academy. Hell, the ramp at the front of the building that had been installed was still being referred to by some members of staff as 'Ben's ramp'. This kid was closer to getting a blue plaque in his honour than Jim was ever going to be, so he was inevitably going to be the one that got the first question when teacher was struggling to get his lesson back on track.

"Come on, Ben. The families. What have we learned?"

"I don't know. They don't like each other?"

Yes, Benjamin. The ancient grudge breaking to new mutiny, with the civil blood making the civil hands unclean does tell us, in no uncertain terms, that they don't like each other. Brilliant. Well done. Gold stars all round. Requires improvement? This lesson requires a defibrillator. Steph, who had been assigned to support Ben in all his lessons and was witnessing this fine example of theatrical teaching, understood what Jim had meant on their first meeting about Ben being 'a bit prickly'.

At this point, the double doors burst open and a short, slightly grubby boy, with his uniform hanging off of him (prospectus material this child was not) strolled into the room and picked up a chair. With no word of explanation to Jim or Steph as to who exactly he was or why he was here, the boy/youth/ragamuffin from a Dickensian novel slumped himself down, joining the collective boredom.

A quick glance at the pre-printed register revealed him to be missing number 15. A kid on Free School Meals, marked as Pupil Premium, and singled out for School Action Plus due to him having behavioural and emotional difficulties. He was targeted a level 4 (in old money, Jim didn't understand the new assessment system). He was Ethan Connoly.

"Ethan?"

"Yeah?"

"Is there an explanation as to why you're only just arriving?"

"Well, I'm late..."

Muted giggles from the circle. Young Mr Connoly's presence had brought a pulse to the room in the same way that a fitness instructor might liven things up by being parachuted into a morgue. He'd got more out of them (they had actually smiled) in two comments than Jim had got from them in the previous thirty-five minutes of utter torture.

To say that this was frustrating for Jim was the understatement of the millennium. He was having to work his socks off just to get them to engage in his lesson. Now the Artful Dodger here had upstaged him just by making an assured entrance and a sarky comment. This wasn't on.

"Well, Ethan, we've only just met but can we make things clear from the beginning? If you arrive late to my lesson, you don't start by sauntering in and pulling up a pew. You start with an apology, then we have a think about you sitting down and trying to catch up with what you've missed."

48

"Oh right. Soz. What did I miss?"

Bugger. You had to ask.

'Nothing' was the answer. They had achieved nothing. At all. Thirty-five minutes of not quite being the Montagues and Capulets. Thirty-five minutes of barely picking up why Shakespeare tells you all that prologue gubbins at the beginning of the play, spoiling all the story for everybody who feels like carrying on watching. Thirty-five minutes of wishing that period two would arrive so they could set fire to explosive stuff over in Science.

Jim was still searching for an answer when the door to the room opened yet again. It was Gavin, one of the Maths teachers, looking like he'd been moving at some speed to get there.

"Morning, Mr Jones. We don't usually see you over in this neck of the woods..."

Or, more precisely, you have NEVER set foot in my room before, so what the hell are you doing here now?

Gavin took a second and caught his breath.

"I'm here to look after your class. You have to go."

Jim managed a befuddled expression, which roughly translated as "pourqoui?"

"You need to get to the hospital. Your paternity leave just started...."

Within twenty minutes he was at the hospital, displaying the regulation amount of panic for a new father who had cocked up the first two hours of his wife's first labour.

"Katherine Tovey?"
The receptionist on the maternity ward looked him up and down.

"You come to deliver her some chocolates?"

Ah, the all-in-black outfit strikes again. It was either Johnny Cash jokes or the Milk Tray stuff wherever he went. He had no time to explain that one was a long-dead country singer and the other was an advertising campaign he had no chance of ever getting a part in at any time, ever. Katie was in labour, Katie needed help, Katie needed Super Jim. Super Jim was here.

"Katherine. Katie Tovey. She's in labour. She's early. Really early. She's not due till November I got a call at school but my phone was dead and I was teaching and I didn't get the message and..."

Not one breath was taken all the way through. Those vocal exercises you did with Year 10 yesterday must be paying off, sir. The receptionist gave a look of indifference to Super Panic standing in front of her, and consulted the mini-whiteboard next to her computer terminal. Tovey. She was in delivery room 3. Been in since 8:30 this morning. Typical bloke, not turning up until nearly three hours after he'd first been called.

"I'll get a midwife to come and buzz you in."

She pressed down heavily on a button on her phone pad and stared at Jim, who was awaiting some sort of instruction. He just looked at her blankly, like those dogs you see on 'You've been framed' that run into patio doors if you throw a stick into the house. God help the kid who he's donated genes to. It'll turn out a right dope if this muppet was anything to go by.

"You can sit down if you want. The midwife will be out to bring you through in a bit."

Jim couldn't sit down. Katie was about to have a baby. THEY were about to have a baby. She might be having it now. Right now, down that corridor. She might need him on the other side of those double doors right now and here he was, standing looking at a poster reminding him to get a flu shot. Had he had a flu shot? Did he need one? Should he be going in without one? Maybe he should mention it to the receptionist and they could get one to him before he went in. Do they do that? Do they have spares of stuff like that lying around on the ward? He didn't know. He was a Drama teacher, not a medical professional. How is that he was expected to know all sorts of stuff like this?

WHY HAD NOBODY COME TO LET HIM IN?!?!

Buzz. Click. Swish.

The midwife, a rotund and gruff looking woman in her fifties, greeted him.

"Mr Tovey?"

"Yes. Right here. Reporting for duty, Captain."

The second blank look Jim had received in as many minutes.

"Sorry, I'll shut up. Drama teacher. Sometimes I just can't help it...especially when I'm nervous like this...."

The midwife sighed.

"Follow me please, Mr Tovey...."

She sincerely hoped that this birth was going to be a short one.

-

Back across town, inside her office, Janet Murphy was sorting through her post. A mixture of junk mail interspersed with telephone message memos, samples of Year 10 coursework and a scruffy looking hand-written letter, scribbled down on the back of a photocopied note she had seen somewhere before. It was from Jim Tovey. Odd that he had decided, today of all days, to send her a message. Had he been told about the changes before she had? So much for her being a member of Senior Leadership, if the heads of department were going to be told things before they were. Whatever it was he had to say, she wasn't going to like it...

-

"Whatever you do, don't push"

She wasn't going to push. That was obvious. How could she? Between the screaming at the top of her voice and the violent way she was squeezing Jim's arm, there was no human on earth that would have enough energy left to push out what all the scans had shown to be even a fairly regular-sized baby. He'd watched 'World's Strongest Man' on TV every New Year's Day since he was about five. Even the mightiest of them would struggle to make this much noise AND have enough energy left to drag a bus down the street. That baby was going to stay put for hours.

"I can see the head!"

Shit.

Squeeze.

"Aaaargh!!!"

Everyone stopped, as Jim gripped what was left of his right hand.

"What? That hurt."

Katie said nothing. Her face said it all, while the midwife just tutted as if she'd seen a hundred of the likes of Jim before. If truth be told, she had seen relatively few like Jim, fussing around as if he was the girl's mother and being attentive to his wife's every beck and call for the last two hours. In the midwives' eyes, he was simply a male and therefore relegated to 'extraneous to need' in this particular situation.

Being a midwife for twenty years, and seeing countless women go through this process alone, had taught her one thing. If it weren't for the sperm, the men were not really needed in this whole process. The ladies came and went, sometimes with a man in tow. But, if push came to shove, they could still get on with their lives without the complication of testosterone.

The confusing thing about this bloke is that it seemed to be the one thing he was lacking. Usually, when men did come into her delivery suite (it had become noticeably rarer to the midwife in recent years) they would attempt (pitifully) to take control of the situation, handing out printed copies of birth plans, demanding TENS machines at a moment's notice, and speaking confidently for their wives and girlfriends on what they thought their partners needed. Usually, a 30-second chat with the mother was enough to throw all that out the door and for someone on the ward to page the anaesthetist, as expected.

The man in black (as the ward sister had now inevitably dubbed him) was doing none of this and had been worse than useless. Everywhere he moved he was in the way, whether it be while they were taking Katie's blood pressure, when they were trying move her onto her side to make her more comfortable or - most annoyingly - when he insisted on holding her hand while they were administering her Pethidine. Why couldn't these blokes just leave them to get on with their jobs? Taking babies out of people was difficult enough.

As it turned out, there was no need to fret too much over the faffing of the Milk Tray man. (They had settled on this as a term of reference for Jim, as the younger nurses on duty had never heard of Johnny Cash). Katie's birthing was simple and went without incident. Yes, she was a screamer but clearly the little one had got the message, as they were in the delivery suite for just under an hour after she'd been moved down from the ward - running pretty close to the record for first births on the maternity ward at Preston General. Everyone took a breath before moving onto the next one, and Mr & Mrs Tovey were transferred back up to post-natal to be very proud parents.

It was a little boy.

They moved the couple back upstairs and, for the next two hours, pretty much left them to it.

The joy of becoming a parent is, of course, an overwhelming experience. Almost transcendental. As the loving parents stared down into the crib at the small, fragile package that they had created, a surge of love flowed through their veins in a way that they had never experienced before. This boy, this tiny little boy, was now an eternal bond between them.

Within ten minutes they were arguing.

"There is no way on earth he's being called Jamie."

Katie took a deep breath and looked to the sky. She had just been through two hours of extreme pain and was not in the mood for Jim's bizarre reasoning about the naming of their son.

"What's wrong with Jamie? My cousin's name is Jamie. And my Granddad was a James. It's a good family name."

"Not a chance. How many Jamies do I teach? They are always little shits. Even the girl Jamies. Jamie Sutherland, Jamie Langridge, Jamie Thompson..."

"I know none of these people."

"They're all Jamies."

"I got that."

"And they've all been, or are currently being, a pain in the arse. We're not calling him Jamie."

Trying to get Jim to understand that this little boy, this helpless little boy, was not going to become one of the little scrotes he teaches everyday was going to be difficult. The school had close to a thousand children in it. Every name under the sun came with its own baggage. Katie had met very few of these children/demons, yet Jim had decided that his powers of veto extended to the name of every child in the western world.

"Okay. Pick out the name of a kid that you do like and we'll see if it fits."

Jim pondered for a second, his mind mentally ticking down his registers looking for a boy's name that would be vaguely suitable. Kyle? No. They were always really lippy. Darren? Definitely not. The poor little mite would end up getting a tattoo before the age of nine if they went down that road... Prince?

"Prince? Seriously? You teach someone called Prince?"

"Uh-huh. Well he doesn't do Drama, but he's a good kid. Top set, Year 11. Predicted straight As. Always neat and tidy. Always really polite."

"Is this kid black by any chance?"

"Well... yes."

"He's not being called Prince."

Jim smiled and winked.

"Bit racist..."

Katie gave him another clump on the arm. Physically harming her husband had been a recurring event during the course of the birth. It had been quite fun.

"It isn't racist not to want to have the only white boy in town, possibly in the whole country, named after one of the most famous black singers in history. The poor kid will be a laughing stock. He's not being called Prince. He's being called Danny."

"Danny?"

Jim thought. Danny Jones. Danny Spencer. Danny Jackson. Middle-of-the-road kids. None of them high flyers. None of them mental cases. Danny could work...

"Not Daniel? It has to be Danny. Cos if it were Daniel, we'd have an issue with..."

Katie wasn't going to let him start again.

"No. It's Danny. Danny is the name of your little boy. Daniel, but we'll call him Danny, James, not Jamie, Tovey. Get used to it. You're going to be using it a lot."

Jim went to the crib and picked up his newborn son, who was rising from his first nap with a puppy-like snuffle.

"Nice to meet you, Danny James Tovey. The baby formally known as Prince..."

Katie refrained from hitting him this time. She knew that their baby was going to have to get used to this sort of thing....

Chapter Five

Ironing with the Munchkins

Janet liked ironing. In a stressful world, in which she had a stressful job, working with stressful people, in a stressful environment, her weekly ritual of shirt-pressing became an oasis of calm in a tumultuous week. She didn't know if it was the rushing of hot steam on her face, the process of making something horribly crumbled look neat, tidy and ordered, or whether she just had a fetish for right angles, but seeing a neatly folded pile of clothes brought a contented smile to her face. Sundays, 10-1, was Janet time. Coffee made in the machine, catch up on the soaps, big pile of ironing. Sheer bliss.

Usually. But not today.

She should have known that things weren't going to go well after the plug blew on the coffee machine. A one-hundred-and-eighty-pound gadget rendered useless by a twenty-pence element that had sparked brightly, before plunging the whole of downstairs into the half-light of a dim Autumn's mid-morning. With her resident electrical repair man out on his weekly round of golf (Bill was actually a mortgage advisor, but in times such as this he doubled as Mr Fix-it) she was forced to accept that her weekly shot of hard caffeine was about to be downgraded.

After rummaging through the downstairs cupboard to find the fuse box (even though she lacked the expertise to fix a plug, she at least knew how to flick a switch and get the rest of the house back up and running again) she resorted to her bland, every-other-day-of-the-week instant coffee. Boring coffee. Not

Sunday morning coffee. The jaunty mood of a perfect Sunday was already on the wane.

She moved the ironing pile from the utility room through to the lounge, and set herself up for the laborious (but entirely satisfying) task of scaling the mountain of clean washing before her. Turning on the television, she hunted for the remote.

This wasn't happening. Where the heck was the zapper? Rugs were lifted, cushions were shifted and coffee tables moved across the room which, although not revealing the location of the mysterious vanishing remote, it did demonstrate to her that the hoovering really did need to be done and she couldn't put that one off much longer. All of this was done in a vain attempt to find the magic channel-changer. She could have been looking all day and wouldn't have located it, as said item was currently sitting in her husband's golf bag, sixteen miles away, witnessing Bill's equally futile attempt to find the pin from the eleventh tee. The TV would remain stuck on the same settings as when it was last switched off. Far too loud and on BBC2.

Not the omnibus edition of Hollyoaks, as Janet wanted, which, frustratingly, was just two channels away, but a musical tale of magical fairies, enchanted beings and a girl lost within a world so many miles from home. The Wizard of bloody Oz. It was DEFINITELY one of those days. Janet, who was a self-confessed technophobe, looked at the selection of manual buttons at the side of the set. She had never had to use them before and, after pressing the top one (bringing up a menu with options that scared her into thinking she might break the damn thing altogether), she retreated back to the iron, resigned to the fact she was going to be spending the next hour or so with Judy Garland and friends.

In Janet's humble opinion, which, if we are honest, was rarely portrayed in anything like a humble manner, *The Wizard of Oz* was the very definition of ridiculous. Musicals in general were pretty annoying, but this one took the biscuit. In fact it took the whole packet of biscuits and rammed them down your throat, making you never again want any kind of sweet, flavoured baked goods. It was the very pinnacle of rubbish. The summit of annoyance.

Who on earth cared if this whining little girl made it back to Kansas or not? She'd run off from her family (for no real reason, as far as Janet could surmise), got herself trapped in a situation she couldn't handle, and was now paying the price for being a complete and utter fool. Right now in the proceedings, of course, she was surrounded by other self-confessed idiots and they were following her, prancing along gaudy roads, singing jaunty songs (paying no attention to the fact that the manslaughter of some poor bystander had taken place just minutes before) as they left the land of the vertically-challenged.

Whoever pitched this idea to MGM was either taking something dodgy or was so incredibly wealthy that they must have paid for the entire folly out of their own back pocket. Surely nobody in their right mind would actually commission this rubbish? She knew there was never any accounting for taste in life, but how this film had ever been ranked as a 'classic' she would never truly understand.

She made it past the skipping and that excruciating section with the scarecrow, but as soon the wailing and warbling of the tin man kicked in, Janet had had enough. This was not relaxing. It was one of those new torture methods that they used in American prison camps to break the resolve of terrorists. She had done enough of Bill's shirts to get him through the week and she would finish the rest of the pile later, when he had fixed the TV – and, of course, the coffee machine. In the meantime, there was Radio 2 and the rest of the household jobs.

She switched on the radio. Steve Wright was away and had been replaced by some fly-by-night Welsh stand-up comedian that Janet had never heard of. She gave in and looked to the sky. Was this finally it? Years of built up non-attendance at church had finally caught up with her? Was her Sunday School teacher going to burst in through the door and show her the true way to repentance, away from BBC soap operas and high-caffeine shots of espresso? Or was it just 'the first rule of sod' working overtime to balance out what had out otherwise been a decent enough week till now? Whatever it was, Janet was forced to count to ten. The radio went off again and she retreated back upstairs with her small pile of perfectly creased ironing.

As she carefully placed Bill's shirts on the bed before retrieving the hangers from the wardrobe, the document that she had been trying all weekend to avoid reading stared quietly at her from the bedside table.

'DRA01 - Specification for the Study of GCSE Drama'.

Considering it was a publication claiming to be related to the glitz and glamour of the performing arts, it looked as dull as ditchwater. She had about as much motivation to study it as she did to pick up and read the phone directory, or even the elongated version of War and Peace that came complete with a biography of Tolstoy and an accompanying glossary of popular terms in Napoleonic France. If it had been the foot high pile of soon-to-be-recycled pizza menus that relentlessly came through the door each day, she would have felt more of an urge to pick them up and have a browse.

This document, this 72-page collection of words and sentences that she had tried desperately to understand all week, lay on the bedside table, staring at her, mocking her lack of understanding. She picked it up, sat down on the bed, and attempted to give it another go. Perhaps now that she was out of the work environment, she would have a clearer approach and be able to fathom what children who opted for a GCSE in Drama actually studied. Even now, however, after she had left it, slept twice and reached her happy place via half a bottle of Merlot last night, the damn thing still read like gobbledygook. This must have been its third reading, but she was struggling to get to grips with even the basic concepts contained within its many pages.

It may as well have been written in a complete foreign language. As a teacher of MFL, who was fluent in two separate tongues other than English, she thought she'd have at least an outside chance of following it. Janet was almost 100% certain, however, that neither the French nor Spanish populations of the world would have made head nor tail of this particular ragbag of sentences that claimed to be an academic document, written (apparently) in the Queen's own English.

What, in the name of Christ, was 'marking the moment'?

The spec claimed in the extensive glossary that it was a "dramatic technique used to highlight a key moment in a scene or improvisation - e.g use of freeze frame, thought-tracking or music"

In the words of a Year 9 choosing their options... Wha?

Another section referred to something called 'cross-cutting'. The specification described this one as "the interweaving of a series of scenes or sequences resulting in a desired dramatic effect". Were these even real sentences? Janet had two degrees and she couldn't work this out. How on earth the examiners of this so-called subject were supposed to decipher whether or not children were demonstrating how to be a cross cut, or if the moment they were in had been marked, she had no idea.

Herein lay the nub of the problem, and the reason why she was utterly baffled by Mick's decision to have her lead the Drama department as part of her responsibilities. She was a linguist. Why had he put her in charge of something she could barely understand herself? Until this year, she had always dealt with heading up the two languages subjects and both forms of English GCSE. It made sense. There was a certain congruence there - an acceptance that she was the one who dealt with language and communication subjects. She wasn't arty. She didn't 'create'. Drama really wasn't her bag.

Now that Petra had been brought in by the trust to lead on Literacy within the school group, there was no space left in English for Janet, so her skills needed to be utilised elsewhere. She had held on to her languages responsibility, obviously, but had now been given two other subjects to administer. Drama and History. History was going to be no issue for Janet at all, and she had met with Andrea, their head of department, within just a few hours of being told of her new portfolio of responsibility.

Andrea, a go-getter of a woman who had herself only come to the Academy last year, had - in her own way - turned around a department which had been coasting through life in much the same way that Drama appeared to be doing now. There was still a fair bit of familiarisation for Janet to do with their curriculum, but at least it made sense. Chronological, ordered, logical sense. Not like the chaotic structure of the hand she had been dealt with Jim Tovey.

In truth, the real problem with Janet's new task was that she was not, in any way shape or form, a dramatic person. She did not do silly voices, she hated putting on costumes, and the idea of 'playing make believe' made her come out in hives. Janet's love of academia had, over the years, given her moments of sheer joy and an ongoing sense of self-worth that relatively few people in her peer group had experienced. She had a love of learning, particularly of foreign languages, and revelled in the fact that she held a skill that relatively few people in her immediate society possessed - having the ability to order a coffee on holiday without resorting to increased volume and extreme mime skills.

The hard study that had got her to this point, those moments of brilliant achievement - her degree, her post-grad, and her rise to being on the senior leadership team at school - were not done on a stage. They didn't happen under the blaze of theatrical lighting or get witnessed by a sycophantic group of followers, clapping and cheering her path to success. Janet's moments (which didn't need to be 'marked') had happened quietly, methodically and with an attention to detail that put her, quite frankly, above all this arty nonsense.

She understood, of course, that in an arts subject that there was always going to be a certain amount of practical work involved as opposed to a proper academic-based subject, but where were the obvious areas of study? Surely, a GCSE in Drama should involve something as basic as learning lines in some way. Where was the unit entitled 'Putting on a play'? She was expecting to see programme content about Shakespeare, Chekhov or that new play with the puppet horse they kept banging on about in the news. All this was nowhere to be seen.

The whole specification document for this supposed qualification was filled with fantastic vagaries. Words like 'explore', 'workshop', 'symbolic' and 'imagery' reigned supreme - with words like 'recall', 'know', 'understand' and 'demonstrate' being relegated to become a mere footnote in the learning of the students (if, indeed, there was any actual learning whatsoever going on in this subject). Where was the rigour? The revision materials? Where were the text books?!

Janet tried to cast her mind back to last year when Jim's GCSE group had performed in her SLT assembly - some piece about drink-driving where the children were all throwing themselves about the room pretending to be the bits of car. She recalled being a little stumped by what was going on at the time, and having to ask her colleagues why it was that Jim had got them all wearing black instead of giving them proper costumes. When she had it explained to her then that they were symbolic of the structure of the vehicle, she remembered distinctly thinking that it would have been a whole lot easier if they had just a painted a car on the scenery so that the audience didn't have to try and figure it all out for themselves. Why insist on making things overly complicated?

Proper drama didn't rely on the audience figuring out these silly puzzles after all, so why did the children have to learn it this way when they were at school? Nobody in Eastenders ever walked into the Queen Vic and asked for a symbolic pint of lager, only to be greeted by twelve fifteen year olds dressed in black, moulding themselves ineffectively into the shape of a pint pot. It didn't make any sense whatsoever. Nobody in real life ever spoke to a lion, broke into song at a moment's notice, or skipped down roads that were painted in such a gaudy fashion that the local council would periodically face a sky-high bill for their cleaning and repair. It just didn't happen.

This was the root of her issue. Including Drama as a subject choice for the children wasn't working. It was all just glorified playing. It was dressing up, putting on a silly voice, singing and dancing. In the same way that being good at running about in P.E wasn't going to get you gainful employment further down the line, being able to pretend that you were a metallic man with no effective cardiovascular system was also unlikely to jettison you out of the dole queue.

She picked up her iPad and scrolled through to take another look over Jim's Drama results from the previous summer. Boys' achievement? Slightly below average. Girls, way below. The differential results between Drama and their other subjects? Around two grades lower. These kids were achievers, just not in Drama. When Mick had confronted Jim on this during their results meeting, he had tried to blame their collective failure on other subjects, as if them furthering their study in Maths or Science was likely to impact on their ability to produce jazz hands on command.

Mick had asked Janet to have a look at whether there might be any evidence to justify Jim's claim that *Gradeboost* was hampering their chances of achieving in their Drama work. There was no way she was letting him go down that particular avenue. The *Gradeboost* programme that she had helped to usher in through English and later Maths and Science, to help pupils in the core subjects, had delivered in spades. No more than one pupil at a time had ever been withdrawn from a non-academic subject to attend the booster sessions and in a cohort of 18, as he had, losing one child at a time was negligible, surely? Plus, there had been no other reports of impact from any other subjects. The musicians and artists still managed to keep their grades up while taking part in the programme, so why not the actors as well?

The only thing that Janet could see from her analysis was that Jim needed to be spending more time getting these kids to knuckle down, and spend a little less time on all this vague nonsense that he kept harping on about. When she did meet with him, there would be none of this codswallop about trying to promote 'collaborative working', 'trust exercises' and 'group ethos'. Trusting, sharing and caring wasn't delivering results.

From reading the GCSE specification cover to cover, (twice over, and the second time with a highlighter pen) Janet knew that essentially a group of pre-schoolers would find some sense of achievement in Drama if they were just guided efficiently in the right direction. Whether Jim Tovey was the right man for that task was another matter, and that would be reviewed later in the year. Janet had been suspicious of him ever since he came to the school, always suspecting that his loud, confident voice and over-use of gesture was simply a cover for what was lacking underneath. Academic rigour and an attention to detail.

It wasn't so much that she didn't trust his abilities as a performer - he had an infectious energy that always engaged people when he was speaking, and he had a fantastic rapport with the children in his classes. Drama consistently came towards the top of league table about pupil subject preferences although, again,

Janet suspected that might be entirely due to the lack of actual achievement taking place in the Drama room, rather than any pride in the acquisition of skills and knowledge.

As she placed Bill's shirts back into the wardrobe, she had a revelation of what needed to be done. It was clear to her now that Jim Tovey needed a line manager who would bring him to heel. Someone to keep his eye on the ball a little more. As soon as he got back from the week off that he had been granted to change nappies, she would bring him into line. No more faffing about with work that children could do as a hobby at a Saturday morning club from now on. If they wanted to 'explore' then they could join the Scouts. Results first, artistic merit second. Under her watch, the Drama department was going to do what every other bugger had to do. It was going to make the grade.

Lancashire Academy
Drama Memo

To: Mick Davies, Head
From: Jim Tovey, Drama
Date: Sep 9th
Subject: Gradeboost effect on last summer's GCSE
              Drama results

Mick,

Further to our results meeting yesterday, here is the analysis of last year's GCSE Drama cohort and those which were on Gradeboost.   The individual pupils' predicted grades are in brackets. Those on Gradeboost are underlined in bold.

The area in which they lost out most was their practical mark, which is worth 40%. I believe that this was caused by under-preparation due to lack of rehearsals. After all, it's really hard to rehearse a group piece when you always have at least one person missing!

Thanks

Jim Tovey
Drama

Drama cohort results analysis

Molly Baker	E (D)
Tom Bakerfield	**C (B)**
Jennifer Baldock	B (A)
Harry Ball	D (B)
Kayleigh Clarke	E (C)
Amir Khan	**D (C)**
Zain Khan	**D (B)**
Saddiq Khawaga	U (D)
Maleeha Malik	B (A)
Terence Matthews	**C (B)**
Brittany Outhwaite	**F (D)**
Corey Patterson	A (A*)
Gareth Pearce	C (B)
James Plummer	B (A*)
Usman Sattir	D (B)
Ameenah Shah	E (C)
David Smith	**C (B)**
Chloe Southworth	**D (C)**
Matthew Surtees	**C (B)**
Ellie Webster	D (C)

Chapter Six

Welcome Back

"Jim, could I have a word?"

That was how it started. With 'a word'. Never before had a phrase been so far from the truth. This would not be a single word. It would be a torrent of sentences, paragraphs of disapproval, and endless passages of stress and worry.

It began fairly innocuously enough, as Janet popped her head out of her office when Jim was passing on his first morning back. She shuffled him into the tiny room next to her languages classroom and sat him down.

Good news! Janet was thrilled to be the new line manager for Drama. It was all decided just before he went on his paternity leave so he didn't get the memo. But wow! Wasn't it exciting? Janet was really excited to have him in her team. Really excited. He knew she was excited as she said the word at least twenty times in the space of five minutes. For someone who dealt so much in the use of language, Jim couldn't help but think that maybe her vocabulary in her native tongue was somewhat lacking.

She was clearly in a good mood, so Jim addressed the memo that he had sent her before he went off on leave.

"Did you get my note about what that science teacher sent to me about the show? I can't believe anyone would have the gall to write something like that."

Janet paused in her response, deflating the mood slightly and quickly making Jim feel less comfortable about this 'little chat'.

"We have to respect his opinion, Jim. Personally, I didn't see the show but I have seen the pictures up in reception. The children looked like they enjoyed the experience."

Possibly the most non-committal response in history and certainly not the 'Don't worry. I've got your back. You'll never see him again' comment that Jim was hoping for. Plus, had she really not seen the show? He wasn't keeping a register of who had turned up each night and he'd been backstage the whole time, but they'd had packed houses for three solid nights. Maybe she'd had other commitments that week.

Janet got down to brass tacks. She was now responsible for MFL, Drama and History. She would meet Jim weekly at this time each Monday morning. Each Friday afternoon he should send her a quick email detailing anything that he wanted to discuss in their meeting, so that they could keep things focused, and she would do likewise.

"So all the arts aren't meeting together anymore?"

Jim couldn't really help being a little bemused. He'd had barely fifteen hours sleep in the last week and had spent most of his time caked in baby poo and sick. He hadn't had the time to think about his department, or his lesson planning. Every time he did, Danny started crying. He figured that he'd get back this morning, get through form, and use his Monday morning frees (he was lucky in that somehow he had been given two in a row on both weeks) to get his shit together and try to hang on until

72

the weekend. Then he could sit down and work out where we were going from here.

Janet, line-managing Drama? This didn't compute. She taught French. In previous years, the arts subjects had all got together and met with Dave (one of the old deputies) who, at the very least, was an English specialist until he retired last summer so had at least had a vague grasp of what creativity was. Dave had been a big supporter of the arts in school. He'd never missed a show, a music recital, or gallery display night. He'd given them the freedom they needed to be creative, but made sure that they kept on top of all those annoying forms that seemed to pile up on their desks. All of the creative artists in school had pretty much been allowed to get along and do their own thing, in their own way, in their own time.

It was a loose co-operative. They helped each other out where they needed to and tried to stay out of each other's hair when they knew there was a busy time approaching. It wasn't broke. Now Janet was here to fix it.

"We're moving on to the next level now, Jim. Everyone has to start being a little more focused on what we're all trying to achieve here, and that's getting the school back up that league table on results day next year. We have to get these E-bacc scores up, or what's the point of us all being here?"

Ah, the E-bacc. The English Baccalaureate. Or the "Bloody E-bacc" as Jenny, the previous head, had referred to it in many a staff meeting. Brought in by a particularly over-zealous education secretary, whose name Jim didn't even dare to say as he thought it might bring him out in a rash. The E-bacc was a collection of GCSEs lumped together in an attempt to drive up standards within schools. Essentially, you couldn't be a 'good' school if your students hadn't passed English, Maths, Science, a language and a humanities subject. For schools that were running with the new 'qualification', the inevitable happened. They all started teaching English, Maths, Science, Languages and Humanities. And nothing else.

"With all due respect, Janet, I'm not entirely sure where I feature in bringing up the E-bacc results. Drama isn't included in the figures."

"Well, this is the trick, Jim, isn't it? We have to look at how we're all contributing. I know you've had issues that you raised in your results meeting about *Gradeboost*. I got the impression that you weren't entirely happy about it being put in place last spring?"

Not entirely happy? He was livid! He was bouncing off the walls! He couldn't be happier if the whole ridiculous concept was killed off and buried next to the AstroTurf pitches, whilst they all, in turn, danced around on its grave.

He'd told Mick that in his results analysis meeting, just before he went away.

Which Janet must know.

Shit. He'd been blind-sided. This wasn't a 'welcome to the team' meeting after all. This was chastisement, stage one. Janet had been on the team that had ushered in the stupid *Gradeboost* programme and he was, as far as he knew, one of only a handful that had voiced any objection to its existence. She didn't let up on him.

74

"E-bacc results were up 8% last year since we expanded the programme, Jim, and that's what we're all judged on, isn't it?"

"That may be the case, but that's only for the subjects that are included in the figures. Every time a kid is taken out of one of my classes, it gets that little bit harder to get them the grades they need in Drama. I did an analysis for Mick of the kids most directly affected..."

He didn't have the piece of paper to hand. If he'd known he was going to be grilled on this, he'd have printed her off a copy. But she'd come at him with the 'friendly chat' thing on the corridor. He'd have to verbally explain it, which was far more long-winded.

"I had a look at your analysis over the weekend but I still couldn't really understand where you were coming from. The five sample children you picked out as underachieving the most in Drama all achieved exactly where we needed them to elsewhere. Your challenge, surely, has to be to bring them up to that grade in Drama as well. They managed to keep their grades up in their other option subjects."

"I would do, but *Gradeboost* takes them out of my lesson. How can I teach them when they're not there?"

"You only lose a child for one lesson out of ten, Jim. It's only the same as if one of them were ill. Plus, as I already pointed out, the other option subjects have mostly kept the grades up. It hasn't seemed to have affected them at all."

Jim had felt the itch under his skin for a few minutes now. It was his blood beginning to boil. This wasn't a good time to catch him. He was sleep-deprived and smelt vaguely of Danny's vomit. Janet was putting up a wall and he was going to either have to leap over it or break it down. The mood he was in now, he was happy to go and look for a bulldozer but, somewhere in his brain, he realised that keeping his job secure at the moment might be a better course of action. He would just have to see how high he could jump.

"The difference between Drama and the other subjects that the kids took is that it requires the kids to be in the room together. If we're doing a piece of scripted drama, as they need to for the practical element, then it needs the whole cast to be there to rehearse it effectively. If you're missing someone, it makes that more difficult."

"For ONE lesson every ten weeks."

"Yes, it might be one lesson per child. But, of my cohort last year, you had eight of them on *Gradeboost* and every one of them went out for intensive Maths on a different week during the rehearsal period. And this distorted statistics idea that it's just the same amount of time lost as if one of them had got ill is not right either. They STILL got ill, the same as any other overworked teenager, so I had that to contend with as well."

Janet didn't get the chance to respond.

"And it isn't the same for other subjects. If Elizabeta loses a kid for lesson in music, she can sit down with that individual at a convenient time and run a catch-up for one about how to play something on an oboe, or whatever it is they're doing. If the ICT guys lose a kid, they can ping off an email and get them to work on it at home. If I lose a cast member, I have the double-whammy of the rest of the cast being put out in lesson time, then having to drag all of them back after school to catch up with the time they missed. It's a nightmare."

Jim was trying his hardest not to make it all sound like a tirade, but it was extremely difficult. He felt like one of those salmon swimming upstream, only to find that there was a bear up top licking its lips getting ready for lunch.

"We can't make the timetable work just for Drama, Jim. That would be the cart pulling the horse, wouldn't it?"

Great. He was now a cart. Lovely.

"I'm not suggesting that, but isn't there a way that we could avoid having the kids taken out of Drama for *Gradeboost* this year, now that we know the effect it is having?"

"I'm sorry, Jim, that isn't going to happen. We're expanding *Gradeboost* to an extra thirty Year 11 pupils this year and I'm not convinced that, without a little more planning, you can't work round the issue you have. If you need more after-school rehearsals, then schedule them."

"I already stay until five, doing extra rehearsals on Mondays and Drama club on Thursdays."

"Well, then, that leaves three spare days, doesn't it?"

"I've only just had a baby. I have responsibilities at home."

"I'm pretty sure you didn't have the baby, Jim, and you also have responsibilities here - ones which you get paid to do. We have a big hill to climb this year and it will be easier if you start coming up with some solutions instead of trying to justify why everything went wrong for your department by blaming something else. We don't want to be looking at competencies when it comes to September next year."

The killer blow hit home. The ace in the hole. Janet was now in charge of his performance management. Her thumb had become the marker by which his career would be judged. As a teacher of drama, he understood her tone very clearly. She wasn't hinting at lack of pay progression. She was talking about showing him the door. Everything was going to be judged on his results next August, no matter what hand he had been dealt.

Finding some time to sleep would have to wait until next year.

Chapter Seven

Bananaman

Twenty-four hours after his showdown with Janet, and Jim was ready to get cracking. He'd teach like he had never taught before. Cards had been laminated, detailed planning (with an actual bona fide, written down, three-part lesson plan) had been undertaken and Jim was ready to face year 11 head-on. He had them periods 1 & 2. Get through form, get to the studio, get back on track. What he was anticipating was a full-on double period of focused and highly differentiated dramatic exploration, devised from news stories he'd picked from various websites last night. What he got was an Australian and some un-ripened fruit.

Alan Cook, in his relatively short time at Lancashire Academy had already made quite a name for himself. Loved by the female population of the school (pupils and teachers alike) for his heroically toned swimmer's physique, and admired equally by the males for just being ridiculously cool, Alan was found waiting for Jim next to his form room, bright and breezy, at 8:30am. This was a full ten minutes before the kids were due in and, even despite Alan's notorious healthy lifestyle, Jim had never once seen him carrying around two – no, wait, three - bunches of fresh bananas. Was some sort of inter-form smoothie challenge going on that he didn't know about?

"You planning on making us all breakfast, or something?"

Jim and Alan had hit it off straight away after the 'incident' on day one with the newbie stealing his parking spot and causing him to uproot a tree. With Alan's laid-back nature, it was impossible not to like him and, as a newly qualified teacher (NQT), he had been assigned to Jim's form for the foreseeable future. This ensured that they had at least fifteen minutes together each morning to get to know each other, alongside some bleary eyed year tens who, all too often, were to be found sleeping their way through morning registers and notices.

It was with a fantastic sense of irony that two of the most physically active members of staff at Lancashire Academy had been left with a form group that wouldn't run for a bus unless the vehicle had free chips on it, but they both saw the funny side. Slamming books on desks to startle dozing (and sometimes hung-over) teenagers was a perk of the job that never made it to the government recruitment adverts.

"Did you not read the email?" chirped Alan, clearly eager to get the morning going.

"I haven't even had a chance to breathe, mate. I got back in and got a grilling from Janet Murphy yesterday. She's taking over line-managing Drama. Then Danny was up half the night again and Katie's struggling to feed. Emails are going to have to wait a bit."

"So you haven't read the lesson plan yet?"

Jim looked blank. It was only 8:30, after all. He may be keen to get going this morning, but lateral thinking wouldn't be on the agenda until well after he'd got himself a big cup of coffee from the staff room. Alan explained what was going on in words that even a four-year-old would understand.

Personal, Social and Health Education day had been moved forward a month as Mick, the head, was convinced that Ofsted were due in for a check up on progress before Christmas. He wanted the kids fully in lesson mode when the demons from the DfE did arrive, so had taken precautions to make sure that all other required lesson delivery had already been completed in advance. The consequence of this was that all the kids were off their usual timetables for that day, completing the age-appropriate resources that the RE, PE and Science departments had deemed suitable for today's incredible learning journey through life, the universe and, well, everything.

It also meant that all the planning Jim had managed to squeeze in between washing poo-encrusted sleepsuits and rocking Danny to sleep last night had been rendered absolutely useless. The news stories and web links he had dropped so efficiently into four different colour-coordinated PowerPoint slides would now have to be redone, and yet another precious hour of his awake time had slipped through his fingers. This had better be worth it.

"Alright, so the planning has already been done? That's a bonus, I suppose. At least I can just follow the instructions. It'll be death by PowerPoint if Debbie Johnstone has had anything to do with it. Which year group did we get lumbered with?"

Alan waved the bananas.

"Eleven."

No.

No way. Not in a month of Sundays could Jim have this much bad luck in one week. At that moment, Steph arrived alongside them to complete the horror.

"Okay boys, I've got a handbag full of condoms. You ready to have some fun?"

Bananas, condoms and teenage kids. A comedy staple in anyone's book. A cliché. A horrible, horrible cliché that no one in their right mind would attempt. Which is exactly why Debbie Johnstone was going to be spending the morning in her nicely furnished corner office, while the plebby teacher minions delivered the lesson from hell in her absence. Debbie thought they would all have fun. Debbie wanted shooting.

In five years of teaching, Jim had managed to avoid this session entirely - even during his training year - and had mistakenly thought that he would continue to avoid the short straw. Steph's giggly excitement was not helping matters. As far as she was concerned, there was no way in the world this session was going to go wrong. It would be fun, informative and a boost to the Personal, Social and Health Education of all involved. Plus, she got spend the morning with that gorgeous PE teacher. Everything would be fine.

She maintained this irritating bout of positive mental attitude all the way through form time and right through the mature and sobering introduction that Jim provided Year 11 with, as it was revealed to them that today's learning objective would consist mostly of learning how birds and bees, two apparently incompatible species, would (in nature's finest sense) get it on.

82

Today was going to be one of the most important lessons they would ever experience in their time at Lancashire Academy. The knowledge they learned in this classroom today would give them the necessary skills they needed to negotiate positive relationships, the consummation of love between consenting adults and, of course, they would learn not just where babies came from but how you stop the little blighters showing up in the first place. All of this, and more, would be achieved. Provided, of course, that Jim could get a grip on his nerves and find a way to stop them all manhandling the fruit.

"Dylan, I've asked you before to leave it alone. If you pick it up again, I'm going to have to move you to another seat."

Dylan was in a world of his own and the temptation to try and break the 'make as many knob gags as you can in a minute' world record was just too much for a boy of fifteen. Steph had figured this out and placed her hands firmly on the banana, reminding Dylan that he had been instructed in no uncertain terms to put the bugger down. While this had the desired effect, it also sent a wave of testosterone shooting most of the way along the back row. Many of the boys sitting at the rear of the room had already had some fairly mature thoughts about Miss Govin since she'd started in September, and now she was putting her perfectly manicured hands all over some phallic squishy fruit right in front of them while speaking in a domineering, yet entirely wholesome, manner.

Dylan replaced his banana on the desk. He wouldn't walk properly for weeks.

Jim turned his attention back to the PowerPoint while Alan gave out the worksheets. The first was fairly simple, as Jim could see. Could you spot an ovary from a clitoris from a womb? It was the starter for 10, the prelude to the symphony, the calm (as it turned out) before the impending storm. By the end of the allotted five minutes, only one member of the class had labelled the diagram at all, and even then Rizwan had only got two parts labelled correctly. He'd pretty much guessed his way around the female anatomy in completing the sheet (something he would actually do in a physical sense four months later, when he had his first experience of drunken party antics with Kelsey Sandringham from Year 10) but he was proud of his work, nonetheless.

The rest of the class were still enthralled by Alan's accent and his inability to say the word 'fallopian' in anything but a comic manner. It was a sideshow, yes, but most certainly an entertaining one. Jim decided it was breaking down the kids' inhibitions about the subject, and it couldn't really do much harm for them to sit back and enjoy the fun. Ten minutes later, he'd be wishing their inhibitions would return and that the walls between nervous teenager and uncomfortable teacher could be wholly resurrected - possibly higher than the walls of Jericho, if that was okay.

"Sir?"

Here it comes. The inevitable.

"Yes, Sadie?"

"Have you had sex, sir?"

Like day follows night, Sadie would walk through the open door that the key stage four PSHE curriculum had opened up for her.

The teacher was there to be shot at. He was the vulnerable figure of authority, and she was top dog amongst the Year 11 girls. She was in his GCSE group, so he had already prepared himself for a morning in her ever-challenging presence, but this conversation was a whole different kettle of fish. He needed to get a grip and make sure he stayed on top of things.

Sadie smiled. It was her job - nay, her DUTY - to press him on his sexual experience, maximising the chances of good old Mr Tovey becoming (a) today's bus time conversation or (b) this autumn's long-term figure of ridicule on social media. One way or another, he was going to get it. Just the scale of his ridicule had yet to be ascertained.

Jim knew this and took a deep breath. He was prepared. Mostly.

"Yes, Sadie, I have. But you know that already, as I've just had my first child. They're not made by magic, you know."

A ripple of laughs and nods from the 'don't pick on us, please' section of the room. Tovey had at least prepared himself mentally for this much-anticipated duel, and his opening gambit held its own. Maybe this wasn't going to be the predicted ring-running that had been much discussed in the toast queue at breakfast time. It was a going to have a bit more ebb and flow than had been billed on the posters. Sex Ed was about to get entertaining.

"You're married, aren't you, sir?"

"Yes, Sadie. I am."

"Your wife's pretty, isn't she? Jenna Asquith said she was. She said she saw her last week when you were buying nappies in Tesco."

"Yes, that's right, Sadie. Babies need nappies or they end up making quite a mess about the place"

Jim put on his best straight-man face as he tried to 'tactically ignore' anymore of Sadie's tracking of his family's whereabouts. Forget CCTV. The pupil grapevine was just as accusatory as any security system that SLT could install to watch the behaviour of people moving about this damned building. They may as well have digitally chipped all the staff to document where everybody who works here is at any given time, just so that the kids could use it as ammo against you later.

"Why haven't you marked my coursework, sir? Is it because you were in the Red Lion till 10:47, and then went on to LA Pizza for a kebab till 11.03?"

It was only a matter of time before 'track my teacher' was an option in Apple's latest gadget range.

Jim tried to pull things back by putting on his very best perma-grin for Sadie who, he now knew, had been put forward by the group as today's challenger in this - the latest round of the teacher embarrassment challenge. The other kids were letting her do all the talking. This was clearly pre-arranged. Jim had a quick glance over to his two colleagues. They just grinned back at him. He was the senior member of staff who'd been rostered to lead this one, and they were leaving him to do the talking from their side. Bastards.

"Is she pretty, sir?"

"Well, yes. I clearly think so. Is my wife paying you money for asking these questions, Sadie?"

There was no letting up here. He'd made the mistake of engaging, leaving her to follow up with a right-left combo that would have a less-experienced member of staff clinging to the ropes by now. Alan had slowly moved himself out of eyeshot, and was beginning to look a bit twitchy. Steph was all too aware that Dylan and his mates hadn't stopped looking at her breasts since she'd forcibly separated him from his banana. There was more than a whiff of a sexual charge in the air.

Jim knew exactly where this was going. He needed to find a way out of this dead-end of a conversation, and quickly. Sadie Masterson was not stupid, and Jim was going to have to be careful with what he said. Careers and reputations were lost in moments like these.

"I think she is really pretty, sir. We saw your profile picture on Facebook and she was with you in it. That was her, wasn't it?"

Bugger.

How had she found his profile? They'd been told to lock down their security and he thought he'd done it pretty well. His pseudonym was surely concrete enough not to turn up in any searches. Nobody outside of his uni friends and a few colleagues knew that he had changed his profile name to 'Professor Caliban' during his training year, in honour of possibly his greatest moment on the amateur stage. Sadie must have detective qualities that MI5 would be interested in. (Obviously they would have to ignore her sociopathic attitude and her compete lack of literacy skills, but she was a dead certain for the double-0 programme, should they ever need someone to replace Mr Bond.)

His pupils had dilated. He'd shown weakness. He'd paused. Sadie allowed the classroom murmur to grow just enough before she jumped in with the follow up.

"That was her in the bikini, sir, wasn't it? Or was it someone else? Have you a got a fancy woman?"

Bullseye. Sadie had gained her no holds barred 'laugh in the teacher's face' moment from the rest of the class, and Jim had to recover quickly. Control was being lost. This was usually the moment that someone from SLT walked in the door.

"Yes, that's very much Mrs Tovey in the picture. Thank you, Sadie. There's no scandal there. Right, these worksheets. Let's see how we all got on, shall we?"

No blind panic, Jim. Just get back to the lesson plan and back to the PowerPoint. Tunnel vision.

"Does SHE have a clitoris, sir?"

Even Alan knew that lines of inappropriateness were being stepped on, if not trampled all over, and did something that he rarely even attempted. He intervened. Well, he tried to but this was way beyond him, even from the start.

"Sadie. That's enough."

"I was only asking him a question."

"Completely out of order. Keep yourself quiet."

The class smiled all at once. Mr Cook, the coolest, but possibly softest, PE teacher ever to traverse the globe had put his foot down and made sure that everybody in the room knew exactly who was in charge of the situation. Sadie Masterson was in charge. The intervention had sounded utterly pathetic.

"I was only asking if Mrs Tovey has a clitoris as well? This is supposed to be sex education, isn't it? You told us at the beginning that we had to ask questions if we were curious..."

Thanks to Alan's paltry attempt at restoring order, things had now got very serious and the volume in the room had risen considerably. Jim followed procedure. It was the only way he knew how.

"Sadie, I'm going to give you a warning now. Any more interruptions and you'll have to take some time outside."

Sadie sat and grinned. She knew the drill. He'd gone straight to the 'escalation staircase' that all the teachers pinned so pathetically to their classroom walls. She didn't know where the one in here was (they'd been put in a geography room for this pointless PSHE lesson, and she'd opted for history) but she was sure that if she piped up again, later on she'd be getting the lecture about why it was her own decisions about her behaviour that had caused her to move 'up the steps'. Could she get away with one more?

You only live once, Sadie. Let's see if we can give it a go....

"Sorry Sir. I was only asking as I wasn't sure if we all had one. Have you got one?"

"Men do not have a clitoris, Sadie, as you well know."

"My Dad says men have a sort of clitoris in their bum. That's why gay men have sex there. Have you ever ha..."

"Outside!"

Sadie was not going to get her chance to get away with just one more. She got up out of her seat and gave a bow (with quite a flourish) to the now applauding and laughing Year 11s who couldn't wait to tell Twitter how Sadie had asked Tovey, in their lesson, if he'd ever had gay sex. It was the event of the week to those that were lucky to have witnessed it live and in person. Tovey had done pretty well in the face of adversity. It had been a pretty gutsy show, but all credit had to go to Sadie for having the balls (figuratively speaking) to ask him.

Jim got the class immediately back on track and motioned to Steph to go and give 'the talk' to Sadie downstairs in the library, which is where they had all agreed they would take any of the kids if they became too hot to handle. Sadie was going to have to miss today's exciting PowerPoint on the many ways that you can or can't get pregnant, but she did have a hell of a tale to tell to the girls when she finally got to see them at lunch.

Steph would have to wait until next year to play with the bananas.

Chapter Eight

Agendas

Never have a meeting that could have been fixed with a round robin email.

That was what Janet had been told when she attended *Leading through Life* all those years back. Why spend hours discussing things that had already happened and were not discussion points at all? It just sucked all the life out of you, after what had already been an energy-sapping day. Agenda item after agenda item designed to swallow up your time and, eventually, your will to live.

Admittedly, meetings these days were a lot more comfortable since the Trust took over. The complete revamp of the staff room and adjoining conference suite made having a meeting in school seem more like attending an international summit. Everyone now had an executive chair, the professional-looking oval table that had been moved in was exceptionally shiny, and the filter coffee on tap was a welcome step-up from the rubbish that they had been scraping together before their conversion to an academy.

Looking back over her shoulder, and glancing into the rest of the staff room area, she was still impressed by the way that the place resembled a small branch of IKEA, with its flash cupboards, industrial size dishwashers (plural - the trust had installed two of them) and American-style fridges. She pondered how long it would be possible for someone to live here, sleeping on the comfy sofas and using the communal kitchen that was in a far better state of repair than her own. If it weren't for the constant drone of teenage children in the background, living here would be almost bearable.

"Let's move to item four, shall we?"

Four? They had been here for an hour and twelve minutes already (not that she was counting) and four was only halfway down the agenda. At this rate, they weren't getting out before 4:30 - which meant sitting, yet again, in the evening traffic. Looks like it was going to be a chippy tea again tonight.

"E-bacc targeting & reporting for Year 10 and 11."

Janet's ears pricked up as, unlike the previous agenda items about cross-curricular numeracy and the refurbishment of the science corridor, this one was very relevant to her. Languages were an essential part of the E-bacc and she needed to make sure that any decisions about targeting pupils for extra revision were going to lead to getting the best out of her current crop. She had 48 in the Year 11 cohort this year and 52 in the Year 10s, so this was going to be important.

She glanced down at the agenda and saw that it was Gareth, the school exams officer, who would be leading the discussion. Gareth was a perfect exams officer, Janet thought. As an engineer, he cared little for 'reasons why little Johnny didn't get his target grade' or 'circumstances that meant they hadn't revised the right topic'. Gareth dealt in facts and figures, black and white, success and failure. His job was to let everyone know where the weak spots were in school, and for the rest of them to try and fix them. Luckily for Janet, the results for her own subject - French - and the other language subjects that she had responsibility for had never been anything less than at national average, so she was confident that anything he was about to say would only help her to get those subjects even further up the tree.

"We've been looking at the E-bacc..." he began, in a manner that told them all clearly that this was going to be a long, drawn-out discussion. "...and we think that it's probably about time that we started to focus the kids' minds on the subjects that we need them to really get the results in."

As he said the word "we" there was a short glance over to Mick, the head, who had clearly had a pre-meeting meeting with Gareth about this particular item.

"We're proposing to put the kids' targets and current predicted grades on a spreadsheet then blow it up onto A2 for a poster outside the dining room. The kids will be able to see where they are in the grand scheme of things. The hope is that it will motivate some of those who are underachieving to be a little more responsive to the extra revision sessions, and to the work that they do in their *Gradeboost* sessions."

Janet made herself tall in her seat. She was responsible for administering *Gradeboost*, after all, and anything that gave those kids more focus toward their results was good by her. Getting a 10% rise in A*-C in the cohort was one of her performance management targets, and she wanted to go and buy a new coffee machine now that her old one had started to go on the blink. Meeting her targets meant getting her pay progression, so this new spreadsheet sounded like a splendid idea.

Gareth passed around an A4 mock-up of what the display might look like, and used his tablet to buzz an image of the same up onto the whiteboard. It was the usual red, amber and green set-up and showed the pupils down one side, cross-referencing with their E-bacc subjects on the other.

There were motivational sticker images around the outside and this year's push slogan of 'Together Everyone Achieves More' was emblazoned across the top. The Trust had pushed the slogan across all of the schools in the chain from early in the year, and now it was starting to be used in everyday parlance throughout communications in the building. Janet made a mental note that she should add it to her email signature, should she ever leave this lengthy meeting and make it back to her office.

All seemed fine. The printing would be done on the industrial-sized laser printer they had over in engineering tomorrow morning, and the poster put up in time for lunch for the kids to see. The Year 10 version would follow the week after. All seemed fine.

Then Debbie piped up.

"Sorry, Gareth, I'm probably being slow but that doesn't seem like all the kids in year 11. There are at least fifty missing."

Janet looked at the clock. She wasn't just going to hit the traffic. She was going to sit firmly in it, stewing, cursing Debbie, and using all sorts of rude words that the her mother had taught her were pure evil. The meeting had already gone on twenty minutes longer than scheduled. How dare Debbie ask a question? Did she not have a home life? She couldn't remember if Debbie was married or not but, if she was, it couldn't have

94

been a happy marriage. Janet certainly didn't want to spend her time with someone who asked stupid questions at inopportune moments, causing everyone to stay behind well after the bell had gone.

"It's not all of Year 11. Just the E-bacc kids."

"So is there a separate sheet going up with all of them on it?"

Debbie knew the answer to this, but wasn't going to let her own knowledge on the matter get in the way of her making a fair point in front of everybody. Debbie was an E-bacc sceptic, and everybody knew it. As representative from Special Educational Needs, she spoke for those who were usually struggling to articulate for themselves. The forgotten few. Those on the margins of society. The thickie kids doing soft subjects. The E-bacc push was all about academic excellence and she was rarely consulted about the way it affected the children in her care.

"All pupils will still see the displays in their own subject areas about how they are progressing in individual courses," chirped up Mick, who had anticipated there being opposition to the idea in advance - hence his pre-meeting with Gareth. "This is to highlight to the whole school how important the E-bacc is to us all, and to give it some gravitas amongst the students."

Big up the E-bacc. That's all they had heard for the previous three years. Get them into languages, inspire them in humanities, steer them towards excellence in academia. For Janet, the head of MFL, this sounded like the mood music for an academic love affair that would develop into a long-lasting, healthy relationship. To Debbie, who taught Health and Social Care and mostly looked after the kids in sets four, five and six, it sounded like she was getting shafted.

"Has anyone thought about how this is going to make the children feel who haven't opted for the E-bacc courses?" continued Debbie, who had never been one for giving up on lost causes.

There was an audible groan from Janet, who then held her stomach as if this were due to a digestive issue rather than disdain for one of her touchy-feely lefty colleagues. She had a dislike for lefties in general, particularly teaching ones with their lapel badges, union posters and a view of the seventies as some golden era of education. Debbie Johnstone was one of those and was pushing all of Janet's buttons at exactly the wrong time.

Debbie knew the stomach excuse was bullshit, and threw Janet a confrontational look that she was in no mood for.

"Yes?"

"You seem to have a problem with what I was saying about how the kids will feel about the poster?"

"I didn't say anything."

"You didn't need to. The way you were rolling your eyes about like a Year 9 in the dinner queue told me everything."

Mick sat back. As the executive head who'd been charged with turning this school around in just six short months by the executive team at the Trust, he hadn't yet worked out the dynamics between the staff who'd been in it for the long haul.

Between them, Debbie and Janet had over thirty-five years educational experience and both, it seemed, were coming from ideologically opposite ends of the spectrum. Whoever won this round was likely give him a marker for the future, when it came to the larger battles of curriculum changes and bringing down the staffing bill. If nothing else, he'd learned one very important thing from fast track management - never take sides because you'll have to screw over all of them at some point in your career.

"We're having a discussion about attainment. This isn't a pastoral conversation."

Janet had been challenged and was now a long way from her early meeting slumber. She had never been one for sitting back and letting some jumped-up Trot tell her what to do. How did the kids *feel*? They were teenagers. It was a Thursday evening. They probably wouldn't be feeling anything! A significant number of them would either be on a PlayStation, drinking cheap cider or, more than likely, fast asleep.

Debbie knew what she wanted to say from the moment she saw this on the agenda and if it were to bring Janet bloody Murphy down a peg or two by her saying it now, then so be it.

"It is a pastoral conversation when you start marginalising the achievements of those who are not in this special group. What about all my kids who are doing HSC? There's only one of them on this list. If I were Hayley Matthews, I'd go away thinking, 'Well, they don't care what I get so why should I bother?'"

"Are you suggesting that we should have run it by Hayley first to see how she feels? Although quite how we'd manage that with her attendance record, I have no idea..."

There were a few smirks from the neutrals around the table. Hayley had been a poor example for Debbie to pull out of the hat. There had been more sightings of Sasquatch around the school in the last few months than there had been of Hayley Matthews. Debbie wanted to justify her example by telling them how Hayley was a young carer and that she couldn't physically get into school while looking after her Mum, but she knew it was off-point and would have given Janet an excuse to scoff some more.

"I just don't understand why we would celebrate the achievements of one group of kids but not the others."

"This isn't about celebrating achievement. It's about giving them a kick up the backside. Look at all those kids on ambers or reds. If it stays that way in August then we all might as well pack up and go home. We'll be forced into special measures and the Year 11s whose feelings you're worrying about will be lining up in the dole queue, probably with some of us standing behind them."

There was a hush. Even Mick wasn't sure how to intervene. Everyone round the table knew it was true, despite Janet having the tact and subtlety of a toddler with a chainsaw. If they didn't turn the school results round before the summer term, their heads would be on the block and the school would be plunged even further into chaos. It didn't matter if Debbie's Health & Social Care group aced the exam, got 100% A*-C, and ran through the streets singing about it at the top of their voices. If the percentage of kids getting the E-bacc didn't go up, then the school would deemed to be coasting. Or, worse, identified for closure.

Mick realised that it was time to bring things back into order.

"I think what Janet is trying to say here, Debbie, is that we have to prioritise and promote the E-bacc if we are going to get the school onto an improvement footing. That's in the best interests of those pupils who are not on the E-bacc programme, too, as we don't want to find ourselves constantly under scrutiny from the Trust and the DFE."

"And what do we do about inspiring the kids doing non E-bacc subjects?"

Debbie hadn't been placated.

"Half those subjects won't even be on the curriculum in five years. We're much better off looking at the longer term."

Janet wasn't going to let Red Deb have last word.

"How can you say that when one of the subjects you are responsible for is probably in the firing line? You're supposed to stick up for the departments you're representing!"

"If you are referring to Drama, then we're already looking at ways that it can contribute to the curriculum in other ways than it currently does. Jim knows we can't keep on promoting a subject that doesn't help the school results more positively."

There. She'd said it. She looked over to Mick for backing. She got nothing in return but she took his silence as an implicit agreement that it was a waste of time backing a subject that wasn't going to count a jot in the figures from now on.

Debbie was dumbstruck. No one had dared to threaten another subject with the axe before, and she knew full well that she was one of those 'outside the club'. It was all very well standing up for your political principles, but she had one daughter in her second year at uni and another getting married in the autumn. If Drama could be under threat, it was only a matter of time before Health & Social Care was next in the chopping queue.

Mick brought matters back to order.

"I think we're getting a bit off-track. We'll see how that one develops when the mock results come in, I think. Now, we're getting a bit behind so let's look at agenda item number five. Sports day. Are we going to have one?"

Janet raised her head to catch Debbie's eye. The stare that greeted her was one that Jack Nicholson would have been proud of.

The gloves were well and truly off.

Chapter Nine

Ancient Grudge Breaks to New Mutiny

By the time November arrived, the battle lines had been very clearly drawn. Drama was under threat unless it started to play ball and toe the party line.

To his credit, and despite not having an unbroken night's sleep in over two months, Jim had provided everything that Janet had required of him with little fuss since he'd got wind from Debbie that the axe man was sharpening his blade. Statistics had been analysed, action plans written, and lesson plans printed in triplicate then passed to Janet and Mick, as requested. The annual performance management meeting had come and gone, with Jim fully understanding why his pay progression had been delayed until GCSE results were able to show any signs of achieving at least parity with national averages. It was tough but (apparently) fair, and everyone agreed (publicly, anyway) that this would be the way to get the very best outcome for the pupils.

From the outside, the Drama department was beginning to deliver everything that was being asked of it but, reading between the lines, it was still very much in the firing-line and poised for the chop at any given second. Jim knew he had to be constantly on the ball if he were to get away with keeping his job at the end of the year.

The trees outside the building were now in an advanced stage of shedding their leaves, and it was clear by the dishevelled look of all concerned on this particular Thursday afternoon that the traditional onslaught of wet, windy weather had well and truly parked itself up for the duration in Central Lancashire. It was tiring just getting to Jim's Drama classroom and it was no wonder that nobody in it looked in the mood to be creative on command. Having Janet parked up in the corner 'informally' observing Jim's and the pupils' every move gave the afternoon an added sense of tension, meaning that Jim found himself bound to overcompensate. He was supercharged with energy, over prepared, and ready to take on his most difficult class of all.

8B.

They were twenty-five minutes into the observation lesson and Jim got the distinct impression from Janet's total lack of emotive feedback that, despite the session running smoothly so far with little in the way of calamitous incidents, things were not going well. She had been silent throughout, only breaking her silence to complete an interrogation of the students working at the far end of the room about their understanding of the lesson objectives. Whilst they were rehearsing, she subtly (in her mind, anyway) went to ask them pointed questions about what they were learning today, how they thought they were making progression in Drama, and what they thought would make their work even better.

She had interrupted almost every group, reducing their concentration on the activity and bamboozling them with questions that were irrelevant to what they had been tasked with doing - that being to recreate the scene where Tybalt, Juliet's cousin, is killed by Romeo who flees the scene, fearing for his own life. It was high drama and a tough job for any thirteen-year-old to get to grips with at the best of times. The last thing it needed was their French teacher (who they clearly didn't like

102

very much) asking them questions that had nothing to do with the task that they'd been given.

Now they were sharing their work with the rest of the circle, looking underprepared and uncharacteristically nervous. A group of four boys were first up, identified in Jim's preplanning as being those at the mid-section of the achievement spectrum. They weren't as breathtaking as Laurence Olivier but they weren't as wooden as Nicolas Cage, either. They were middle-of-the-road lads. Good kids. Triers.

"Fantastic work! Brilliant effort, lads! Give them a big clap!"

Janet got up from her chair and sharpened her pencil.

Jim could feel himself being over-zealous to try to rebuild a bit of atmosphere in the room. Under the circumstances, he felt it entirely necessary. 8B gave a ripple of applause that wouldn't have been out of place at a low-ranking golf event. It was polite enough, but said more about the effectiveness of the drama they had witnessed than any attainment mark Jim could give them as their teacher. Everyone agreed. It was alright. I suppose.

Except for Ethan. Ethan didn't agree with everyone. Ethan hated it.

"Ethan, what do we do when someone performs for us?"

Ethan stared. Not a cute stare like Paddington might give you. This was more of a psycho-killer look, confirming Jim's earlier suspicions that he was simply babysitting this particular lad before Broadmoor was able to take him on in later life.

"Ethan?"

A single, solitary clap followed. No one said anything. No one made a fuss. No one wanted to get stabbed. Janet put her pencil down on the table, and watched.

"Okay, moving on then! Let's evaluate what we've seen in the boys' performance, shall we? How did James and Imran use their facial expressions to show how Tybalt is feeling about Romeo?" The elephant in the room was not going to get in the way of Jim having a good lesson today.

Silence.

Ask a specific kid. Not Ben again Tovey, you can't just keep going to him, especially as he hasn't got Steph here to help him out today. Choose someone new....

"Grace? What do you think? What sort of facial expression would you expect to see from Tybalt at the start of this scene?"

More silence. Then enlightenment.

"He's angry."

"But why?"

Jim knew he had to get the kids to develop their answers a little bit more if he was going to get through this observation alive. One or two-word responses weren't going cut the mustard. Grace had been better than this when he'd thrown a few pre-emptive questions out to the class last week. Why the silence now?

"Come on, Grace. Why is Tybalt feeling so angry towards Romeo?"

"I wasn't in last lesson. I was at the dentist."

Grace didn't like Drama. He kept making you talk in front of everyone and she hated her voice. It sounded all croaky and the boys started whispering to each other every time she gave an answer. Plus, she hated Mrs Murphy being there because she was the same when they were in French - trying to make her talk in front of the class all the time. She hoped he'd hurry up and pick on someone else. But the questions kept coming.

"No, you weren't. But do you at least remember when you read the play with Miss Davies in English last year? Something happened at Juliet's party? Do you remember what it was? Can anybody help Grace out a bit?"

Jim knew that he was beginning to sound a bit desperate… but he was sure that once he got them on a roll, the free-flowing discussion about the nature of Tybalt's rage and its translation into performance during Act 3 of Shakespeare's great tragedy would result in a diamond mine of speaking and listening marks. He might also get that moon on a stick he'd requested for his birthday. If he could just get one of them to open up for a sentence or two, they'd be off. Unfortunately for Jim, it was Ethan who decided to take up the challenge.

"He's pissed off with Romeo after he crashed Juliet's party."

Jim's shoulders dropped. SLT had put a zero-tolerance order on bad language this term and he was going to have to follow the escalation plan he'd been given last week after the INSET day. Wonderful. In an observation, too.

He hated writing referrals and he hated dishing out detentions even more. It was such a waste of his and the kids' time. It wasn't going to cure Ethan's potty mouth and would just mean that Jim was home half an hour later on Wednesday, when he was supposed to be picking up Danny from Katie's mum's. Let's face it; he wasn't relishing the idea of spending some one-on-one time with Ethan either, as he wasn't entirely sure he'd see the other side of it alive.

Jim considered for a moment whether he might have a case for saying he'd misheard what, in fact, he had heard very clearly. Was there any way he could get away with turning a blind eye? He took a quick glimpse round the room and over to Janet, who was now using her freshly-tapered pencil to scribble away on her observation sheet. It was also written all over the kids' faces. "You heard him. Now you've got to deal with it, Buster." Thanks, kids. Love you, too.

"Ethan. Could you not use language like that, please?"

"Well, he is. I'd be pissed off if someone who hadn't been invited turned up at my house and started getting off with my cousin."

Damn. He'd repeated it. Now it really needed writing up and the lesson was heading down a very dark alley.

"Ethan, come and sit over here next to my desk, please, while we try to evaluate the piece."

Escalation staircases and damage-limitation measures buzzed through Jim's head as he glanced at the clock. They only had ten minutes left until the end and he could still get to his plenary if he nipped this one in the bud by ploughing on. He repeated his instruction for Lancashire's answer to *The Omen* to shift seats, but Ethan wasn't playing ball. He just stared. Jim knew the start of a sit-in protest when he saw one. He wasn't going to shift for Jim. He wasn't going to shift for anyone.

No one moved. The word 'awkward' popped into many of the children's heads, and would be prevalent in most of their Facebook statuses when they reported on the incident when they got home.

Was it possible to hear someone smiling? Jim was sure that he could hear Janet's grin ringing in his ears as she scribbled away at her desk.

"He was like this in Maths, sir. He swore at the supply teacher."

Jenny, who loved moments like this where she could demonstrate her civil duty by ratting on whoever she could, decided that this was an appropriate time to bring up Ethan's previous misdemeanours during period four, directly before lunch.

"He got put next door into Mr Khan's room".

The word smug was invented for moments like these.

"Will you just shut the fuck up, you fat dog!"

One comment from Jenny was enough to put Ethan straight into the red zone. He wasn't going to take it from a suck-up like her, even if it did mean digging a hole further for himself and plunging poor old Tovey into a living hell. He knew Tovey was being watched for some reason or another by that French teacher who sometimes did their assemblies, but he wasn't going let Jenny make him out to be some sort of criminal just because he'd got done for talking in Maths this morning.

"Outside, please, Ethan."

Jim acted quickly. He needed to defuse this before it descended into a full-blown shouting match in front of Janet. Surprisingly, Ethan got straight out of his seat and headed for the door - but not before he managed to get his parting shot away.

"This class is thick anyway. They all sit here pretending not to know anything when we already learned why Tybalt hated Romeo in English last year. Tybalt's annoyed because the families are feuding and Romeo's made his uncle look stupid. Not that you'd have guessed from the gormless face that James put on when he was supposed to be acting. He can't act for toffee. And if you'd answer the fucking question, Grace, then we could have told him that and moved on to something more interesting. And, Imran, you need to speak up cos we can't hear you when you're talking. There's no point in acting if no-one can hear it."

Ethan took a breath and seemed to falter a little, showing the faintest of tears in his menacing twelve-year-old eyes and giving Jim a chance to finally interject.

"Can you wait outside please Ethan?" Jim repeated calmly.

"Yeah. Sorry, sir"

Ethan walked out, but didn't wait behind as asked. He walked straight down to the all-weather pitch and ducked under the fence to go to his grandma's.

Jim spent his free lesson during the final period of the day writing up the behaviour referral form and passed it straight to Janet for immediate follow-up. It was out of his hands now, and Ethan would need to have a home/school liaison meeting before he could come back onto a full timetable. The observation lesson would go down on his teaching record, and would trigger Jim getting the third-degree about his classroom management from Janet and probably Mick for many weeks to come.

At the end of the school day, Janet tried to phone the number listed on the school system for Ethan's home but didn't get an answer. This shouldn't have been surprising, as Ethan's mum had had her parole turned down just a week before.

She wasn't going to be home for at least another six months.

Lesson Observation

Summary Sheet

LANCASHIRE

ACADEMY

Teacher: Jim Tovey	Observer: Janet Murphy	Date and time: Thu Nov 16th, Period 5
Year group & ability: 8 (English Set 2)	Subject: Drama	No. of pupils: 27 (11M, 16F)

Support staff or teaching assistants:
None present - Stephanie Govin rostered on with class to act as support but required to administer support in Year 10 exam invigilation so not present.

Focus: Understanding the themes of anger and revenge in Shakespeare's Romeo & Juliet	Context: Practical lesson - 7th of 9 in unit. Pupils recreating a version of Act 3 Scene 1 from the Shakespeare play.

Summary of lesson:

Children arrived slowly after lunch, lining up outside the drama room. JT ushered them into the room quickly. No uniform check done. Two pupils not wearing blazers. A number were chewing. One boy tripping up others as they entered went unnoticed. Lesson aims displayed clearly on board as pupils entered. Register taken quickly, but with children being asked to answer in Italian accents (relevance to lesson?)

Starter activity completed quickly - game of wink murder followed by discussion of how to die realistically. Some boys acting very silly, laughing and joking during the game. Again, unsure of relevance to lesson aims?

Core - Scene reintroduced from previous lesson, although some pupils seemed unsure about the reason for rehearsing when questioned. Most pupils said they enjoyed the lesson, but few were clear as to their current target levels. At the performance part of the lesson, one group of boys was able to share their work. Evaluation from the rest of the class showed little depth of understanding.

Swearing incident from one of the boys in the audience. JT slow to react and was unable to follow the escalation staircase effectively. Situation quickly descended into a shouting match between pupils. Offending pupil sent outside the room but walked away from the building instead.

JT attempted to regain class focus but children seemed unwilling to participate further. One pupil at the back attempting to text on phone while JT was questioning pupils at the front. (I confiscated phone at the end)

Plenary not delivered.

Key strengths

Pupils enjoyed starter activity

Agreed areas for development

Uniform & chewing policies need enforcing, numeracy and/or literacy aims need to be included into future lessons, behaviour management requires improvement, lesson tasks should be focused on achievement. Pupil assessment needs development.

Overall grading

Lesson does not meet the relevant teaching standards - Category 4 - Inadequate

Chapter Ten

A Christmas Cracker

"Back pain. Back to back. Back side. Back side? What? Back in the USSR! BACK IN THE USSR!"

"Ten seconds!"

Steph was into this in a big way. Christmas had come around, and this was her 'Bridget Jones at the lawyers' quiz' moment. Her own chance to shine in front of her colleagues and friends and show them that, despite her social tag of 'the ditsy one', she did indeed have a skills set. Parlour games had been a staple at home since she was tiny, and charades was her specialist subject.

Being one of six children who had four sets of aunts and uncles (all with their own broods too) had given her a lot of experience when it came to family parties. The TV was rarely on at these gatherings. There were too many people about and too many games to play. Want a tail pinned on a donkey? Steph's your girl. Have an urge to see human beings throwing themselves shamelessly to the floor when the music stops? Steph's your first port of call. Christmas parties really were her thing.

This evening was also the first time in her three months of working at Lancashire Academy that she'd felt as if she were on the same level as the others on her table. All too often, she felt like she was 'just the Support Assistant' or that her lack of a teaching degree somehow made her inferior to those who had gone off to university to learn the ancient craft of standing up in front of people and talking. It wasn't just that her teacher colleagues mostly earned three times her starting salary for doing their respective jobs - after all, their job was undeniably more stressful than hers and the hours they put in utterly sucked. She wasn't going to begrudge them that. But the thing that really got to Steph was the way that some (a minority but a significant number, nonetheless) really looked down their noses at the Support Assistants who were attached to their classes. The ones she was sat with tonight were some of the nicer ones but there were others, noticeably some of the younger teachers, who acted like they (a) owned the place and (b) were a class above everyone else - especially the SAs.

She remembered how, in an early meeting, she'd heard a teacher being told that the Support Assistants were the most expensive resource in the classroom and they should always be used to their best ability. She understood what they were trying to get at, but she still didn't really like the idea that she had the same social status as an overhead projector.

They weren't going to beat her at charades though. Tonight she was on fire.

"Back to the Future!"

A rapturous round of applause for the Queen of the Party. Stephanie Govin, take your bow.

"Thank you! Thank you! In your face, PE!"

The fighting talk had started before the game had even begun, but now was definitely the time for an upgrade to trash talking. After the debacle of Denise clearly mouthing the words of the answer to Geoff in the last round, the gloves had definitely come off. How she thought she could get away with silently whispering 'New York, New York' to her team and nobody else noticing was quite unbelievable.

This section of the Christmas gathering had been divided into two teams. PE had three staff on the table and the arts lot matched them with Elizabeta from Music, Jim from Drama and some Art teacher whose name Steph hadn't managed to learn yet. PE had Geoff, Denise and Alan (that dishy Australian guy) on their team. As the two SAs on the table, Steph and Safeerah split themselves down the middle and the challenge was laid down. With crackers pulled, they were now adorned with stupid hats, fuelled by cheap Prosecco, and destined for battle.

Being an event involving the PE department, and with Geoff never quite being able to put to one side his mantle of 'glorious leader', there had been an insistence that there was to be a competitive element even to cracker-pulling. Within minutes, teams had been formed, house rules established and scoring systems devised. Luckily, there had been a little Argos pen in one of the crackers, so Geoff had even sketched out a rudimentary scoreboard on a paper napkin. If Preston were ever to be awarded the Olympics, Geoff would inevitably find himself on the Steering Committee.

The score was now 3-2 to Steph's arts team (nobody said it, but she had clearly risen to the challenge of being unofficial team captain against Geoff's Titans of PE) and they had one charade each left. She was feeling confident after getting the last two right, and now she had her trump card to play. Step forward the Drama teacher. The master of mime. A giant in the world of gestures. This would go down as a stunning victory.

Jim hated charades. If there was ever a parlour game that could be classified as a busman's holiday, this was most definitely it. He spent his entire working day gesticulating and teaching people how to use expression effectively when broadcasting to a live audience. Tonight (as with every other day during the holiday period) he wanted a break. Looking at the way Steph was pumped up, however, he wasn't going to get one.

"Go on, Jimbo! Bring it home!"

There was a drumroll on the table, making the glasses shake and causing at least half the room to turn and pay attention - despite the overly loud PA system blasting out "All I Want for Christmas is You" in a vain attempt to festivise the cheap, slightly undercooked meal they had been served. Jim wondered if Mariah Carey was forced to play charades at Christmas. Probably not. Maybe making millions from four minutes of Jingly Bells and a video in a short Santa skirt would be Jim's ticket to avoid this sorry routine in the future. In the meantime, he stood before his team, tiny cracker ticket in hand.

Relative quiet descended around the table as Alan shouted, "Go!" and simultaneously started the stopwatch on his phone. (Geoff had insisted on a time limit of a minute per mime to crank up the tension even further). Jim turned over his piece of paper and looked at his team, who were staring at him in a way that no one on the planet would ever describe as comfortable. There were army experts working on roadside bombs in the Middle East who would be feeling less pressure than this. Five seconds had already passed and he hadn't even got past the 'how the bloody hell am I going to do this?' stage in his head.

Those Magnificent Men in Their Flying Machines

Seven words. His team had drunk nearly two bottles of Prosecco and had to count twice, despite him holding up an accurate number of fingers.

First word. Impossible to do. Second word. Impossible to do. Third word. Point at all the men on the table.

"Men!"

Go, Steph. Twenty-five seconds gone already.

Sixth word. Do a stupid flying gesture.

"Airplane! Aeroplane! Air Force One! Birds! Birds of a feather!"

Shut up, Elizabeta. You're useless at this and you're wasting time. The supply Art teacher (whose name, it transpired, no one actually knew) just sat quietly watching. This version of Pictionary without pictures was not interesting him in the least. He was only here for the cheap table wine.

"Flying!"

Thank you, Steph. Jim didn't know if charades could ever be entered as a specialist subject in Mastermind, but he'd tune in to watch this girl give it a go.

"Twenty seconds left!"

Machine? How do you mime machine? The closest he could even think of was a robot. But that would send them miles off track.

"Fifteen seconds!"

Jim looked around the team. Elizabeta was bemused. Art guy was pouring himself another glass of red. Steph looked like she was going to explode if he didn't speak soon.

"Just do something! Anything!"

It was the robot or bust. Like every kid in the eighties, or your dad when he got on the dance floor at a wedding, Jim attempted the world's worst impression of a machine that he could manage.

"Robot! Peter Crouch! Metal Mickey! Terminator! Terminator Two! Terminator Three..."

Elizabeta continued her run of being useless.

"Machine!"

How the hell did you get that, Steph? That was nothing like a machine. I mean, he got the jerky movements right and made his face pretty emotionless as he got himself into the role but...

"Time up."

"Those Magnificent Men in Their Flying Machines"

The palpable disappointment around the table was felt throughout the room. Steph was heartbroken. Now it was 3-3 and PE were bound to win.

"Why did you skip the second word? I'd have got it from that."

116

Jim couldn't believe how seriously Steph was taking this.

"Seriously? Magnificent? You'd have got that? How do you mime that?"

The master demonstrated.

Second word: Four syllables. First syllable. She mimed reading a magazine as if at the hairdressers. Shorter. Mag. OK. Second syllable. Sounds like...sniff.

"I'd have got the full word from magnif, then it was either your film or Magnificent Seven."

Jim had to hand it to her. She had a special skill.

Geoff, fuelled by the copious amounts of premium lager he'd preloaded before they hadn't even got to the venue, opened up his mouth.

"Sack the Drama teacher! Inadequate! Give him a four!"

Jim's face fell through the floor. He didn't sit back down in his seat. He quickly excused himself and took some time out in the toilet.

Alan stared at his head of department. There's no way that he could have known but, even so, did he always have to be so damn bullish about people? Did he not realise that sometimes things might run just that tiny bit easier if he'd just keep his mouth shut?

"What? It was a bit of banter? Jimmy knows I'm only kidding."

117

Steph glanced at Janet who, from an adjacent table had been keeping a quiet eye on Jim's table throughout the whole process. She caught Steph's eye but didn't react, choosing instead to take another sip of her third gin and tonic, making the inexperienced Support Assistant the one to blink first. Steph quietly explained the situation to the rest of the table. Janet couldn't help but raise a tiny smile.

Fifteen minutes later, Jim had not returned. Alan knew that he hadn't left the building, but dessert had now been and gone without Jim in attendance. Geoff should, by rights, be the one making the apology to him but that didn't fit with his own plans for the Christmas party. His primary reason for being here was to buy drinks for the more accessible members of SLT and secure some funding for sorting the drainage out down on the rugby pitch on the bottom field at the school. He had no time to counsel an over-emotional arts teacher. It was left to Alan to attend.

"Jim? You in there, mate?"

The cubicle door swung back and Jim was out like a shot, full of pretence and stage smiles. He'd have got away with it, if weren't for the fact that tears had clearly been streaming down his face. That, and the fact that his eyes were as red as the cracker hat that he'd failed to remove.

"I'm fine. Honestly."

"Bollocks are you fine. Look, Geoff didn't know about your obs last week. He wasn't making any kind of dig. I'm sure when he sees you he'll..."

Jim wasn't going to let him go on. The last thing he wanted right now was to have some non-existent battle with Geoff about the so-called 'banter' that he clung so preciously to as a social habit. Jim didn't really understand why, in recent times, putting people down and making them feel bad had been given this new title (after all, it used to be called just plain bullying) but right now there were so many bigger things for him to worry about.

"I told you. I'm fine. I didn't come out here because of what Geoff said. Well, not entirely. I just had a bit of a wobble and a panic. I've got strategies to deal with it now. Just needed a few minutes."

Alan knew about Jim's 'strategies'. Breathing exercises, meditating, that sort of thing. He'd never really suffered from depression himself, not that he knew of, but had seen plenty of people - particularly blokes back home - taking the alternative route of bottling it all up and pushing on through. It never ended prettily. Jim had already mentioned that he'd been to a fair bit of counselling in the past and knew how to make it through a flashpoint like this one, but it was the bigger mess that Alan was worried about.

"Have you sorted out about getting another observation done?"

Jim didn't cry again, but wanted to. That word had become a trigger that made him want to run for the hills, with every second of his day haunted by it. That, and the number four. The number which told him he was inadequate. The one that told him he wasn't up to scratch. The one that told him he wasn't going to pay the mortgage next month and that they wouldn't have food and clothes for Danny. And what would Katie say?

And how would he tell his Mum if he wasn't teaching anymore. And…

Alan put a hand on Jim's shoulder to try and steady him. He couldn't remember how much of the table wine Jim had downed during the main course but he was certain that, right now, Jim was looking like he might keel over at any minute. Despite his protestations, Jim was not a man who was in a good way. He took a deep breath and finally answered Alan's question.

"She won't let me re-do the lesson before Christmas. Says it will get in the way of the special assemblies and it won't be a true reflection of my teaching."

"Oh, but one lesson with a set of Year 8s from hell who everyone knows are arseholes is? Can you not get someone else to come in and have a look?"

"Yeah. They have to now. She'll be bringing in someone else from SLT as she can't escalate it if she hasn't at least had a second opinion. Don't worry. I've already been through all this with Elaine. I went to see her straight after. Safeerah looked after her year 7s for the last ten minutes of her lesson and she took me through it all in the English office."

Alan just nodded. He'd had little contact with the bullish English teacher who was also both his and Jim's union rep, but he knew if she was involved this was going to be a ding-dong of a spectacle. She was old-school and knew their rights as teachers, inside-out and back-to-front. Jim was in good hands with Elaine.

"I guess I'll just have to try and plan something amazing over Christmas and sort it out when we get back."

He went to leave, thinking that the conversation was over, so was surprised when a rough, slightly hairy Australian hand prevented him from doing so.

"You bloody won't. This is your first Christmas as a dad. You're going to go home and forget all this shit, and certainly about that bloody woman out there. You had a crap lesson. Some French teacher doesn't like your style. So what? The sky hasn't fallen down yet and you have so many more important things to stress over. You getting anymore sleep?"

"Better. He's managing two or three hours now."

"Right. So things are not all shit. Do me a favour and focus on the stuff you really need to. You're brilliant at your job. I talked to some of the guys in P.E. They told me how cool that show was that you did last year. They'd be nuts to try and push you out."

Jim didn't realise that people in other departments would still be discussing what they had done with 'Fiddler' last year, and the positive review made him smile just a little. It reminded him of a moment where things didn't feel quite so apocalyptic.

"Now, are you coming to have a beer?"

"I'm going to have to. I agreed to get a cab back over to our end with Steph and Safeerah, and it doesn't look like the party queen is going to be leaving any time soon."

"Yeah, about that. Steph... Is she available, do you know?"

Oh no.

"Yes, she's single. But drop what you're thinking as I'm not going to pay an extra tenner for my cab fare just because you turned on the 'Mr Lover Lover' routine."

Two manly slaps on the back later and all seemed better, for now.

The boys returned to the party. Pints would be pulled and Shakin' Stevens songs sung on karaoke. Geoff offered a hand of apology and Alan flirted outrageously with Steph, who was still on cloud nine from pulling a surprise victory out of the bag with the remaining charades players. Janet would make her excuses early to go and be miserable at home, allowing Jim to let himself get caught up in a room which didn't contain any of his usual day-to-day worries.

He knew it was only temporary but, at the same time, it felt very much like he was still attached to a team. He didn't know if it was a winning team yet, but it certainly felt better than crying in a toilet cubicle on your own.

Chapter Eleven

A Much Needed Break

You are in loco parentis. You must care for them as any reasonable parent would. That was what Jim had been told during his training year. Care for them. Nurture them. Love the children like they were your own.

Well, his own had given him a cold. A horrible, runny 'why is there so much gunk in my sinus?' cold. A cold that came with pressure. A stinging, drilling pressure that that had left him looking like a grumpy version of Mole from *Wind in the Willows*, and made him flinch every time a loud noise or bright light was within thirty yards. Right now, if he got hold of one of the little germ-infested buggers he'd throttle them.

Boy, did his head hurt. In a really, really annoying way. Annoying mostly because the physical symptoms alone didn't seem obvious enough to those around him to allow him to stay in bed. Katie had taken his temperature and it was barely up. Not even enough (in her opinion, anyway) to be considered Man Flu. However, there was no denying it from his point of view. The niggling pain just below the right hand side of his temple was continuously boring its way into the back of his eye. If it didn't stop soon, he was sure it would become some kind of tumour. In fact, he may be having a slow-burning aneurysm right now. Then she'd be sorry for doubting him.

Why was it that the only time he ever got ill was during the holidays? He'd dragged himself through the whole term where, fair enough, he felt run down by the end of only the second week. But that was only to be expected, with all the shenanigans at work and becoming a father for the first time. Now he'd actually got a prolonged break, his body had turned on him and he felt as if he didn't want to even drag himself out of bed.

Christmas Day had come and gone, and they were all now in no man's land - that time of year when days lose their usual meanings - so being dosed up on ibuprofen simply compounded Jim's stupor. What day was today? Three days after Christmas. A regular sense of time had gone out of the window along with his health and as he stood in the kitchen, trying not to look at the pile of unmarked Year 11 coursework in the dining room, he realised just how much he was dreading going back in the New Year to start it all over again. He tried to figure out exactly how long he had left to recover physically before the stress-and-pressure cycle of going to work began all over again.

Eight days to mark fifteen pieces of completed work. The unfinished pieces would be dealt with on the first morning back, with a break-time detention for the six pupils who thought writing one paragraph of evaluation was going to cut the mustard. If he started tomorrow, and did two a day, he'd still be okay. Tomorrow would be a better day for work. Yes, tomorrow. Right now, he had to try and reclaim the inner workings of his cranium before they exploded and made a mess over his already grubby kitchen, which still contained the unwashed pots and pans from last night's feast of mash, sprouts and cold turkey. The smell was not helping the nausea, but there was no way he could tackle the dishes right now.

Sandra, his loving but very high-maintenance mother, came into the room clattering the washing basket onto the kitchen floor. Jim woke from his stare into the middle distance. She was 'helping' in the best way that she knew how. He knew that his mum always meant well and that her being around for the festive season was the best thing that could happen for all of them at that moment. That was very clear. Sandra needed company to keep her on the road to sobriety over the tempting Christmas period. Jim and Katie needed adult help to ease the stress of two months without sleep.

Right now, however, as he tried to focus his weary, stinging eyes away from the winter sunshine that was bursting through the window, the last thing he wanted was Central Lancashire's answer to Mrs Doubtfire fussing around and doing her best to 'perk him up'.

As she loaded the machine with vomit-encrusted sheets and bodysuits (Danny had developed a habit in the last two weeks of puking as soon as he was laid horizontal) Jim decided that the help she was about to offer may well be the straw that made the camel's head explode. Telling her what to do and when to do it had never really been Jim's strong suit, but he knew that he'd rather hit himself repeatedly in the face with a hammer before he'd allow her to switch on the washing machine.

"Mum, leave the washing for a bit. Or put it on a timer, will you? My head is killing me."

Nice try.

"It's only a few bits. They won't take long."

It was almost as if he hadn't spoken at all. Sandra was already onto pouring detergent into the drawer (the wrong part of the drawer, too - they never used the pre-wash section) and had no intention of taking domestic advice from her son. As much as Jim had been the primary carer in their relationship since his teens, Sandra was very much of the opinion that she was the mother here. And what she said went. Right now, the washing needed doing and, if he had a problem with that, there were other rooms in the house for him to whine in.

"Seriously, mum. The pain's been getting much worse since Boxing Day. Can you leave it?"

Click. Whirr. Ouch.

"It's only a quick cycle. It'll be on for half an hour. Go and have a lie down for a bit. I'll see to Danny if he wakes up."

Jim squinted disapproval at his mother in a way that would be best described as 'contained'. She had become both impossible and stubborn in her later years, doing things to 'help' that only ever led to him being left tenser than if she hadn't bothered in the first place. Whether it be from the zealous way that she insisted on ironing ever fabric item in the house (including items such tea towels, pillow cases and socks), or the way that she had a knack of making home-cooked food that was utterly devoid of taste and flavour, Sandra's brand of domestic bliss was more than enough of a reason for a judge to be lenient, should Jim's patience finally snap.

"Mum, please can you turn it off? My head…"

"I've told you. Go upstairs and have a lie down. This is what I thought I was staying with you for. To help."

No, mother. You're staying here because last year when you were on your own, you ended up getting so lonely that, in the middle of February, we were still dealing with the consequences of you almost falling off the wagon and having a mini-breakdown.

Jim didn't say it out loud, but the words hung in the air above his head for some time after, like a thought bubble in a cartoon strip. He kept them there because, as far as he knew, Sandra was still on shaky ground nearly ten months later. He did wish, though, that she would sometimes realise how much extra brain space she was taking up in his broken and soon-to-explode head.

"I can't go and lie down. I already promised Katie that she could have some time today, and she's fast asleep. You heard Danny last night. Four times she had to get up and feed him. It's only fair that I do the day shift."

"But you aren't doing the day shift, are you? You're sitting here moaning that you've got some life-threatening brain condition that apparently only you have ever had. Now either go and lie down on the sofa, or grab a tea towel. I'm getting this place cleaned up."

This was going beyond stubbornness. It was almost...he didn't dare say it...self confidence. Not since his dad had died had Jim ever witness his mother actually get to grips with a situation in a manner that you would usually see from a regular human being. Normally, if people around her were stressed or worried, she would internalise their stress and get in a complete flap. Years of sending her to groups and counselling sessions had taught Jim enough about his mum's fragile psyche to know that her current behaviour was a little out of the ordinary.

As if to stop him wasting more time deconstructing her life in his head, Sandra noisily dumped the pans that were lined with dried potato into the sink, and started to fill it with water. There was no attempt to be subtle or to leave Jim in peace. Was she being vindictive? That was unlike her. His mum was a lot of things but nasty was never one of them. Just as he was considering what on earth had happened to make her so loud, upbeat and organised, he got a tea towel in his face.

"Get up off your bum and dry these pots."

It seemed like ages since they'd done such a menial task as doing the washing up together. It took Jim way back to holiday times when he was small, before Sandra had her first breakdown and while his father was still alive. Christmas Day always used to be a routine family affair, with his mum sitting with her own mother in front of the TV, both ending up boozing and snoozing their way through the rest of the day in the living room. Meanwhile, Jim and his dad would be out in the kitchen, cleaning up the remnants of dinner and telling cracker jokes until they just weren't funny anymore (but, of course, they never had been). To a ten-year-old boy, the combination of bubbly water, bonding with your dad, and the sense of doing something that usually only the grown-ups do, was fantastic.

Now that he was doing that same job with Sandra, a tear was forming in his eye, and it moved from a trickle to stream within a few moments. He hated this. The uncontrollable crying was something he could live without. It's really hard to get through day-to-day tasks when you're busy wiping your eyes, and this was the second time in a month that he'd broken down in front of someone else. And this time, it had been caused by something as inconsequential as some dirty dishes.

In all the years he'd been walking (and, more lately, stumbling) over the earth, he realised that he'd never once stood at a sink anywhere doing the washing up with his Mum. It was a stupid thing to make him cry. An event that should have no bearing on life whatsoever. But it did. Just as on results day while he was on holiday, Jim also found himself blubbing helplessly into the arms of a caring woman. This time it was his mother. But he didn't care. He was sick of fighting it.

As Jim tried to explain to Sandra why the waterworks had appeared, he revealed as much to himself about the stress he was under as he did to his Mum. On the face of it, he was upset because of the Christmas thing. Dad's accident had been at the end of November and he remembered clearly having to skip the school Christmas play to go to the funeral the week after. Since then, festivities had always been tinged with a slight hint of sadness, no matter how much tinsel was put up.

This year was much worse, though, and he felt like he had the weight of the whole world on his shoulders. No matter how much he tried to forget school and Janet and Ethan and Year 8 and results and his observation and the e-bacc and all the paperwork, they kept piling up in his thoughts. It was relentless. The lack of sleep was just compounding the stress, giving him the added fun of thinking (while he was grappling with Danny, who steadfastly refused to sleep in anything that even resembled a pattern) about whether kids like Sadie Masterson had a hope in hell of passing their GCSE.

Jim was very much back on the edge. Just as he had been while they were away on holiday in the summer, high up on that waterslide, he started to consider if he was really cut out for all this. His colleagues seemed to absorb the stress, lap it up and press on. He thought about Andrea, the Head of History, who had come over to him just before they broke up to ask him about coming out on a trip with her Year 9s. She seemed so utterly together wherever she was in school. It seemed as if she could teach, mark, plan, and belt out a song and dance number, yet still walk around the place looking immaculate and full of boundless energy.

Since Janet had taken over both Drama and History in September, Jim had heard nothing but praise for Andrea. Like a younger brother whose sister who'd already aced the system, Jim felt as if he was always being compared.

'Why can't you be more like History? Their schemes of work are already differentiated into three levels of ability, as you can see in their immaculate workbooks. AND they've tidied their room...'

Sandra listened to ten minutes of teacher talk before she decided to intervene. It wasn't that she didn't care, but she just simply didn't follow some of the things he was talking about. She didn't know what an SLT was (but it sounded horrible). And as for the kids he was teaching, Sandra was glad that she wouldn't get the chance to get a hold of one of the little scrotes or she'd have ripped their head off. Action had to be taken.

"Is this the marking you have to do?"

Sandra picked up the meagre pile of paper that sat on Jim's work desk in the corner of the dining room, and plonked it unceremoniously in front of him. The sound of fifty sheets of A4 hitting the table should have caused him to flinch, yet his life-threatening headache appeared to have subsided for now. Maybe it was the ibuprofen finally kicking in. More than likely was the ability that unadulterated crying had to wash away tension.

"I'm not doing that today. I'll find some time tomorrow..."

"When, exactly? Do you think Danny is going to suddenly stop puking so that you'll have a window to mark some work in the next twenty-four hours? Pick it up and follow me."

Jim wasn't liking this. Who was this woman who had replaced his mum and was taking charge of the situation? So many things had happened to him recently that he wouldn't rule a body takeover experience out of the equation. It had been that sort of year. For the time being, he followed her through the lounge and into the hall, where she grabbed his keys and tossed them over to him.

"Get your coat. You're going out."

"With my marking?"

"Yes, with your marking. There's a Travelodge in town. You're going there tonight and getting this marking done."

"Don't be ridiculous. I can't leave Katie on her own with Danny. And the house is a mess..."

Sandra wasn't letting up. Her son was in a place she'd been in many times before. He was one step from desperate, and needed dragging back to somewhere that resembled reality. When she needed someone all those years ago, drink had been her crutch but it had betrayed her in quite a spectacular way. There was no way she was giving him the option of finding himself on that road. He needed straight. He needed narrow. He needed out of this house.

"I'll talk to Katie when she wakes up. And I'll do a much better job of cleaning up than you would in a million years."

"But what about you...?"
She knew where he was heading with this, and she understood his concern, but he didn't have all the facts at his disposal. Not yet, anyway.

"Look at me. Do I look like I'm in a place where I'm going to go downing a bottle of gin the moment your back's turned? I'm in a good place at the moment, Jimmy. And besides, Katie's far more effective at keeping an eye on me than you've ever been. She's like a hawk. Take me off your list of things to stress over, and go somewhere else for twenty-four hours. Go to the Travelodge. It's got a shower. It's got a desk. It's got a Debenhams next door where you can spend those vouchers I got you for Christmas on a change of clothes. Get this off your mind and then maybe we can have a good time at New Year."

Without letting him argue, she opened the door and motioned towards it. There was a moment where she thought he was going to cry again, but he kept it together and rewarded his mother with a hug that sons reserve for only the very special people in their lives.

As the door closed behind him and he gripped tightly hold of his coursework, Jim took a moment to try and breathe in the cold winter's air. His cold was still very much in attendance but the pain in his head had almost completely vanished. The dull, heavy pain that had been wracking itself through his body just minutes before had already lessened to just an uncomfortable niggle.

Perhaps it was true. His mother had become a witch doctor. He got in the car and drove the ten minutes into town. By the time he got there, a room had already been booked for him. Less than an hour later (still fully clothed) he was asleep, recharging his body for an exciting evening of marking fifteen evaluations on how his students thought they had performed whilst rehearsing their very own low-budget version of *The Woman in Black.* For the first time since he could remember, he found the marking quite easy.

Back at home, Sandra made another cup of tea and chatted to Katie about breast feeding, sleep deprivation, and how she was going to break it to Jim that a very nice man called Peter was about to become his stepfather.

SPRING TERM

Chapter Twelve

Swashbuckling for Beginners

Within four days of the new term starting in January, the world appeared to have done a full one-hundred-and-eighty degree turn. Things were most definitely looking brighter. Having some time away to mark his coursework had, of course, helped but there generally seemed to be a can-do attitude about the place when Jim returned to work.

Danny had settled into a routine at home, not yet sleeping through but at least giving his parents a straight run of four hours at a time before demanding to be fed or changed. Jim's mum seemed rejuvenated and, although it was more than a bit weird that she was seeing someone new after all these years, he was finally able to check her off his daily list of things to worry about. Whoever Peter was, he had made his mum happy. And, when they finally did get to meet, he was sure they'd get on well. Jim felt the best he had in months, but this morning had really put the icing on the cake of what had already become a very good week.

The staff room was buzzing in a way that was more than a little overwhelming, and it was close to throwing Jim completely off his stride. As a performer, he was well used to being the centre of attention but he usually had on a hat and some sort of glittery make-up to divert from the fact that it wasn't really him up there. Today, though, it was all about the Tovey boy and how good a teacher he was. As the school's solitary practitioner of Drama, he probably should be used to being the one in middle of all the fuss. When you're not ready for it, though, it can be a little disorientating.

Mick had taken the time to personally come over and shake Jim's hand. Little Jimmy Tovey. He had got a 'fantastic' and a pat on the back from the big boss man. In front of half of the school, too. Was there a catch? Was he missing something? Elaine from English was relaying the story of Jim's immense success to a group of Support Assistants who were gathered around the kettle. Even Janet, the woman for whom positivity seemed an entirely alien concept, had very publicly walked over to him and said, "Well done." Well done! From Janet! This day couldn't get any more bizarre if it tried.

And the cause of the fuss? An assembly. An assembly which, for over three months, Jim's form had fought tooth and nail not to perform.

The original plan had been for them to take their turn in presenting to their year group during Dyslexia awareness week, back in October. As was usual with Jim's working life, Year 8's jabs had to take precedence in the hall and the assembly that day had been postponed. The rota wouldn't come around to them again until after Christmas, with the kids believing they'd got away with it. Jim broke it to them that they'd be resurrecting the piece just before they finished in December, leading many to label him The Grinch for giving them lines to re-learn during the holidays.

It had finally arrived. The morning for sharing this fine piece of work. The morning for them to do what they had all been dreading. Perform this stupid play about slidexia that stupid Tovey was making them do. Why was he making them perform?

Everyone else just read stuff off sheets of paper when they had to do an assembly. Why did they have to get the Drama teacher as their form tutor? When they had Mrs Liebewicz for form they didn't have to do assemblies. It wasn't fair. Stupid Drama. My dad says it's a waste of time. Etc. Etc.

From Jim's point of view, it was a shoddy piece at best. He was lucky that, as he knew how to use the lights and sound system in the hall, he could at least attempt to cloud over the extraordinary lack of passion with which 10JT were approaching their subject. It was clear that his form group would rather have been doing anything other than raising awareness about Dyslexia, three months after the rest of the country had already done so.

As well as the lights and music, Jim had given the kids the handheld mics to help combat the inevitable lack of volume you get from nervous, unwilling teenagers. He had also worked out how to get a video clip projected up onto the wall by the doors to give the piece a bit of pizazz. It wasn't a Jean Michel Jarre special, but it would do. Smoke and mirrors was definitely the key to getting this show up and running.

The running order for the ten-minute masterpiece was simple. Start with a blackout. Then lights up to full. Cue kids running into hall shouting "Argh!" at the top of their voices, wearing eye patches (£3.99 for a pack of twenty from a distinctly dodgy Hong Kong importer on eBay – bargain). Bit of physical theatre as they get in positions that look like a ship. Then to the dialogue. Azeem and Gemma do a quick eight lines from Pirates of the Caribbean before Adeela shouts "Cut!" through the mic and tells everyone in role how well the scene went. Everyone freezes. Bobby and Arouge tell everyone that Azeem and Gemma are really Orlando Bloom and Keira Knightley, and that they both have problems with Dyslexia. Cut to YouTube clip of Orlando (the real one, not Azeem) explaining how he spends extra time learning his lines. Big ending with slow-motion mimed sword fight where Azeem and Gemma triumph. Adeela thanks everyone for coming and tells those who suffer to with Dyslexia to "keep battling on" - complete with prop sword in hand. Black out. Applause. Oscar nominations in the post.

As is usual with these things, nothing went to plan. The video clip was delayed because Jim's laptop had timed out and he had to login again. Azeem completely fluffed his bit of dialogue and made up some rubbish about feeling seasick, which threw Gemma completely. Gareth and Terry were (predictably) pratting around at the back when they should have been standing frozen looking like a mast. As with all directors, Jim wanted the ground to swallow him up every time something went wrong. But, like all professionals, they got their heads down and ploughed on to the end. There wasn't going to be an Olivier award coming to Jim for this one.

After the final blackout, a huge pause. Jim started clapping for what seemed like ages, on his own, in the dark. He briefly considered keeping the lights down and trying to run away but, as that was neither professional nor practical (the latter swinging it for him), he stayed in his seat. Then, massive relief...

Year 10 clapped. And CHEERED. Year 10 never cheered. About...well….anything. Labelled the 'difficult' year group even before they had arrived in Year 7, they were easily the most miserable group of individuals that Jim had ever come across. If you told them the world was about to end in the next ten minutes, they'd probably shrug their shoulders and go back to their phones. In the dictionary under 'malaise', Jim was certain that there was just a picture of a hundred and forty glum fifteen-year-olds. Asleep.

To hear them cheering and being positive about something without any kind of prompting was like hearing the Hallelujah Chorus being played at a hundred and twenty decibels. Talk about a rubber stamp for your work. He looked at his form. They were smiling. As usual, Jim had forgotten to bring the camera so he tried desperately to remember what it looked liked for future reference. The confused beam that would emanate from his face for the rest of the morning began to show.

10JT took their bow professionally (except for Terry, who tripped over the edge of the stage curtain) and returned to their seats as Janet moved back to the regular business of their assembly. Namely, moaning about ties, and letting everyone know about the rooming changes that they would later claim not to have received so that they could be five minutes late for Period 4. By the time they left the hall, they were docile again and ready to fall into their daily slumber in Maths. But they did, at least, have some pirate stuff to talk about at break.

"Fantastic assembly, Jim. I watched it from round the back of the curtain. Really impressive."

Mick had never spoken directly to Jim before outside of their official (and, as it turned out, calamitous) results meeting and, to be honest, it came as quite a shock that he was there at all. If he'd known the head were coming, he'd have added a bit more razzamatazz to the sword fight. He knew he should have tried to do that bit where they leap onto the stage in unison. His mind was wandering... The head's speaking to you, Jim. Say something.

"Thank you. I didn't know you were coming, Mick. I'd have saved you a seat out front."

Jim desperately tried not to sound like a creep but it was hard. People were going to get fired by the end of this year, and his natural instinct was to get down on his hands and knees and look subservient.

"I wasn't planning on coming in. But once I heard the yelling and charging about in the corridor, I figured I'd be missing something if I didn't. I wasn't expecting that, though. Pirates in the assembly hall! Did you get any photos for the website?"

"No, sorry. I wasn't expecting..."

"Ah well, never mind. Next time, eh? I think we're all just impressed with how you managed to get her up there!"

Jim tried hard not to pull his 'I don't know what on earth you're talking about' face but it was very difficult. Mostly because he didn't know what on earth Mick was talking about.

"Amazing! Well done, Jim!"

Janet's Head Teacher radar that functioned solely when Mick was in the room had gone off, so she clearly had to become a part of the action. If reincarnation did turn out to be true, Janet would most definitely come back as a leech. And one with a particular penchant for the blood of authority.

"Weren't they good? And Adeela!"

"What about her?"

Jim was beginning to lose track of where this conversation was heading.

"Well, she spoke! I've never heard her speak before, Jim! Well, I mean I've heard her speak and I've taught her for years but I've never once heard her as confident as that. I ask her questions in class all the time and she just crumples and mumbles. That must have taken you hours!"

He didn't know how much all of this was put on for the head's benefit, but Janet was laying it on thick. Jim decided just to stand there and take it all in. Mick made his motions to leave.

"Going to have to shoot off, Jim. I'm meeting the finance committee. Just wanted to say, "Good work.""

And with that he was off. Like Batman into the night. But with a nice tie. It would be another three months before Jim would have such an in-depth conversation with the big boss man.

Janet also made her exit apologies (apparently, she actually had a class to teach. Yes. Jim was surprised, too) leaving him his free period in which to ponder the reaction of the crowd. He quickly flicked through his registers on his tablet. He'd taught Adeela for Drama the whole time she'd been in school, since Year 7. He honestly thought that her presence on the SEN register was an admin error that nobody had got round to fixing, so he had just ignored it.

She was down on the list as having speech and language difficulties due to English being her second language. Sure, she was quiet but she always joined in with the games they played or took a line here and there when the kids were performing in the studio. It had taken a bit of patience and time to get her up to speed but once she felt comfortable that nobody was going to shoot her down for speaking, she was fine.

How had he got her to speak so confidently in front of her whole year group?

He'd asked her. It was as simple as that. The girl at the centre of all the fuss appeared at the staff room door.

"I've put the sword with the other bits behind the curtains, sir."

"Thanks Adeela. Well done. How do you think it went?"

"Okay. It was a bit scary."

"Good, though?"

"Yeah."

She smiled and went off to her Maths lesson on her own. She didn't really have anyone to walk with, as she had no friends in her set. As she turned the corner, she gave a little fist pump to herself. On the other side of the wall, Jim did exactly the same.

Chapter Thirteen

Birdwatching

Just one week later, and the morning that had left Jim floating on cloud nine was already becoming just a faint memory. He was possibly now at cloud seven, but was all too aware that things were descending quickly. The inevitable drop was coming.

Normal routines had been resumed and his paperwork was piling up. Despite Danny's concerted effort to behave a little less like the girl in the exorcist with regards keeping down his food, he was back to being grumpy during the night as he'd picked up Jim's cold over the festive break. There was no way Jim was going to find time to get the GCSE entries done, fill in the annual review forms for the SEN kids in his class, and look over the plans for Andrea's history trip he'd promised to go on. Not this afternoon, anyway. Year 7 reports were looming as soon as he'd finished this single lesson with his Year 10s.

Jim turned his weary eyes to the window and looked out over the yard. It was a full ten minutes after the bell had gone yet the kids still weren't even all in the building yet. This was the sort of thing that Mick was going to have to get to grips with before OFSTED came back. The general malaise about the place was picked up on in the last report and was cited as a reason that the school had barely scraped its 'good' rating. Finding a way to get the teenagers inspired and motivated to get to lessons is, of course, akin to herding cats - with more than a few slightly feral ones, at that. It would take some work. That was for sure.

The gulls were circling already, even before the last of the heel-draggers had crossed the tarmac, but Jim could clearly see them eyeing up the crisps, butties and half-eaten bananas that now littered the four corners of middle courtyard. Squabbling, pumped up kids replaced by squabbling, pumped up scavengers. If it weren't so utterly nauseating to watch, it might be considered poetic. A post-modern version of the circle of life being played out before his very eyes.

As he watched the birds ripping the remaining life out of what was once a tuna mayo baguette, Jim wondered whether this sorry sight might feature in Jenny Anderson's Year 7 biology lesson on the food chain. How on earth might you classify the species 'Yeareightus' in terms of its position as key provider of sustenance for the avian population of Lancashire? Even Attenborough would struggle to narrate that one.

"Give it back!"

Jim's attention was quickly dragged back into the room. The relative quiet of a child-free lunchtime was over. Year 10 were completing written evaluations this afternoon so the fold-out desks had been moved into the middle of the room, making it almost seem like a regular classroom. If it weren't for the higgledy-piggledy manner in which the kids had arranged the desks, Jim might even consider himself to be teaching a 'proper' subject.

"Sir! Tell him!"

Jim did not know what he was to tell or, quite frankly, why Gemma thought that he would be a suitable person to deal with her current injustice. He didn't have a clue what was going on. His attention was clearly on seabirds and their daily diet. He wasn't doing behaviour management right now.

"Sir!"

146

"What is it, Gemma?"

"Don't listen to her! She's lying!"

And so it began. Lewis had taken her planner. Steven had seen him do it and was only too happy to tell everyone. Lewis had given it to Azeem, who did not know how it had got into his blazer pocket at all. That's why Azeem hit Lewis. Which is why Lewis hit him back and why Jim shouted louder than he had done in months. He prayed to God that Janet was teaching and not standing outside the door, otherwise he'd be called in for another 'chat', with her pretending that this wasn't a competency conversation but that SLT was just worried for his welfare.

"If we're shouting, we have to ask ourselves if we're really in control, don't we?"

Screaming at the very top end of his range also buggered Jim's voice for the rest of term. Schoolboy error, Mr Tovey. Never yell, especially when you're only in the second week. You need to keep it fresh for the Easter term when things are getting really tense. Five-and-a-bit years in the job and he still hadn't learned. It's all about pacing yourself.

When he got home that night, Jim would reflect on his lesson with 10A that afternoon and give himself a damn good kicking. They'd told you about this in the behaviour management at INSET last Monday. Be there, be smiling, be ready to start from the get-go. Give them something to do as soon as they get in the door so they don't have time to get distracted. BE ON IT. Somewhere in the pile of paper on his desk were the notes from the training session. Nowhere on the beautifully printed PowerPoint slides did it say anything about looking out of the window, pondering the eating habits of seagulls.

That's why you got a 4 on your last observation, Jimmy my boy. You don't concentrate on what you're supposed to be doing. Too busy with your head in the clouds, floating about with the birds. You've got to get your head back in the game. All the time. Every time.

These kids take no prisoners, that's for certain. 10A don't care that, just two weeks into the new year, you're already shattered and you didn't get enough sleep again last night. Ofsted won't care that Katie is getting depressed and struggling to deal with Danny's crying, so you're the one doing the night feeds. As Janet told you quite clearly at your review meeting, there isn't a box for that. You need to pull yourself together, Tovey. This is only January.

Regaining his composure, Jim spent the next forty minutes delivering a masterclass in how to get a group back on track, resolve conflict, and inspire young minds to reflect on their own strengths and weaknesses through exploration in the dramatic arts. If an inspector had bothered to pop their head round the door, they'd have seen what an outstanding lesson actually looked like. As it was, the only people to witness it had their heads buried in their books, transcribing what would later form the basis of their strongest exams answers when they finally reached Year 11.

The lesson ended and the class made their way to period six, leaving the tables stacked. Not in the tidy manner which Jim wanted but in a pile which, quite frankly, screamed for a risk assessor to come in and shut the whole place down as 'an imminent threat to the health and safety of all involved'. Tidying them properly would have to wait until later. Right now, he had to get on with those reports.

He'd already started the Year 7 progress reports during his lunch break and was about halfway through, so didn't feel quite as uninspired as he may have been when he first realised just how much of a chore it really was. He opened the screen to the reporting system and began punching the digits.

1,1,1,2,3,1,1,1,2,3,1,2,1

A,A,B,B,B,A,C,D,A,A,B,C,B

Within ten minutes of this, Jim's fingers were hurting. His eyes were hurting. And his soul was hurting.

Continually pressing the same series of buttons would cause him to get RSI, he was sure. He would be at the GP's over half term, complaining that his wrist was going to break. Or worse, maybe his whole arm would fall off while sitting at his workstation. That wouldn't be good for the Academy's corporate image, would it? A terrible headline in the local paper. "Teacher loses arm in report writing shock". Maybe it was time he took a break.

He looked down at the class lists. Six and a half done. Three and a half to go. When he had a spare moment, he would have a wander up to Gareth, who had organised the timetable, and punch him squarely on the nose. "Having all ten Year 7 groups will be a blessing", he had said. "You'll only have to plan one set of lessons and do them ten times over", he had said. "It'll be the easiest year you've had". He. Had. Said. Let's not mention the insanely long parents' evening, or the day when you have to complete ten sets of data entry in one free period. He went back to pressing his buttons. Numbers one to four for progress, Letters A to E for behaviour. Input. Input. Input.

Jim did not feel 'blessed' as he waded through ten sets of mid-year reports. He had already got pupil blindness (he'd forgotten the faces that matched the names appearing on the spreadsheet) and was relying solely on his mark book for making accurate and systematic judgements about the attainment of the pupils in his care. Which would be fine, if it weren't for the canyon-sized gaps that were all too frequent in said mark book.

He would never accept an entire cohort of kids without knowing them in advance again, that was for sure. There was something about this group of Year 7s that Jim struggled with, and he had three groups among them that he had put on a Drama behaviour report at the start of the year. Those three groups had produced so little work of quality that he had spent at least six lessons of the winter term just working on teamwork skills and games. What had the world come to? How do they get like this? Young people today don't have any respect. They're getting worse, these kids....

He had whipped them into shape, of course, and just about got them on side now but this meant they were a long way behind where they should be on the scheme of work. Hence the gaps. Jim could fill in those gaps using his common sense and professional judgement, but those judgements took active brain cells - something in which Jim was sadly lacking after delivering his uber-lesson on self-evaluation to Year 10.

The door of the studio opened. It was Janet. Of course. Why on earth would it be anyone else? She had not been anywhere near the department all week but, as reports were due tomorrow, she had begun her vulture-like circling. With lightning reflexes, he shut the book and closed the reports screen with his other hand. It was quite a juggling manoeuvre - a feat of amazing manual dexterity of which Cirque de Soleil would certainly have been proud. The move also ensured that Janet didn't have a clue how he was winging it with some of his assessments.

"Everything ok, Jim?"

"Yes, fine, thanks."

"Just thought I'd pop up and let you know that we've postponed the SLT meeting this week so we won't be able to meet on Monday. I didn't know if you'd got the email from earlier."

Liar, Liar, your bum is most definitely on fire. Huge plumes of acrid smoke spelling out the words "I am a big fat liar" are circling you, Janet. She knew full well that an email went round first thing this morning and she had seen already that Jim had responded to it. You are not here on any mercy mission this time, Princess.

Janet was here for one reason only. To cover her own backside. The last time she had let Jim deal with his reports himself, he had forgotten to do it. She had been named and shamed at the SLT meeting by Gareth, who had gleefully listed the departments that hadn't got their reports finished by the deadline. Drama was top of that list and, as usual, there was a problem with the Technology carousel subjects filling in the wrong boxes on the system. Janet wasn't line manager for Technology but she had been lumbered with Drama. She wasn't going to be publicly singled out for chastisement by Gareth again.

Being on paternity leave was the excuse Jim gave for forgetting to do them and, against her better judgement, she hadn't made a big deal of it at the time. Paternity leave? It wasn't as if he was the one having the baby. The one thing she had learned in education over the past twenty years was that letting your personal life take precedence over your career was never a good idea. You had to stay focussed in education or you just didn't get the results. More precisely, she had learned since moving up to being senior leader that if you didn't get the results, you didn't keep your job.

She bit her tongue about the baby issue, just as she had been advised on the *Leading Through Life* course she had been put on when she was first promoted to senior leadership. People got funny if you bemoaned them their 'parental rights'. Jim revelled in his ability to breed, with his desk being covered in pictures of little Tommy or whatever his name was. Maybe a little more time working and a little less time putting up pictures was needed around here. Janet didn't have any children but she was certain that, if she did, she wouldn't force pictures of them down the throats of everyone who happened to be passing.

"Reports?"

"Year seven? I'm on it."

"You know they were due today."

Were? She was speaking in the wrong tense. That would imply that the 4:30pm deadline was a past event and at the last time he checked it was... 2:17pm. He'd already worked through lunch and was now using his planning, preparation and assessment time for, well, assessment. Jim had managed half a dozen Skips and a Toffee Crisp during lunch so he was dining on the job, but he was definitely doing what he was told to do. If she'd bugger off and leave him in peace, he may actually get them in before the deadline. There may even be a trumpet fanfare in his honour. Plus, he might get a handful more crisps.

This was, of course, one of the twenty-eight reasons he hated having Janet as his line manager (Katie had mistakenly made him sit down one night and list them). He was in the process of doing, in advance, the shockingly dull job that he hated doing - something that he felt he should be applauded for - but she still made him feel like he was making a compete hash of things. Admittedly, missing half the marks for his classes wasn't exactly textbook assessment policy, but at least he was typing in the stupid letters into the stupid system making his stupid hand hurt.

"So, when will I be able to check over them?"

Four-thirty Janet. That's when the deadline is! Now go away back to your over-sized office with your posh chairs and leave me in peace, you soul-crushing pen pusher! As ever, he remembered to scream it in his head, while contorting his face into the perma-grin that seemed to be obligatory when he was in *her* presence. She'd been his boss for four whole months now. He knew the drill.

There followed the kind of awkward silence that can only ever be understood by two colleagues who don't like each other, or two strangers who are trapped in a lift. The "What do we say now?" moment. She had come to ask a pointless question simply to impose her authority. He had responded in non-committal sentences, and had no way of answering her latest question in a manner that didn't involve the words "You dimwit".

Time went by.

Then... Serendipity.

The phone rang. He glanced down at the call display. It was Gareth, probably calling ahead to check that Drama wasn't going to have to be named and shamed for not meeting a deadline. Again. Gareth the rock was on the phone, with Janet the hard place standing behind him. Did everyone get this level of intimidation over admin tasks, or was it just reserved for Drama teachers?

It was at that point that the planets aligned and created a magical moment in time. It didn't seem so at first but, in years to come, he would look back at these next few seconds as some of the sweetest of his entire career.

"I'll just get that."

Jim tentatively picked up the receiver. No talk of his reports. No discussions about deadlines. Was Janet there? Someone had seen her in Jim's part of the building. Yes, she was here. He'd put her on. The receiver was held out and taken in a bemused fashion by Janet. Jim shuffled his chair back and took it all in.

"Yes? Oh hi, Gareth.... Yes, Jim and I are just doing Year 7 Drama reports now... MFL? No we're all done over there. We had a meeting Tuesday and I got the girls to fill in their reports while they were there with me...Hmm...No, we finished all of them... Yes... All four columns.... 1 to 4 for behaviour and A to E for...."

Jim couldn't help but smile.

"....No we discussed this last week at SLT. The system was changing to reflect.... Well yes, that was for Key Stage 4 but surely we're doing.....Well, that doesn't seem a very sensible way of doing things....Well, yes I'll talk to Mick about it...."

The smile became a grin.

"ALL of them? That's eight classes... The girls are both teaching the option groups this afternoon... Okay, okay. I'll get onto it."

Receiver down.

"You're going to have change your reports, Jim. Seems we're...."

He didn't even let her finish her sentence. With one click, he reopened his reports screen and pointed at his immaculately formatted report, with letters and numbers all in the right places.

"Good. Fantastic. Well, I've got to go and talk to Sarah and Dominique about theirs. Thanks, Jim."

With that, she was gone. Off to spin the affair in a way that would make her two colleagues in MFL look incompetent at the SLT meeting the following week and would ultimately lead to Dominique taking another extended leave of absence due to stress.

Jim went back to punching in his numbers. For some reason, his hand didn't hurt anymore.

Chapter Fourteen

Problems Looming

Seventeen, Eighteen, Nineteen....

"Sir! Is there a toilet in the museum?"

Bugger. One. Two...

"Sir! Is there a toil..."

"Yes, I'm sure there is, Jacqueline. Can you please sit in your seat so I can make sure we've got everybody?" Jim thought he'd made a very good job of not sounding like he wanted to hit her over the head with his trip folder. Twenty-one miles of constant wittering in the seat behind him had left him a teeny bit on edge, but no amount of inane chatter was going to get in the way of him doing an accurate check on the number of the Year 9s who were sitting/standing/falling about in front of him on the coach.

Jim was fully qualified in Off-Site Safety Management and felt completely in control. He'd done a half-day course three years ago (a proper one, not one of the whole-staff INSETS that SLT try to pass off as 'professional development') so he knew his stuff. Count them on the coach. Count them off. Count them when they're queuing up. Count them when they're sitting down. The ABC of never losing a kid when on a trip. Always Be Counting.

Thirty-two kids. Three members of staff. Just like when they had pulled away from the school gates. He knew somewhere in the back of his mind that an escape from a coach during a motorway journey was unlikely, but he'd taught 9F1 last year and knew them to be scheming little buggers. If he hadn't checked, he'd probably get a phone call later from a bemused coach driver saying he found a small boy under the seat and could I please come and pick him up from the depot? Martin Fitzroy could definitely squeeze himself under one of those seats.

Always. Be. Counting.

As they got to the museum entrance, Jim reflected briefly on how he'd managed to get himself running this little jolly in the first place. He was the Drama teacher. Why on earth was he running a KS3 History trip to a textile museum on a cold, wet January afternoon? He'd like to say it was because he had a fondness for history, or that he enjoyed watching the kids have a real learning journey as they experience our culture first-hand. It wasn't. It was because a young teacher had pulled a puppy-dog face at him when he'd had a long and tiring day.

Sucker.

Andrea was only in her second year at the school but, through a combination of retirements, incompetence, and being a textbook passive-aggressive, she had quickly risen to become Head of History. For the school, it was a win-win all round. Andrea would develop her outstanding practice from her own lessons and spread it amongst an ageing (and often blundering) History staff. Plus the school would get someone who was cheap. Everyone's a winner, baby. That's the truth.

As no-one in the Humanities faculty at Lancashire Academy had organised a trip in living memory, getting the kids off-site to a textile museum was somewhat of a coup for Andrea, and would ensure that her target number three on this year's Performance Management would be well and truly met. The museum was booked, the coach price haggled over, and relevant forms and contact details filed in triplicate. All achieved with the relentless vigour that comes from a new teacher. And someone who doesn't have kids of their own.

When Andrea sold the idea of the trip to Jim, it was suggested that it was because he was seen as someone who had experience of running these things, what with him doing all those theatre trips and doing that course last year. She made a very convincing argument that Jim had bought into straight into. She also seemed desperate not to ask Peter or Graham as they spent most of the day making inappropriate comments about the length of her skirt - an attitude that Jim was sure would ultimately get them sacked. She had asked so nicely and had offered to buy him a donut when they got to the museum cafe. Oh, go on then.

Suckerooney.

Jim was actually the only male member of staff who was not teaching on Wednesday afternoon, so did not require cover. Couple that with Andrea's unforeseen bout of glandular fever and you get a full explanation of why Jim, along with two ineffective and demotivated Support Assistants was herding thirty-two Year 9s in the rain. Dedicated as Ginny and Safeerah were to the children in their care, it was cold and they were going to be on their feet all afternoon. Jim gave them a sympathetic "I know" smile but received little in return. This is not how Andrea had sold it to them. They were less than impressed. The unofficial Support Assistants' Union would be hearing about this in the staff room at break tomorrow. Jim gave the ladies in the front seats a big smile. They didn't scowl but it wasn't far off.

It's something you did when you were seventeen, Tovey. That's why it always rains on you.

"Right. Everyone has their worksheets, yes?"

Nods and a few groans of 'Yes' came from 9F1. They were top set and had been through this drill a hundred times before. After all, they were one of the only classes at Lancashire Academy that were trusted not to break the coach or swear at the public when allowed out of their cage. They'd been on four trips to everyone else's one in their year group, so were well-versed in the rigmarole of getting on and off the coach, being counted incessantly, taking photos for the website, and holding the door for people who looked like they might be museum staff.

They knew they were privileged to be here. They knew they were representing the school. They weren't to leave litter on the coach or use bad language in the museum. Did all the teachers write this speech together? Tovey was usually more human than the rest of them but even he'd turned into a drone today.

"Can we just go to the museum please, Sir?"

"Yeah, I'm bursting!" Jacqueline was now looking more than perturbed.

Jim sighed and realised they'd better get on with it, or SLT would end up paying for a £325 trip to a car park.

"Fine! Stick with your groups of five and we'll gather at the front entrance. Jacqueline, go ahead with Mrs Thompson and the rest of us will all go into the museum together when you're back. Please walk sensibly across the car park. Thank you, everybody!"

Jim used the age-old teacher trick of bunging 'thank you' on the end of a sentence as a way of making clear that this was not a polite request, but premature thanks for a task that he would be grateful to them for delivering. Saying 'please' suggested subservience to them and he was most definitely the one in charge today. He had no idea if such psychological double-bluff tactics actually worked on teenage kids, but he'd been given this tip when he was a newbie teacher and it had stuck with him.

The driver opened the doors and thirty-two children exited, en masse. Jacqueline, who clearly had a bladder like an over-cooked haggis on Burns Night, managed to break her PB for the one hundred metres. There was shouting and arm-waving, and one of the boys definitely said a naughty word to the coach driver as they were getting off. It was clear that not one single instruction had been listened to. The SA's gave a simultaneous shrug that simply said, "You're the group leader, sunshine".

As soon as they were inside, Jim's mood lightened. The museum was surprisingly interesting, with enough artefacts for the kids to touch, and a discovery trail that made them inspired enough to read a little about strange Victorian contraptions. Looms (which are not the easiest of things to sex up) were given a bit of razzmatazz by the young lad who was in charge of the tour. He projected well, did a bit of role-play as a mill owner, and kept thirty-two kids engaged long enough for Jim to check Facebook on his phone. This was definitely a kid who'd done GCSE Drama. Jim liked him.

The bit about catwalk fashion and how materials are used engaged the boys (it may have been the life-size cut-out of Kate Moss that did the trick but they were definitely listening to the audio tour) and a group of girls actually got a chance to use one of the smaller looms and weave something that looked vaguely like a scarf. Worksheets were filled in, snacks were consumed in the cafe (with a minimal amount of litter) and not once did he have to speak to any of them about getting 'giddy'. He'd even got a decent photo of everyone smiling for the website. Even Mrs Thompson.

As they all flopped back onto the coach, Jim pondered whether or not he should start to relax a little. Was his chosen profession really as stressful as he was making out? Maybe Katie was right. Everybody goes through tough times at work, and he had been more than a bit picky at home lately. Maybe it was because crunch time was approaching, with exam season on the horizon. That, of course, was under extra scrutiny this year. Perhaps it had something to do with trying to work out what was going on with his Mum and this bloke Peter she'd been seeing. Whatever it was, tension in the house was running pretty high.

Knowing you are tense and doing something about it are, of course, two very different things and there didn't seem to be much he could do to keep his emotions in check. His fuse had become much shorter of late, leading to Katie taking the fairly extreme step of banning the TV news at home. Full stop. Every time a politician mentioned education reforms, Jim started a tirade of abuse, and she already had one bawling male to deal with.

Jim had brought home more than a couple of arguments about work issues, causing them to spill over into more domestic disputes. But he'd honestly thought that was to be expected when people have a new baby. Things were bound to get a little tense. Especially when Katie insisted on putting the carry-cot right by the front door. There was no way he could get through that little gap with his work bag and all the folders he had to get into the car. Why have you done that, Katie? It's ridiculous! What do you mean I'm shouting....?

"Sir?"

Oh, Hurrah. Everyone had decided to sit back in the same seats. Jim would have the joys of Jacqueline on the return leg to school. Surely her bladder couldn't be an issue now. They'd only just set off. As the coach driver turned out onto the motorway, Jim switched round to speak to his very own personal Jiminy Cricket.

"Yes, Jacqueline?"

"Your phone's going off."

He glanced down at his phone. It was the museum.

Alarm bells rang and his heart sank as he turned back to look at the kids on the coach. Without having to count, he instinctively knew that there were only thirty-one children.

In a Lancashire museum, three volunteers were working hard to free Martin Fitzroy from a loom he'd been stuck under for the last forty-five minutes.

162

Chapter Fifteen

Choices

Jim knew he was supposed to be concentrating on the stage. In his struggle to stay awake, he found himself looking at anything but. He drifted from being attentive member of the audience to daydreamer - something he had chastised so many pupils for over the years. His daydream became a ponderance, the ponderance turned philosophical. Within seconds Jim's head was elsewhere, reflecting on how we got here and trying to fathom out the point of it all.

Becoming an academy had been a very strange metamorphosis.

The 'Craic' (as any good Irishman will tell you) is more important than anything if you want to grab yourself a bit of success. A pub with no atmosphere isn't going to sell any beer, and a workforce that are down in the dumps are far less likely to go the extra mile when you need them to. It doesn't matter how many training sessions or procedures you put in place, you'll get nowt out of your people if they'd rather be at home, poking themselves in the eye with a sharp object. And if the people you've employed are hating it, you can be damned sure that those who are forced by law to attend every day for ten years are going to be pretty cheesed off as well.

Since last May, when the Trust had officially taken the reins and changed the name of the school from *Deepdale High* to *Lancashire Academy*, morale had been on the wane. Last year, after the school had been marked by the inspectors as 'coasting', there had been a real camaraderie about the place - a wartime spirit that can only result from poop hitting the fan at high speed. They knew they had to do something to improve results, bring up attendance and shuffle the school into the modern era (Deepdale High had been a run-of-the-mill comp since the late sixties) but no-one envisaged the aggressive corporate takeover that happened before they'd had chance to blink.

No sooner had the school been downgraded, than wheels were put in motion for its conversion to an Academy - the government's flagship policy of bringing in business chains to 'sponsor' schools that needed improving. Growing Acorns would take over the management at the school and immediately promised that no-one's job would be at risk, that everyone would get the support they needed to turn the ship around, and that investment in the pupils would be the key to making the new Lancashire Academy the shining light in their chain. With Growing Acorns, these children would be nurtured and would grow strong and tall. Now, nearly twelve months after the takeover, Jim had thought of plenty of places he could plant one of their acorns, but none of them were possible to enact in front of lower-school children.

From his experience of the Growing Acorns chain, he had discovered that the key to academic success appeared to be the ability to transform a school from a place where children take a guided tour of life on the way to adulthood, into an exam factory that topped the league table and looked fantastic on a spreadsheet. Experiences had been replaced by tests, pupils had become stakeholders, fun had been consigned to history. (Although obviously not the History department. Janet wouldn't be having any of that).

164

Jim's visit to Church Street Primary last year should have given him a hint as to what a soulless vacuum his place of work would become but, as usual, he was a little slow on the uptake. In the weeks following the announcement of the conversion, each member of staff was sent to one of the six other establishments that formed a part of the chain. The aim was simple; to understand the 'group message' that the trustees were trying to develop. After sorting out his form one Tuesday morning, Jim had driven the three miles across town to Lancashire Academy's latest feeder school. A sparkly 'new build' that had squeaked in through the bum-end of the last government's rebuilding programme, shortly before 'austerity' became the new black.

Jim signed in at Reception, using a very swish computer system that took your picture and asked important questions about who you were, why you were here, and whether you were blocking anyone in on the already over-stacked car park. (He was). He was then greeted by a woman in her early fifties, who was clearly unimpressed by his wink to camera and accompanying thumbs-up that formed the image for his visitor pass. The unimpressed receptionist pointed out the chairs where he could wait until someone came to collect him. He sat down. They were waiting for new Reception furniture, she said, so for now he'd have to make do with the chairs they'd brought through from the library. Whilst waiting, he got chatting to a Roman Centurion. As you do.

Primary schools are always awash with adults playing dressing up; it comes with the territory. World Book Day had, over the last twenty years, opened the door for all sorts of costume shenanigans in Britain's primaries. But there were some, like Jed (the gentleman who Jim found himself with in Reception), who were ultra-professional and went the whole nine yards. This wasn't just a bloke in a fancy dress costume. This was professional historical re-enactment at its most serious. Jed had a full suit of Roman armour, a shield, feathery helmet and risk-assessment-busting sword. He had also brought with him two huge IKEA bags filled to the brim with fairly authentic and well-crafted replica shields. The sight of Jim wearing his Drama blacks and Jed in his full-on tribute to Caesar, sitting on two tiny primary-school-sized chairs more suited to eight year olds, would have made a great caption competition.

For someone who clearly must enjoy his job (well, what was there not to like about being a Roman commander every day of your working life?) Jed came across as somewhat jaded. As the conversation progressed, it became clear that this was not the first school that the big Roman guy had visited in the Growing Acorns chain.

"Just watch out", he whispered to Jim, like a downbeat Nostradamus. "This whole Academy thing will change teaching. I've been doing this job for fifteen years all over the North and I've seen all sorts of schools, from little village parish places to massive inner city schools. The ones that still do their own thing, and aren't run by businesses, never keep me waiting. They always make sure I have time to get my head together and a place to set up my stuff. I get in, I get a coffee, I get in character for the kids, we have a great time. Whenever I've been to any in this chain, they haven't the time for any of that. In most schools, I'm made to feel like some sort of visiting magician. You know, the teachers big it up and give me the wow factor. I've been to this lot twice. They make me feel like a plumber. It's not that I don't feel like I'm needed, but really I'm just the hired help for the day. I tick a box for them while they get on with something else. Still, I'm getting paid so I guess I can't complain."

At this point, the stern-looking receptionist told Jed that assembly was now finished and the children would be brought down to the hall in five minutes. He could go and set up his history thing. The centurion picked up his bag of replica shields and wearily made his way to the beautifully crafted atrium, which appeared to double as an assembly hall. Jim pondered how much more the school might get out of the kids if they spent as much money on teaching the staff at the front desk how to smile, as they did on architects.

After ten minutes of waiting on his own with Miss Personality UK, it became abundantly clear that the Deputy Head, who was supposed to be giving Jim a guided tour of the school, was going to be a no-show, at least for the immediate future. Phone calls were made, information gathered and the bad news broken.

"He's had to go into an emergency meeting with a parent. He's going to be at least half an hour."

"Don't worry. Maybe I can just wait in the staff room and grab a cup of coffee? I've got some work I can be getting on with anyway..."

A short delay shouldn't cause too much hassle. He'd been granted cover for his lessons that morning, so was free to stay till lunch if he needed to. He'd stay out of the way with a nice warm beverage and get his guided tour when someone had a free minute. He was informed that they didn't have outside visitors going into the staff room but she could bring him a drink and he could work in the library. She disappeared into the small kitchenette behind Reception for about a minute, and returned clutching a specially printed travel mug with 'Visitor' emblazoned on the side. He wouldn't be shouted at for mug-pilfering today - something he was accused of daily at school. He was usually guilty. He took the drink while she pointed to a tub on the corner of her desk.

"It's 30p a cup. You can put it in the pot."

Er...Right. Paying for a coffee? The *guest* paying for a coffee? They really had been working on customer service this month!

Jim fiddled around in his pockets. He only had a £2 coin. The coffee was made already. No turning back.

"Looks like I'm going to have to get a bit of change...."

Looking in the pot it was nothing but 5ps and 10ps. He counted out what can only have been a pound's worth of change before the tension of the situation got to him and he took the financial hit.

"Staff bring their own here, you see, and catering deal with any pre-planned meetings for the school Directors. Do you want anything else? No? Ok. The library is just over there."

Walking across the corridor, he got a glimpse into the staff room with its huge-windowed wall, giving the impression that the staff were an exhibit in some sort of zoo. The behaviour that he witnessed from these animals, however, was nothing like that of the species with which he usually shared a habitat. Their heads were down. They were working. No chatting and no laughing. Just very, very professional-looking people doing very, very professional-looking things. Where were the in-jokes, the laughter, the race to find the most hilarious homework grammar errors? These were obviously some sort of clone teachers whose genes had been spliced to have their camaraderie tendencies removed.

Jim thought back to his own days at primary school. Was it ever this quiet? Was it ever this ordered? Had Jim been given a sub-standard education without knowing it?

As he parked himself in the library, he checked out a large display board with details of who was really running this show. The Growing Acorns Executive Board of Trustees (a little bit of vomit found its way into Jim's mouth) was made up of a totally un-unique group of Caucasian fifty-something, greying individuals who, in another life, could easily masquerade as the Village Green Preservation Society. There were seven of them. Five serious-looking men and two equally stern women, one of whom appeared to have an OBE. He didn't recognise her from watching Sports Personality of the Year or the BAFTAS, so he assumed she must be a political party donor of some kind.

All but two of the Magnificent Seven appeared to have a business background, and it was clear that they had been very successful at it. If you're looking for strong leadership and a profit in a competitive world, these were definitely your A-Team. They all had specific areas of expertise on The Board - one was responsible for Curriculum Development, another for Academy assets (which Jim assumed meant buildings and the like). There was one trustee, a sharp looking man named Terry Balderstone who had clearly made the decision to go for the 'distrustful estate agent' look. Short and stocky with silver hair, he was a man whose responsibilities within the Trust included Economic Growth.

Jim tried to imagine how you could possibly 'grow' a school and get more cash flowing in. Yes, you could scrimp and save here and there - go back to Turkey Twizzlers for lunch, buy your exercise books in bulk, that sort of thing - but it was hardly going to push Branson off the Sunday Times Rich List.

To Jim, the only two ways in which a school could increase the amount of money it made were clear. Either you bring in more private money to sponsor things that the school did (if the country's football team could be sponsored by a fast food restaurant, then there's no reason that the same company couldn't sort out lunches for a group of ravenous kiddies) or you could push for the size of the school to be increased. Economies of scale were always the best way to turn a quick buck in any business, but that would mean a drastic increase in the size of the pupil population - something that even someone as powerful as an estate agent has little control over. Maybe estate agent guy was some sort of modern-day child-catcher and was dragging them in, one by one. From his photograph, he looked the type.

When it eventually happened, Jim's tour of the school that morning was an uninspiring affair that simply reinforced his long-held perception that primary teachers had it so much more difficult than he did. As he exited the building, he caught a glimpse of Jed with a group of Year 1 children in the atrium, desperately trying to control them with hefty wooden shields, and observed that he would have had a little more success if he'd attempted to juggle with bowls of jelly. It probably wasn't helping Jim's new Roman friend that the class teacher had seen this as an opportunity to relinquish responsibility for a few minutes and was marking, head down, at the back of the room. Jim didn't blame her. It would mean the poor woman might just be able to grab a whole evening to herself at the other end of the day, but it was a bit harsh on poor Caesar.

Fast forward eleven months. Jim found himself sitting in his own school assembly hall, alongside Years 10 and 11, daydreaming about how it had all come to this. How had the school he had joined just five years ago changed so drastically that he now felt like he was attending some sort of daily corporate function? When did it all become such a grind? Had they lost their way that mu...

"What do you think, Sir?"

Back in the room, Jimbo.

A hand-held radio microphone was thrust up Jim's nose, and he remembered where he was and what he was supposed to be doing before he had drifted off. Oh yes. He remembered now. He was in theatrical hell. Attention was turned back to the rest of the audience.

"Let's open it up. What do you think Abdul should do, everyone? Should he take the drugs...?"

Jim stared at the actor and waited for some kind of response from his two options groups who sat quietly behind him. There was a long, eerie silence. The actors on stage had achieved something that teachers regularly struggle to do and parents just dream of. They had managed to get a group of teenagers to be absolutely silent. Pin-drop silent. 'Don't you dare shove that microphone up my nose' silent. As this was supposed to be a 'stunning piece of interactive theatre', however, it did cause a tiny problem with the running of the show. 11B remained tight-lipped and steadfastly uncooperative. They had been beaten into submission by half an hour of mind-numbing theatre, and were talking for no man. Especially the annoying man in front of them.

"Come on, everyone. What do we think Abdul should do here? What are his CHOICES? Does he know what his CHOICES are?"

Shoot me now. I'm done.

If he hadn't been so damned angry about it all, there's every chance that Jim might have felt a sense of solidarity for the actors who had been trying very hard for the last thirty-odd minutes to engage his GCSE groups on why illegal drugs are very bad things indeed. It wasn't the theatre company's fault that they'd pitched the performance at the wrong age group, or that their script was terrible, or that the soundtrack would have better suited to an episode of Downton Abbey, or that the stereotypical characters weren't believable and the plot twists were farcical. Oh, hold on. It WAS their fault - and they were getting paid bucketloads of cash for the privilege. Jim was not going to be anyone's saviour this afternoon. They could dig themselves out of their own creative black hole.

It was at this point that Jenna (bless her cotton socks) jumped in to go some way towards saving the situation, but there was no disguising the disdainful tone that she managed to squeeze into just a few short words. Should Abdul take the drugs, Jenna?

"No, he shouldn't. Of course he shouldn't. That would be plain stupid."

There was a slight giggle from a few Year 11s on the front row who, unlike the actor on stage, had completely understood the true meaning behind Jenna's less-than-subtle comment. The rest of the audience stared into space, numbed into submission by what had, so far, been thirty-two minutes of utter theatrical dross.

Jenna looked towards Jim, partly to check that she hadn't over-stepped the mark with her biting words and partly to give him a look that said, "What the hell is this rubbish you're making us watch?" For his part, Jim responded with his own carefully crafted expression of "Please don't blame me. This really wasn't my idea."

And it wasn't. The blame for this one was going to sit squarely at Mrs Janet Murphy's door. She'd been the one who'd returned from the Growing Acorns arts provision meeting, bringing with her news of 'such an exciting project that would be coming to Lancashire Academy as part of a national tour'.

Someone had clearly negotiated money to commission a show and send *Youth on Tour* on a trek across the UK. As there were now 9 schools in GA's chain, and they had links to some of the larger chains down in London, this made it a pretty big deal for the three actors who were employed to write and star in 'Choices' - their ground breaking show about young people being pressured into illegal behaviour. (No one, it appears, had ever thought of tackling this as a topic for a play before). Janet had heard that St Cuthbert's up the road had used this company already, so it was only right that she got them in to their school as well. As Janet was also Jim's line manager, there was pretty much nothing he could do about the whole sorry affair.

"It's all about drugs, Jim. Choices. PSHE issues all rolled into one. And they do it through DRAMA."

The way she had accentuated that word made it sound as if she had coined it entirely by herself. All that Greek tragedy business, the Shakespeare stuff and the glitzy world of the stage musical was just a minor distraction from the new, exciting art form that she was bringing before him. Never before had a word been so completely stolen and misappropriated.

Drama. By Janet. Calvin Klein.

It was decided (not by a panel of experts, but by Janet herself on her way into work the next morning) that this would be the piece of theatre that Year 11 were to write a review of. That particular section of the course had been marked down by the board in the previous summer so, as part of her 'support' for Jim, she had found a new way of approaching things. It didn't matter that Jim wanted to take them to Manchester to see *Wicked* because, actually, Janet had found something much better. The reviews for the show by *Youth on Tour* would probably be the best that anyone had ever written.

"They're going to all the schools in our chain, Jim. It's got lottery money attached to it so it must be good, and it means we don't have to have any more issues with off-site trips."

You leave one kid trapped under a loom in a textile Museum and that's your lot. He wouldn't have minded, but it wasn't even his trip. It was Andrea's. Why wasn't she being made to watch some dross piece of non-theatre as punishment for getting glandular fever and dropping him in it? Life was just a big bundle of unfair.

"I think you're going to be very impressed, Jim."

Impressed. Yes. That's the word she used. How much was he going to enjoy trotting that sentence out for her at the end of the day? How much was he going to enjoy rubbing her slightly pointy nose (it did have a very odd, carroty, snowman-like appearance) in it once this lot had packed up and gone home?

After this, there was no way she could ever tell him to do anything with any authority, ever again. This was a failure on the most epic of scales. Maybe he should start drafting her resignation letter right now. This day would, he was sure, be marked in the future as a red-letter day by Drama teachers up and down the land. Today was the day that Janet was shown up, very publicly, to be exactly what she was. Great at talking French but bobbins at managing Drama.

'Abdul', the central character in the cringe-worthy play, had moved on to his big death scene. As this was a play about drugs, it was obviously accompanied by a pointless five-minute monologue. He reiterated that he wished he'd made different CHOICES. We all wished that, my friend. You could have chosen to stay in bed this morning and save us all the hassle. But no, you insisted on coming. The solo violin played, our heroic lead took his final hit of heroin, and everyone was put out of their misery.

10A and 11B, being well-trained Drama monkeys, responded exactly as they should - with a ripple of polite applause. Some of them stretched as if awakening from a twenty-year slumber, while David gave Robert (who had actually fallen asleep) a sharp nudge. Jim turned and looked at his class for some immediate feedback, and knew that they were of the same opinion. This was 45 minutes of their lives that they would never get back.

Janet stood up and made her way to the front, where 'Abdul' was packing his Heroin paraphernalia into a wash bag. What a wonderful glimpse behind the facade of theatre as the three actors from *Youth on Tour* Theatre Company packed away their travelling circus. Go on. Trip over that big box of props, Mrs Murphy. That would just put the icing on a perfect day. She avoided it, but Jim still had the mental picture and couldn't help but smile. He sat back in his seat, ready to take it all in. This was going to be good.

"Well I have to say, Year 11, that was...."

Here it comes.

"...absolutely Amazing!"

.........Wha?

"You are so lucky to have the people here from *Youth on Tour* come in to perform for you today. What very talented people you all are. Can we give them another big clap please as I'm not sure we really gave them a proper thank you? Did we, Lancashire Academy?"

She forced them. Forced them to clap harder.

"I'm really expecting big things from you all now, Year 10 and 11. With so much excellent drama to write about, you'll all be getting your target grades for your review section, and next lesson Mr Tovey will be going through what he expects you to write about."

Will he?

Jim wondered how even he could produce 2000 words about a show that had no lighting, costume, props or sound, and that was possibly the worst written piece of role play that he had ever experienced. How the hell did she expect his class to do it?

"Thank you everyone for being a very polite audience. I'm going to show our actors the way back to Reception."

She led them towards the door, leaving a bemused Jim with a group of bemused (and now terrified) teenagers. As soon as *Youth on Tour* had left the hall, the room erupted.

"It was rubbish!"

"Why did he have to keep saying CHOICES over and over again?"

"I was asleep. What happened?"

"Are we all going to fail?"

Like any good General, Jim stepped up to the plate and gave his troops the most rousing speech he could, under the circumstances, using the wisest words he could think of. It was at times like this that morale needing boosting so he said, with all the conviction he could muster...

"I don't know, guys. I honestly don't know."

There was an audible sigh.

"But don't worry. One way or another, we'll sort it..."

And he would. Somehow.

Chapter Sixteen

Dramarama

As sure as night follows day, the realisation that, from a written work point of view, they were utterly screwed was followed the dawning that the practical exam for GCSE Drama was a mere seventeen school days away. There was no time to evaluate the theatrical lessons they had learned from Abdul and his pals the week before. There were performances that required some serious rehearsal.

"And your names, please?"

"What?"

"Your names?"

"You know our names."

"I know I do, but the examiner isn't going to. You'll need to say your name and candidate number before we start. Remember - today I'm the examiner, not your Drama teacher."

Jim tried his hardest to look sympathetic but he had been through this a gazillion – no, scrap that; two gazillion - times already. Name, candidate number. Look confident, smile. Look professional. Look like you do this every day. Drill it into them every lesson, so it's second nature when they get to the end of year 11. Then they can't go wrong in front of the examiner.

Jenna had forgotten.

"I thought they had it written down on those entry sheets we did."

"They do, but you have to say it again here."

"Why don't they just look at the paper?"

"Because this is for the camera."

Tick, Tick, Tick. The exam day drew ever closer.

Jim didn't want to lose his temper with Jenna. She didn't understand the exam board administration system, that was all. She chose Drama because she liked acting and pretending to be someone else. She liked dressing up in costumes and putting on make up, waltzing around the place in a voice that wasn't her own. Jenna hated numbers, which was probably why they'd put her in Set 3 for Maths. Numbers didn't make sense to her. But she had to say one now or she might end up failing her Drama exam altogether.

"Just say your name, candidate number, and who you're playing. Clearly, for the camera."

"Are you filming this? You didn't tell us you were filming it!"

Oh lord, no. Not this. Murmurs went up all around the room as 11B looked at one another. He hadn't said they were filming. Where was the camera? I haven't done my hair. I don't like being filmed. Are you going to show it in assembly? It's not going on the website, is it?

"No!"

Jim had to nip this one in the bud.

"We will be filmed on the day and it will be seen by the examiner, and that is it. No-one is being put on the school website. Today we are PRETENDING that the camera is here."

A huge sigh of communal relief. Don't frighten us like that, Tovey. We're vulnerable creatures and we scare easily.

"So, where am I looking?" she asked.

"Straight ahead."

"At the window?"

"That'll do."

"Isn't that higher up than where the camera would be?"

The coiled spring became ever tighter. Was she doing this to wind him up? It was now seventeen minutes into the lesson and they hadn't even got past the introductions for group one. Had he not stated clearly enough to them how important it was to work swiftly this afternoon? How we didn't have any more time for flapping about? Seventeen days, guys. Seventeen days! These plays were not going to perform themselves.

"Jenna. Please. Just do it. Name. Candidate number. Role you are playing. Straight ahead. Go."

Group one lined up at the front of the stage, shuffling nervously. In turn (and in somewhat military fashion - Jim was going to have to work on chilling them out a bit) they gave the appropriate information to the window that wasn't a window, but an imaginary camera that wasn't filming. Jenna was last in the sequence.

"My name is Jenna Asquith. I am playing the role of Susan, the Hotel Inspector and the homeless girl. My candidate number is... I've forgot it. What was it?"

Jim had his spreadsheet in front of him. He glanced down and immediately noticed that she still wasn't on the list, despite numerous emails asking Gareth to correct it. Jenna had transferred from his other option group halfway through Year 10, and Gareth still hadn't moved her over on the system. He'd have to go into the office and print the other class list to find her number. He opted for cutting a corner.

"Just make it up. Say it's 1234 for today and I'll look it up for you in future."

"I think it's something like 7013. Or 7103. They all begin with 7s, don't they? Is it the same ones that we had for our mocks before Christmas..."

"WILL YOU JUST GET ON WITH IT!!"

Silence.

Jenna didn't cry, but Jim knew that she was on the brink. She hated it when anyone raised their voice to her, and got nervous when anyone became angry in her general vicinity. When voices were raised at home, she shut herself in her room and put her headphones on. She didn't have the tools to deal with it here.

183

The group hurried into their positions and performed a lacklustre version of their show, inhibited by the worry that the man who was usually their rock in these situations had turned rogue on them. The show (albeit in embryonic form) had potential, but today suffered from lack of voice projection and was devoid of any gestures whatsoever. Fear does that to any performer, especially ones who have hormones rushing about their body in a way not dissimilar to rush hour at Piccadilly Circus.

As the show played out in front of him and an equally inhibited audience, Jim's attention was again drawn to his spreadsheet. It was a sea of red and amber boxes, screaming the word 'failure' at him like some sort of visual loudhailer. If these numbers were the same in August, he was done for. Last year's results were bad enough, but he was 17% down from his target with these guys. He had to find a way of getting those Amber kids to Green before the exam came round, or Danny would find himself celebrating his first birthday with a dad who was joining the mass ranks of the unemployed.

As he stared at the sprawling mass of coloured numbers, he noticed that four of the starred names (he'd given 'free school meal' kids a different notation so he could point them out easily to a snooping Ofsted inspector) were coloured amber. Mick had mentioned in briefing that there was some money left in the pupil premium pot that needed spending before April. Anyone on free school meals got access to pupil premium money. Could he do something to boost those four? Four more Cs would narrow the gap to just 5% down, and may be enough for him to show some sort of progress from last year.

Jim's train of thought was punctured by a ripple of applause as the show came to an end. Jim clapped as an instant reaction, but as he raised his head he realised that all was not well. Jenna ran to the door crying, finally feeling able to let go of her pent-up emotions. Jim looked up at the rest of the group, giving them a perfunctory 'what happened?' gesture as he tried to establish why the tears were flowing now rather than ten minutes ago when he'd actually raised his voice. Sadie, never afraid to speak up in this sort of situation, spoke on behalf of the group.

"You didn't even watch it, Sir."

And she was right. He hadn't seen a thing.

Jim followed Jenna into the corridor to apologise, console and win her round, but it meant that another fifteen minutes of precious lesson time had been lost. Time was ticking and the rest of the lesson would now be behind schedule. By 3:25pm, there were two groups still left to perform and the kids from Drama Club had already started to lurk about outside. He would have to carry it over to their single lesson in the morning, and written work would have to wait. Again.

As the Year 11s drifted out of the studio, and the dedicated souls of 'Dramarama' moved in, Jim caught up with one of the groups who were first up in the morning, stressing to them the importance of being on time so that they could finally get through these rehearsal runs. They promised faithfully that they would be there on time and that, no matter what, they would get these pieces performed. Less than eighteen hours later, Jim would swear, very audibly and very loudly, as he stood in the empty studio whilst those faithful children sat in an over-running assembly, powerless to keep their promise.

For now, though, he had more pressing matters. Recreational Drama. He returned through the double doors of the studio, ready to crack on.

Ow. Ow. Ow.

Jim had to physically put his hands over his ears as he entered. He had no idea how children - those small delicate things that we all coo over in their prams, could create such a nerve-shredding sound. First thing this morning he had struggled to get his low ability Year 7s to raise their volume in their Speaking and Listening assessment, desperately trying to mark the inaudible mumbling of nervous children with low self-esteem. How he longed for those moments now.

Like a weekly alarm going off, the noise told him that it was time for Drama Club. And the first rule of Drama Club? Everybody talks about Drama Club. All the time. REALLY LOUDLY. In front of him stood a group of high-ability, high-volume, gesture-tastic (real word) monsters that Jim had willingly brought together to create amazing pieces of theatrical art. They were keen. They were ready. They were making more noise than would be acceptable to an environmental health inspector.

But as with all good performing monkeys, they were well-trained. In his self-appointed role as organ grinder, Jim stepped into the centre of the maelstrom and silently raised his hand. Only Zain noticed this simple, non-verbal signal and he knew what it meant. His hand went up, his mouth was shut. Jenna and Amy followed suit, followed by two others, then two others. Within fifteen seconds, the whole room had their hands up.

Except for Gemma, who would continue talking days after the apocalypse before noticing that there was no one left to respond. Jim loved these nights. They worked on things that he wanted to do in lessons. If he asked the kids at *Dramarama* to create something (Katie had come up with the name), they did it. There were no schemes of work and no deadlines. If it took them ten weeks and all they came up with were ten improvisations that were never performed again, it wouldn't matter. No one checked it, no one graded it, no one wanted a measurable outcome from it. It was a haven from the daily grind, and every week the kids skipped out of the door and went home smiling. Behaviour management went as far as decibel control, and that was it.

This week he had gathered three big sacks full of stuff from the costume and prop store. They'd done some script work last week, so he wanted to do something a bit more creative. As well as a selection of hats, wigs, bits of costume and a couple of props, each bag had a printout of a famous painting. One had a copy of Van Gogh's *Starry Night*, the second Constable's *The Haywain* and the last a slightly faded version of Munch's *The Scream*. (His printer at home was getting desperately low on coloured ink - much to the annoyance of Katie, who thought he should do all his printing on site.)

Without any hassle, the kids got into three groups of six and Jim handed over their 'sacks of intrigue'. He gave them twenty minutes and off they went. Then Alan appeared and the kids all stopped. It wasn't because Alan was a big, mean, tough teacher - the sort that commanded ultimate respect from the children and instant subservience. They knew Mr Cook was a walkover. Nor did he hold any great position of power within the school that gave him a false sense of empowerment. The reason they stopped and stared was simple.

Alan taught P.E.

A P.E teacher? In the Drama room? This was a creature who'd strayed far from its heartland. It was like seeing a penguin in the Sahara. It simply did not compute. They just stared.

"Come, on you lot. You've only got twenty minutes!"

Jim got them all back on track and went to the door, where Alan was waiting. They had become quite a recognised team of late - Alan helping Jim with his lesson plans, Jim giving his Aussie mate a crash course in Lancashire dialect. That sort of thing. They saw each other every day in form, but that was over on the other side of school in the 'proper' classrooms. There were very few occasions when Alan had been into the Drama studio and it was usually because he wanted something. And he did. Jim would do anything for a mate; he was that kind of man. Right now, though, Alan was pushing it. This was going to need some serious payback.

"It's just for half an hour..."

Jim usually associated the Antipodean accent with rampaging Aussie cricketers, lauding it up over their feeble Pommie cousins. But today, Alan sounded more like Kylie Minogue begging someone to give back her straighteners. There was more than a whiff of 'pathetic' in the air as he explained how, essentially, he had cocked up his diary by setting a detention on the same night that he had an NQT training meeting. Could Jim babysit the detainee? Of course he could. This way he could have a whole week of getting GCSE marking done during form time and Alan would do all the donkeywork, taking the register and giving out the morning notices.

Jim calmed his Aussie friend and sent him on his way, settling the criminal child in question next to his desk. It was the first time that Ethan had been back in the Drama studio since well before Christmas, when he'd stormed out of Mr Tovey's lesson then got himself excluded the following week for punching one of his fellow year 8s in the dinner queue. Through a combination of suspensions, days of 'illness' and plain old bunking off, he'd been able to avoid a confrontation with Tovey about the swearing incident and he was relatively pleased that the Drama teacher wasn't bringing it up now.

"What's the detention for? They don't give out many detentions in P.E. Most people usually enjoy P.E"

"It wasn't P.E. It was Dance."

Ah, yes. This old chestnut. Dance, despite being an art form participated in by millions across the globe, and most definitely worthy of being a subject in its own right, was relegated to a six-week block within a subject that really didn't want to teach it. Of the four Physical Education teachers at Lancashire Academy, one specialised in Rugby League (Geoff had played three seasons at St Helens, don't you know?), one was a young, inexperienced Aussie Rules player ('walkover' Alan), another played hockey to county level (never get in Denise's way when she had a stick in her hand) and the other was Ellen. Ellen's Commonwealth bronze medal was displayed proudly in the PE office. For the shotput. She was no Darcey Bussell.

The staff hated teaching the subject, and the kids knew it. Relegating something to 'not-a-proper-subject' status was never going to produce dynamic, beautiful pieces of contemporary dance. Instead, the pupils learned pre-choreographed routines by rote, literally going through the motions. Not surprisingly, in the same way that a car with no brakes is likely to come a cropper, Ethan had come to blows with Alan during the very first lesson of Dance.

What a shocker.

"Can I join in?"

"You're supposed to be on detention."

Jim was unsure where Ethan was headed with this, and wasn't going to let the purity of his untarnished drama collective be threatened by the teenage equivalent of the Angel of Death.

"Yeah, but it's boring just watching everyone"

"Detentions are supposed to be boring."

Listen to yourself, Tovey. Did you ACTUALLY just say that? Had the system really brought you that far that your way of making people realise the error of their ways in one part of their life was to make them bored in another? Yes, letting the Tasmanian Devil loose on your angels was risky, but when did Drama suddenly become a 'safe' subject? Did Olivier used to play it safe? Did De Niro do any risk assessments before getting into the ring for *Raging Bull*?

Jim flipped an imaginary coin in his head. It came up tails. Just to be sure, he did it again. Same result. We were good to go. With more than a tremor of doubt in his voice, Jim pressed the go button and let Ethan loose on the room.

"Okay, Ethan. See if Gemma can find you a part in her group. They've been working on it for a few minutes now, so you might just have to slot in."

"That's alright. I just don't want to be sat on my arse doing feck all."

Ethan Connoly, ladies and gentleman. Eloquent to the last.

The resulting piece of drama was never recorded, but Jim knew that it represented something quite special in both his career and Ethan's life. The group's *Starry Night* piece was now blessed with a visiting spaceman from another planet, who entered their scene (complete with Green Wig and Electric Pink Bobble Hat) and halted their improvised star-gazing. He would tell them (in a beautifully crafted Welsh accent) that we were all being watched, just as we were all watching the skies. He told them not to be afraid and left a bag of marbles as a sign of peace. As the alien left, they all played the game and the marbles exploded, killing them all. The play ended with maniacal cackling from a green-haired Welsh alien. Ethan had the audience in the palm of his hand. They were in absolute stitches.

At the end of the session, as the usual crowd went skipping out of the door, Ethan came over to Jim's desk to grab his bag.

"That was great, Ethan. You coming again next week?"

"I don't know. Am I allowed?"

"Everyone's allowed."

A pause of weighty consideration.

"Dunno... Maybe."

Ethan was as non-committal as ever, but that wasn't surprising. The way Ethan lived his life, a week in advance was a long time to be making plans.

"Just out of interest, what were you in PE detention for? Do you not like Dance?"

"No, it's not that. I told him his choreography was shit."

Jim laughed out loud. It probably was. Ethan's judgement seemed pretty good on these things.

Chapter Seventeen

Half Term Break

Katie wasn't impressed.

As she was holding open a door and trying to placate a bawling five-month-old at the same time, it was hardly surprising. Jim bundled through the double doors to the studio, almost tripping over his box of props. If she weren't so annoyed with him, she may have laughed at his Chaplin-esque attempt to be organised. Watching him perform physical comedy at college had been one of the main reasons she'd fallen in love with Jim in the first place, and this morning wasn't dissimilar to a French farce. However, in the name of solidarity to all women with crap husbands, she kept her game face on. She was cheesed off, and he needed to know it.

"Sorry!" he repeated, for easily the tenth time in as many minutes. He wasn't sure if he was apologising for the situation or the utterly stupid design of the doors but, whichever it was, he sounded suitably grovelly.

Katie knew his apologies were genuine, but this whole sorry saga simply proved what she already knew. Her husband was a class-A mug. Why he was CHOOSING to spend time in a school that wasn't even open, she had no idea. She acknowledged that this was being done out of necessity, but utterly resented the idea that he was not getting paid extra for being here over half term. If she were asked to do overtime at the office, she got time in lieu. What did Jim get for his extra effort? Zilch. Her husband was a very giving man. And a living, breathing doormat.

It's certainly didn't help that Lancashire Academy seemed like one of only a handful of schools in the country who were completely out of sync with the rest of the educational establishments, in that they were having their half term this week and not last. Katie's mum would happily have had Danny for the morning and avoided this whole sorry mess, but she and Katie's dad were instead on a flight to the Maldives, taking advantage of the cheaper flights on offer during term-time. Well, the sensible schools' term-time. But not Jim's. Oh no. Jim's school had to be different.

"How long is this going to take?"

Katie decided that being practical about things was the safest way to avoid an all-out argument.

"There should be two groups coming in, that's all. I'll have to have a run through with both of them, plus we need to work on a new scene for the boys' group. They've got a piece of silent role-play to finish, which will take a bit, plus the other group haven't sorted their cue sheets yet so..."

"How long?"

She was giving him the smile. The one that said "I'm supporting you right now, but if you say one more thing to wind me up, I'm going to chop you up into tiny pieces". He knew he had to get to the point.

"Three hours."

That was about half of the time he actually needed, but with an active volcano standing next to you, you don't push it.

"Fine, I'll be back at one. And then I get a break and you can look after your son, for a change."

With that, she turned on her heels, effortlessly moving through the double doors that only a minute ago had been Jim's nemesis. He swore she just did these things to show off.

"Morning, Sir."

Continuing the slapstick theme, Jim jumped in the air, almost falling over the props box for a second time. Where had Robert come from? He swore some of these kids had Ninja training in their spare time. Had Robert heard any of that conversation/argument? Was his personal life about to become the latest social media phenomenon amongst bored Lancashire Academy teenagers at half term?

"How long have you been here, Rob?"

"The caretaker let me in. My Mum dropped me off at 9:30. I've set up the studio."

What was Niall doing letting him into the building before any of the staff were even on site? So much for safeguarding. It was typical of the double standards of this place that one of the kids could be let into the building unsupervised, yet Jim had to get a signed letter of consent for the boy to even be there in the first place. Jim had no doubt that Robert being a relative of Niall's had something to do with it - he was a great nephew or

195

something - but that shouldn't really make a difference when it came to deciding who was in or out of the building.

"I've set up all the sound cues and dug out that DMX cable you couldn't find last lesson, Sir. Thought I'd get started before everyone got in and started practising."

Jim's mind was immediately put at ease re: the Facebook gossip. He considered Robert's character. He was polite. He was efficient. He was a tech nerd. In social terms, this made him a complete outsider; he had a selection of close friends, but not enough for him to be considered in any way popular. It also meant that, for years, Robert had learned to keep his own company pretty well; he exuded a confidence that many of the louder students would be envious of, if only they'd take a moment to stop trying to impress everybody else.

Although they didn't have a thing in common (Jim had never really got the whole superhero thing that Robert spent most of his lessons blathering on about and, for his part, Robert hated performing) he had always felt an affinity towards the boy. Robert had chosen Drama so that he could go on to be a lighting technician at college and he spent most of his time in the studio, experimenting with all the various pieces of kit that Jim had acquired over the years. As Jim had little idea of how most of the stuff worked, past plugging it in and pressing the 'on' button, he was happy to let Robert tinker.

Robert wasn't going to let on that Jim was having marital trouble to the Facebook massive, and this was confirmed as the rest of the kids drifted in slowly for their rehearsal. "A prompt start at 10am" was how Jim had described the session in the letter home. It was now 10:13am and they were about three quarters of the way there. Jim was pleased to see that those who had arrived had already got down to doing something constructive.

Robert helped the boys put the music together for their silent role-play, while the remaining pupils in group two were distributing their time evenly between writing out cue sheets and frantically texting Sadie, who had failed to turn up the rehearsal for the umpteenth time. When they finally did get through to her on FaceTime, some rude words were said (which Jim could obviously not hear due to it being half-term) and Sadie was soon on her way into school.

The boys' silent role-play went well, portraying with consummate ease the events of the 1914 Christmas truce to a mash-up of *Altogether Now* by *The Farm*, and *Firestarter* by *The Prodigy*. This was despite the tension of the scene regularly being broken for long periods by Rizwan failing to control his urge to dance to the soundtrack. Jim pointed out that the poignancy of the slow-motion, hand-to-hand combat scene was somewhat compromised by having a raving teenager in the background.

"It's a bangin' tune, Sir. It'd be a crime NOT to dance to it."

Self-expression. You gotta love it. Rizwan promised sincerely that he wouldn't do it on the day. Sadie eventually rocked up at 10:40, with no one but Jim even mentioning the fact. Yes, this was half term but professionals in the theatre always started promptly... Yadda yadda. Alright, Sir. What'evs.

Sadie would not be listening to Jim this morning. It was nothing against him personally, but he was over the age of seventeen and therefore invisible to her. Sadie didn't do authority. She only did

Drama because her only other options were Dance and Art. She wasn't going to get sweaty or have paint under her nails for anyone, so Drama it was. During the first term, he did ask her why Music hadn't seemed a viable option but he had only made that mistake once.

"I ain't doing Music cos that bitch Collins takes the GCSE class and she accused me of spreading shit about Gemma Wallace when I wasn't. I just said she had a fat head cos she ratted on my sister about that whole thing about her and her mates with that girl in Year 8..."

It was settled. Sadie was doing GCSE Drama.

Sadie's choice of rehearsal attire this morning was questionable at best; a pink crop top with the words "Watcha lookin at" (no punctuation) emblazoned in silver lettering across the front, some black skin-tight leggings and a pair of cream Ugg boots with fluffy leopard-print trim. It was a look clearly taken straight from the catwalks of Milan. Whether it was appropriate attire for a run-through of a piece of Theatre in Education about legal highs and their potential dangers Jim didn't know, but at least she was here. Her hair and make-up had clearly taken her at least two hours, explaining her tardiness to the rehearsal. Jim had said it was a non-uniform affair when he wrote the parents' permission letter, and she had taken him at his word.

The rehearsal went well, with each group getting two full runs of their pieces on the stage. They were a bit stop-starty (professional theatrical term) mostly due to it being the first time Robert had been able to add in the lights and sound – a lot of scenes plunged in and out of darkness as he tried to get his levels right. It was now 12.55 and Jim gathered them all together on the front row to give them a pep talk and let them know how much he appreciated them coming in during their holidays. He knew how much of a hassle it had been to get himself in, so he really did want to thank them for doing the same. He didn't get the chance, however, as he was upstaged by a screaming five-month-old.

Katie bundled through the double doors without any of the grace that she had left with three hours earlier. She placed the blubbering Danny in his seat down by the now-empty props boxes, stood by the door and sent a heavily loaded look of expectation in the Head of Drama's direction. Jim could tell from her face that she had been to hell and back, and it was time to bring that day's theatrical proceedings to a halt.

"Okay everyone. That's your lot. Enjoy half term. Stay safe and do try to get some revision done in your proper subjects!"

The kids laughed. They knew full well that some of the other teachers didn't rate Drama as being a bona fide academic pursuit, and that they should be concentrating on 'more rigorous' subjects rather than prancing about pretending to be other people. Plus, they'd heard some woman on the news going on about how arts stuff wasn't going to be worth anything anymore and it would never get you a proper job. But they'd still rather be doing this than learning trigonometry formulae. At least with having the skill of being able to talk to people, the pupils could work out how you could actually use that in a job. Working out angles on triangles just didn't seem as useful.

They gathered their things together to the soundtrack of uncontrollable baby wailing, and made their way slowly to the door. Jim made a beeline for Katie. He knew he had some major sucking-up to do.

"You been okay?" he asked, knowing full well that the response was not going to be particularly positive.

"Well. He screamed in the bank, he screamed in Aldi. He needed a change and peed all over the place when I took him in M&S, then he's screamed pretty much all the way here. So, all in all, no. This is the last time you can do this, Jim. I can't do it on my own. He just won't calm down. I don't know what I'm...."

She stopped and listened. The crying had stopped. Mr & Mrs Tovey, parents to baby Danny (commonly known as that screaming kid), turned around to see two teenagers, one dressed all in black and one dressed all over the shop, taming the beast that both teens knew to be Sir's son. Sadie was giving Danny a tummy rub while Robert pulled big faces and blew raspberries. For the first time in his short life, they heard from their son an audible giggle.

"How are you doing that?"

Katie pounced on them. She wanted to know the secret to parenting and this was the best demonstration she'd seen so far.

"Doing what?"

Robert was a little taken aback by the wide-eyed woman with the wild hair who'd just gone into full interrogation mode.

"The crying. How did you get him to stop crying?"

"Oh, that's easy."

Sadie interjected as if she'd raised five kids and was the next Miriam Stoppard.

"You give them a tummy rub. My sister's kid loves it. It's to do with wind, or something. You've got a baby brother haven't you, Rob? Does he get wind?"

"Yeah, but I just spend hours pulling faces at him. He just sits there, drooling and giggling. You walking up to the shops, Sadie?"

"Yeah, alright. Cheers for the rehearsal, Sir."

And with that, they were gone. Robert with a female companion, Sadie with someone who could make her look fabulous on stage by pressing some buttons. Without knowing it, little Danny had started the journey to a long-term teen relationship that would easily beat Robert's previous record of four and a half days. Danny closed his eyes and nodded off for his first nap in over six hours. Jim looked at Katie, who was struggling to understand exactly what was going on, then down at the sleeping baby who looked as if he was settled for the rest of the afternoon.

"Looks like my shift has started well. Let's get home. eh?"

Jim picked up the car seat, easing it slowly through the double doors in complete silence. His mark books and the props were still all over the studio, but they could wait until he got back after the holiday. Half term had started.

He would not pick up anything to do with work until next
Monday.

Chapter Eighteen

Crunch Day

The earth continued its relentless turning, time shifted cruelly onwards and, just seventeen broken sleeps later, crunch day arrived. GCSE practical exam day for Jim's Year 11 Drama group.

While some of them were still tucked up in their beds (they were teenagers, after all) Jim was up and ready, ensuring that every detail of the day ran smoothly. With this part of the course worth more marks than any other, it was fair to say that Drama practical day was a red-letter one in Jim's calendar. It was make or break day. It had to go well. Jim focused his mind on the getting the basics right.

Biscuits.

Biscuits. Biscuits. Biscuits.

Jim stood in the empty assembly hall, rummaging through his rucksack. He had them. He knew he had them. He'd been in Morrison's at 6:30am. He most definitely had biscuits in this bag.

Like Mary Poppins, he worked his way through the contents of his sack of wonders. Desk lamp, extension lead, gun, juggling balls, carrots, blonde wig, Heroin (well, icing sugar in Clingfilm), make-up bag, plastic cocktail glasses... Ah! Biscuits! Jim realised that the contents of his bag would look more than a bit suspicious to a passing police officer, but for a Drama teacher this was everyday stuff. He placed the props on the stage and went back to the staff room to sort out the refreshments for the imminent arrival of their examiner.

As he removed the Classic Variety Pack, there was far too much movement within what had been (in the supermarket aisle, at least) a very rigid packet of biscuits. He knew he should have carried them separately. So much for buying the posh ones to make a good impression. He may as well give the moderator a pile of crumbs and a straw to hoover them all up. There was no way his kids were going to pass this exam now. The biscuits were wrong.

Everything was wrong. The layout of the room, the biscuits, everything. It didn't matter any more that the kids had been working really hard for eight solid weeks on these pieces of drama. The baked goods were not up to scratch. A disaster was looming.

He looked at the clock.

7:22am

At least three quarters of an hour before the first kids would be here, and at least an hour and a half before 'Mrs G. Winters' from the board would arrive.

Returning to the assembly hall, he plugged in the lamp and extension lead to make sure she could see her notes in the darkened room. He knew that Robert should probably be doing this stuff as he was being examined on his lighting skills, but Jim needed to keep busy. As it was, Robert would move it to the

204

other side of the desk as soon as he came through the door. Jim checked the time again.

7:24am

He was going to need to find something to do for the next hour.

He decided to go and find Niall, the caretaker, to remind him about today's goings-on. Jim had been forced to move some tables out of the assembly hall first thing this morning, and it was out of courtesy that he sought out their resident ray of sunshine to tell him. Not that Niall wasn't quite a cheery man, in general, but being the site manager for such a large school (Lancashire Academy had around 1000 kids) inevitably came with a huge amount of stress. Some of that stress was caused by irritating Drama teachers who left random boxes of clutter around the building. Over the years, Jim had learned to keep Niall sweet.

It didn't take long to find the rapidly ageing caretaker pushing a chair-laden trolley towards the assembly hall.

"Morning, Jim. Bit early for you, isn't it?"

Jim's tardiness had become a running joke in school since Danny had arrived.

"Drama exam day."

Niall nodded. He knew how important the exams were for the teaching staff, and how they lived and died on the results. In his thirty-two years at the school, he'd seen many a teacher fall by the wayside with exam stress. Right now, though, he could do with a hand shifting these chairs.

"Do me a favour. Could you hold some doors for me?"

"Sure, no trouble. Which ones?"

"What do you mean?"

"Which door? Where are you heading with them?"

"Behind you. Into the hall."

"But the Drama exam is..."

Both paused briefly before the inevitable realisation dawned. They were about to stumble upon a gargantuan problem.

What followed was a series of images in slow motion, tinted with more than a hint of surrealism. As the blood rushed directly to the head of Jim Tovey, PGCE (Head of Drama), the room went dark and he was alone in a spotlight. Floating chairs, desk lamps and giant biscuits surrounded him, while a group of children dressed in black walked around slowly, repeatedly whispering the word 'Inadequate'. In his vision, Janet & Mick appeared with clipboards, shaking their heads and noting his failings. As the whispering grew to chanting, Jim found himself running helplessly towards the door, where he could hear Danny crying, louder and louder and louder. "INADEQUATE!" chanted the children over and over again, until Jim relented and closed his eyes.

Silence then blackout.

If it were being marked according to the exam criteria, his hallucination would have got band three at best.

"Jim?"

"Hmm?"

"You alright?"

"The Drama exam, Niall. Today. The hall's been double booked, hasn't it?"

Rude words were exchanged, not in the heat of battle but between two comrades who had been screwed by the common enemy of poor communication. With Megan in the office being off with her back for the past six weeks, no one had thought to sync the diaries. Jim had a Drama exam due to start in an hour and thirteen minutes. Niall had a first aid course to set up. That explained the tables in the room, and the imminent arrival of the chairs.

"What time is the first aid due to start?"

"Two-thirty but there's about ten people coming up from Clitheroe Academy and a few from St Bernadette's. We can't cancel it, Jim. This woman from the Red Cross is driving all the way up from Telford...."

Two-thirty was fine. They had six groups to see; even with a runover or two they would be finished by half one. Jim began to think this might not be such a problem, after all.

"We'll just put the chairs and tables behind the curtains and I'll get the kids to help me put them out at the end. How's that? Everyone's sorted."

"It's not just the chairs and tables, Jimmy boy. There's twelve resuscitation dummies sitting in reception. They just arrived by courier. Where the hell am I going to put them until two o clock?"

And so it came to pass that the audience size for the Year 11 Drama exam grew by twelve people of restricted height and movement. When Jenna entered the hall (the first to arrive, as always) she was greeted by a dozen emotionless attendees which, if she were honest, freaked her out and would give her nightmares for weeks. As Mr Tovey seemed jumpy enough already, she kept her fears to herself but throughout the morning she kept one eye on the front row.

Robert and Sadie were the next to arrive together and both found it hilarious to start a puppet show with the silent twelve.

"Do you reckon we'll fail if they don't clap?" Sadie pondered, as the rest of Year 11 began to drift in.

"One more dummy in our Drama class… Will anyone notice?" replied Robert who seemed, for the first time in his life, to engage in what could only be described as witty banter with the rest of the group.

Sadie gave him a playful nudge on the arm before going to her bag to sort her costume. Jim, who usually failed to spot these things, noticed for the first time that those two seemed to be getting on rather well nowadays. Were they...? Not now, Jim. You've got six shows to run.

For the first time in his five-and-a-half years at the Academy, every single one of his year 11s arrived on time for their exam. These really were a good group. All were quickly dressed into their base black colours and group one had set themselves up ready for the examiner's imminent arrival.

Jim glanced at the rapidly advancing clock. It was 8:42am. Robert was in position at the lighting desk and had set the room in a warm and welcoming pre-show state. Jenna and Lucy were ready at reception to meet and greet the examiner. David stood dutifully by the video camera with its accompanying pile of spare tapes and batteries. Everyone was set.

As the girls ushered Mrs G Winters into the assembly hall, there was nervous anticipation of what could be the finest moment of their theatrical careers so far. They had created these pieces, they had devised the stories, bared their souls, built the characters and rehearsed them until they were blue in the face. They had gathered costumes, props and special effects. They had tested lighting and sound states, and given up so much of their time after school, all for this moment. They had done test runs for the Year 10 group last week and got a really good response, even though a few things had gone wrong in the dress rehearsal (just as they should). They were damned good and they knew it. Now they just had to show it to this random stranger from the exam board.

Jenna used her very best Deputy Head Girl voice to welcome their visitor.

"Here is your table, Mrs Winters. Would you like a biscuit?"

"I'm very sorry. I have a severe allergy to anything containing gluten. Could you take them away, please?"

Jenna looked solemnly at Jim, who was wincing on the other side of hall. He was right. Everybody was going to fail...

The following day, he found himself sitting in Janet's office, trying to explain why. But he was still struggling to get to grips with how events had panned out himself.

"So, Jim. How do you think it went?"

This was a trick question, and Jim knew it. How did it go? In the space of five and a half hours, they'd had pretty much everything that life could throw at them.

Nerves aside, the first performance piece had gone pretty well. The girls had devised their own adapted version of John Godber's *Shakers*, but had updated the play's location from a 1980s urban cocktail bar to a Friday night at Wetherspoons after a United match. The piece had been dreamt up entirely by Karen Gosforth who, despite being a fairly quiet member of the group, had written the piece almost single-handedly.

It helped that Karen's dad was the licensee of the River's End and that, when they were in Year 10, Jim had taken the group to see a student version of Jim Cartwright's acclaimed pub play *Two*. But writing a twenty-minute, four-hander adaptation of someone else's work was no mean feat, and Karen deserved some credit.

As is always annoying with these things, Karen would get little credit for her writing as she was only marked in the exam on her contribution to the play through performance. She wasn't the strongest performance candidate, even within her own group. This didn't bother Karen much; performance wasn't really her thing. She'd chosen Drama because she loved plays and wanted to be a writer. If she scraped a C, she'd be happy.

Janet and the rest of the Senior Leadership Team would, however, be fuming. As Karen was such a strong candidate in her English class, her target grade for Drama had been set at A*. The realistic C that Jim was talking about on this spreadsheet would put her four full grades down on where they considered she should be. Was Karen a victim of the system? You'd better believe it.

After trying (and failing) to explain Karen's situation to Janet, Jim moved on and went through what he thought the kids in group one would have got for the performances. He showed Janet the marks that Sameerah from St Bernadette's had given them when she visited the school for the dress rehearsal last week. It was standard practice nowadays for teachers to double-mark almost every task.

Absolutely everything was about accountability, and double-marking the work meant they were covering each other's backs for when the actual results came back from the board in August. Jim would be returning the favour in a couple of weeks when Sameerah's group would be jumping through exactly the same hoops. But, for now, he was left explaining to Janet the marks they'd agreed upon, whilst also trying to explain exactly what each mark meant.

"That's what we think they would have got for the performance, in that column there. But, of course, this is all very speculative. You have no idea how an examiner will feel about the pieces she managed to see...."

Jim pointed on his tablet to his nicely colour-coded exam spreadsheet, which he'd spent a good two hours tweaking last night to try make this meeting as painless as possible. Imran, the school network administrator, had given him a crash course in how to do conditional formatting in Excel. Jim had used it to make his results spreadsheet so easy to read that even Janet (a self confessed computer-phobe) could follow it. He had even printed her a copy. It couldn't be easier to understand.

Jim had enjoyed using conditional formatting. It was simple. You put numbers in the tables and pretty colours came out, explaining what exactly your numbers mean in terms of success or failure. The issue right now, of course, was that neither the numbers nor the resulting colours were looking at all pretty. In fact, they looked down right ugly. What the colours did do, though, was make it a simple for even someone like Janet to understand.

Janet didn't understand. Try as she might, it looked like Dulux colour chart of primary colours. Why was this helpful when grading an exam? It might be suitable when planning to paint a child's bedroom, but where did it tell you if these kids had passed or failed? This was just typical of Jim. Style over substance, every time. It was what she found really frustrating about all the Arts teachers in school. Everything they did was about 'the craft', continually banging on about this piece or that piece of the kids' work. They didn't understand that neither she nor Ofsted were interested in the artistic merits of what 11B had

212

produced yesterday. They need figures, they needed A*-C grades, they needed EVIDENCE.

"Are they going to hit their target grades, Jim? That's all we should really be interested in. Are all these red kids going to fail? Are they all like Karen?"

There was another one of Jim's (by-now) trademark pauses. Harold Pinter had nothing on him for injecting silence into everyday pieces of dialogue, especially when he was attempting to talk shop with Janet. It was as if they could only do four or five sentences of interaction before both remembered that they despised each other's views on how to teach. So they invariably stopped every now and again, just so they could remember not to get on with one other.

"Janet. If I'm going to explain these grades to you, I need to talk about the pieces and about what happened during the exam."

Jim tried as much as he could to lose the 'butt out of telling me how to teach my subject' tone of voice but, from the way she screwed up her face, he could tell that he'd been somewhat unsuccessful. He ploughed on, regardless. There was no way that granny was going to continue her egg-sucking lesson without him at least letting her know the circumstances of how all these eggs had turned rotten in the first place. And these eggs were bad.

Group two had got off to an excellent start, with Jenna and Lucy playing out really well their comedy Fawlty-esque duologue about the hotel inspector and the grubby chef - even getting a few smiles out of the examiner. Everything was going okay until

10.15. Things seemed to be going according to plan, and Jim's early-morning jitters had settled.

That was when the fire alarm went off.

There was a moan of disbelief and Jim moved quickly onto the stage floor area, directly in front of Mrs Winters.

"Right, everyone. Please can you move yourself sensibly to the doors and line up!"

Sensibly. Twenty-two teenagers, many of whom were in costume and most of whom were at a heightened level of exam stress, were being asked to do something sensibly. Was that possible? It shouldn't have been impossible, but it was never likely. As they pushed aside chairs to get to the doors, and shifted from silence to full-blown chatter mode at a hundred miles an hour, Jim could already find himself trying to answer the questions they were going to ask as he escorted them out of the building.

"Will Lucy and Jenna have to start again?"

"What do we do if all our props get burned? Do we have to make them again?"

"Is she still marking us when we're outside?"

Jim followed the evacuation procedures and directed Mrs Winters to the spot on the far side of the top yard, where the day visitors would be counted by the office staff. He glanced out of the window. It was pouring down. He hoped to God that someone from the office had brought an umbrella or he'd have a very soggy examiner.

With Mrs Winters out of the way, he turned his attention to the rest of the group who needed to be taken to the meeting point just outside the entrance to the central block. This situation was now nearly thirty seconds old and had moved swiftly from calm disbelief and sheer bad luck, to an all-out panic. He had to calm them down before....

Crash.

An arm bounced across the floor. The united motion of stop, turn, giggle couldn't have been better executed by Year 11 if they'd rehearsed it a hundred times. The source of mirth was obvious. The battered remains of a resuscitation doll clattered across the stage and landed in the examiner's bag, which had been left by the side of the desk.

What wasn't so funny was the way that Sadie was now clutching her ankle after being attacked by said dummy just moments before. She had insisted on sitting next to the first aider's mannequins throughout the morning, playing puppets with them from the start. Now they had got their revenge. Robert was first at her side, clearly worried for her health (Those two WERE an item, Jim knew something was going on) and, as Robert helped Sadie to limp out of the building, it was clear to both of them that she was going to need some serious medical attention in the next few minutes.

Jim and Robert took an arm each and slowly made their way with the rest of 11B to the meeting point. Under instruction from Robert who, it turns out, was pretty good in a crisis situation,

Lucy had brought a chair from the hall for Sadie to sit and cry on. He gave a quick shout to Alan to do his form register then began to deal with the Sadie situation, using his limited knowledge of injured ankles. In hindsight, the P.E teacher would probably have been a better bet for dealing with this rather than the form register but, to be honest, Alan had looked pre-occupied and not entirely with it as they came out of the building. Jim was also in exam mode and had to deal with everything himself if he wanted it done properly...

"And the fire alarm is the reason that you are giving for all these grades being below expectation?"

Janet no longer hid her lack of belief in Jim. This was now a no-holds-barred attack. She wanted him out and he knew it. She hadn't been on site on the morning of the exam, but she still spoke as if the fire alarm episode was merely incidental and - if he were worth anything at all as a teacher - he'd have prepared them better for this examination.

"Well, for starters, Sadie being taken to A&E threw that group completely because Jenna had to improvise the lines with them. Add into the mix Robert being completely knocked sideways by his girlfriend being taken off in the ambulance, meaning the lighting and sound cues were off, and you get an idea of what we were up against. Plus, we couldn't get going again for an hour as the power in the hall had been cut off to reset the alarm system. That's why we've got Armageddon on a spreadsheet."

"Why did the delay make a difference to the performances?"

"It made us run until well after lunch and Niall had to do the first aid in the science rooms. The first aiders turned up, wanting their dummies back, and walked straight in during the middle of the final piece. It put the kids off completely. I don't think the day could have gone any worse if we'd tried."

At that stage, the lesson bell rang. An end to the meeting and an excuse for Jim to escape before she asked him another stupid question, to which he knew he would give a stupid response, thereby getting him the stupid sack.

"I'm going to have to go. I've got that group now and I need to work on their preparation for the review piece with them. They're going to need as many marks as they can from this essay."

Janet responded with the kindest words she could muster.

"Yes. They can't afford to screw the next exam up as well, Jim. You're going to have to put in some serious damage limitation to sort out this mess."

Cheers for the support, Janet. You're a rock.

Jim didn't want to prolong these moments, but still had a burning question that he needed her to answer. It had been bugging him ever since he got home after the exam, and no one on the staff seemed to be able to tell him what had happened. Hopefully Janet, being amongst the inner circle of school bigwigs, would have the information he needed.

"The fire alarm. Do we know who set it off yet?"

Janet didn't even show him the courtesy of raising her head as she tried to make sense of the printed copy of Jim's spreadsheet.

"We're still working on it. It's one of the Year 8s, that's for sure. It was set off somewhere between MFL and the gym, and they all had P.E then. The cameras on that corridor were broken so there's not much chance of catching them now, though, is there?"

Not if you complete the investigation, Miss Marple. But no way was Jim was letting this one go.

Chapter Nineteen

A Short Note

Junk, junk, SEN form to give to Debbie, junk, coach booking form, junk, reward sticker sheet, junk.

Filing was fun. Jim loved filing. It was what got him up each morning. Nay, it was what drove him to become a Performing Arts teacher in the first place. The very idea that he could be given ten to fifteen pieces of paper a day (that he would probably never read) to sort into little piles, was such an amazing incentive to become an outstanding practitioner of Drama. How he had gone through the first twenty years of his life without this unimaginable joy was anybody's guess, but here he was - just fourteen days since his last 'file-a-thon' (his official name for this hour of the fortnight on his timetable) - and the 'pending' pile was at least a foot high.

He daren't think about the poor trees that had sacrificed themselves for this pointless, soul-destroying ritual. He dwelled not on the number of work hours put in by countless individuals who had lovingly gifted him these pieces of paper, only for him to sling them in the recycling bin. The only thing he was thinking about was that the quicker he could chuck this lot away, the quicker he could get on with doing what he actually needed to do – try and fix that squeaky stage block that had been driving him potty for the last two weeks.

He continued his flick and sort.

Did he want to organise a trip to New York to see a show on Broadway? Yes, he did. But there wasn't a chance of that happening after the debacle of the textile museum trip. He'd been through hell to get permission from the governors for his trip to see *Wicked*, so a proposal for a transatlantic excursion would probably not go down too well. If he couldn't get out to see a show twenty miles down the road in a coach, he doubted SLT would be amenable to him taking a group of kids halfway round the globe.

Into the green bin.

Did he want a new pack of subject-specific reward stickers with slogans like 'Arts Champion', 'Award Winner', and 'Star Performer'? No, he didn't, as the pile of freebie ones that he ordered at the back end of last year were still sitting in his drawer since he'd realised that the majority of kids in his classes felt utterly patronised (and he utterly patronising) every time he tried to award one. The looks of 'Really sir? A sticker? I'm fourteen' were still fresh in his mind. Screw it up, lob it in the bin. Three points.

There was the odd gem in amongst all the detritus. He found two pay slips (nothing boosts the morale like seeing how little pension the government was giving you nowadays), the 'Numeracy News' that Gavin Jones (Head of Maths) had been banging on about in briefing for the last week, and an abridged copy of *Much Ado About Nothing* that he'd been meaning to get photocopied to try out with Drama Club for the upcoming Shakespeare festival. Pay slips in pocket, Maths newsletter pinned to the board (at least he could make it LOOK like he'd read it to those passing through) and play script in his bag to read tonight.

Next. A small piece of folded file paper. Ripped from an exercise book and folded in half. Jim unfolded it. A girl's handwriting (it was legible). It contained one simple, short and (as it would turn out) career-defining sentence.

Sir. It was Ethan who did the fire alarm.

No name on the paper. It was clearly one of the Year 11s as it referred to what had happened on exam day. Only they really knew how annoyed he was about the alarm going off, and only they would have found out who had been the one to make them all get drenched outside. What was he to do with the note? He hadn't touched this pile in two weeks and it was at least halfway down the mound of paper. Had he left it too long to be able to deal with it? Plus, he had no proof of Ethan's involvement other than this one scrap of paper.

The exam was on the 17th March, which was twelve days ago. Jim logged into the register system and browsed until he found the one he wanted. Scrolling through the lists, he found the information.

Connoly, E. Tuesday morning. 17/3. P.E.

Exactly where Janet had said the alarm had been set off. Jim looked for the staff teaching code attached to the group.

A.C. Alan Cook. Everyone's favourite Aussie. Or at least he would be if he could confirm that Detective Inspector Tovey finally had his man.

Jim was at the doors of P.E in a matter of seconds, clutching the accusatory note. Alan was in the midst of an athletics session, trying to enthuse a group of Year 10 girls to throw themselves backwards over a high jump bar. There was a real air of disappointment. Alan was clearly failing to enthuse and they were definitely failing to jump. If he'd had the time or inclination, Jim would have witnessed a prolonged and painful display of teenage failure, putting most of the girls off organised sport for the next twenty years. Jim didn't waste any time getting to the point.

"Ethan Connoly."

Being a dramatist made Jim particularly astute when it came to reading faces, and Alan's had a definite look of "Oh Shit" about it. The note was bang on-target. Alan knew exactly what this was about.

"Is this about the fire alarm?"

"You knew it was him?"

Jim's blood pressure was rising already. This was now turning from a hunt for a lone gunman into some sort of organised cover-up. He didn't like what he was hearing one bit.

"No. No one saw him do it."

Alan was starting to look more and more worried – panicked, even. Jim did wonder quite why he was getting so agitated. After all, this was 'Who set off a fire alarm?" not "Who shot Kennedy?" He doubted there would be a Hollywood blockbuster about this particular incident.

"He was supposed to be doing hockey with the rest of the Year 8 boys, but didn't have any shorts with him. I was going to let him just do it in his school trousers but Denise and Geoff keep getting pulled into the head saying they've all got to be in sports kit if they're doing P.E, and we have to set them a detention for not having the right equipment."

This still wasn't adding up.

"So why didn't you just give him some spare kit?"

Jim knew it was standard policy for kids to be given stuff from lost property if they turned up without a kit, so that they looked vaguely presentable when they trooped out onto the school field. Sure, it was ill fitting and occasionally tatty, but most of the time that meant that the kids remembered their kit in future. In this case, apparently not.

"He wouldn't wear the spare kit. Told me it'd make him look like a pikey. He wasn't going to budge. I had 35 Year 8 boys trooping down to the all-weather pitch in the rain with Geoff, and I needed to lock up. So I got him out of the changing room and told him to follow me down to the pitches. I warned him that if he didn't hurry up he get another detention. But he didn't follow me. He just wandered off."

"You just let him go??"

Jim was reaching boiling point.

"I'll be honest with you, Jim. I completely forgot about him. By the time I got up to the pitch, James Leach had already been clumped over the head with a hockey stick, so I had to take the session while Geoff sorted out an accident form in the office. Ethan was the last thing on my mind. It wasn't until the alarm went off and I saw all your guys all standing about in their costumes that I figured it might be him. Even then I didn't have any real proof..."

Clang!

The high jump bar hit the ground under the full force of Bethany Holt, who had clattered into it at great speed. She clutched her arm and shot a look at Alan that said, "You did this". The P.E teacher did his duty, helped her up while dishing out the industry standard amount of sympathy (i.e. none), got her back in the jump line, and turned his attention back to Jim.

"You understand why I couldn't say anything, don't you? I'd only just scraped past my induction after having Geoff observe me with those Year 7s. If someone on SLT found out that a kid I was supposed to be watching had buggered off and started the fire alarm, I'd have been screwed."

Solidarity, brother.

A quick hands-up gesture of submission was enough to tell Alan to stop digging this particular hole. Jim turned on his heels and walked away, giving Alan the distinct impression that he wasn't angry. Just very, very disappointed. Alan would apologise properly, and attempt to make it up to his friend on Friday afternoon for their end-of-the week pint but, right now, he was in the doghouse.

As it was, Alan's incompetence and inability to fess up about the alarm had already left Jim's mind. He was currently in the red zone and emotions were running through his veins at a rate of knots. He would go back to his desk, find out where Year 8 were currently housed, and get to the bottom of it. Right here, right now. Then he would march Ethan to Janet, where he would explain what had happened and, for a change, she would have someone to blame whose name wasn't Jim.

As fate would have it (in hindsight, it was definitely fate and not at all luck) Year 8 were in the dining room, waiting to be shuffled into the hall for a special assembly that was scheduled to start ten minutes earlier. Each lower school year group were, in turn, being lectured to by the new local PCSO about their conduct around school and the estate. He reminded them that the people in uniform who they saw when they were leaving school weren't just traffic wardens with an attitude problem, as one particularly erudite Year 9 had shouted from the top deck of the bus just yesterday. Rather, they were highly respected members of their community. They also reminded each and every one of them that their friends, the 'actual' police officers (one of whom stood menacingly in the corner), were armed with big sticks and handcuffs and could throw them in a jail cell at any time, if they so wished.

Year 9 were in the hall getting their 'community briefing' (aka the 'show of force' revue) but it had overrun by ten minutes as someone had forgotten to change the batteries on the radio mic since the Drama exam two weeks ago. Another item for the list of things that Jim would be to blame for in next week's meeting with Janet.

Waiting outside in the dining hall, Ethan was sitting at the end of the row, kicking Jack Sutherland underneath the table. Jack Sutherland was kicking him back. There was no malice involved and neither knew why they were doing it, other than it seemed like a good way to pass the time until 'Stick Insect' Anderson (whose Science class they had all been dragged out of) was ready to shuffle them into the hall. The Neanderthal minds of pubescent teenage boys remained a mystery but, as they were not actually bothering anyone else, Jenny Anderson had chosen tactical ignoring as her way of dealing with their under-the-table kick-a-thon. As Jim strode into the room on the final part of his mission, it was clear to her that the Drama teacher wasn't in the mood to be patient.

"I need Ethan."

He hadn't intended to sound quite so abrupt, but the red mist was down and he really wasn't in the mood for pleasantries. There was no questioning from Jenny who, like her counterpart Alan in P.E, was also an NQT. She really wasn't up for crossing an experienced Head of Department who looked like he was about to thump someone.

"Ethan! Stop trying to take chunks out of Jack's legs and get over here! Mr Tovey needs to speak to you."

Ethan gave one last kick under the table, a killer blow to the goolies that caused Jack to howl in pain and the waiting class to descend into fits of laughter. The Tovey vs Connoly celebrity death match was about to start and now had a full arena of baying audience members, warmed up and ready to go.

"Did you set off the fire alarm?"

Ethan looked away and sniggered. First blow to Tovey. He'd caught him unaware. Connoly responded with the best weapon in the teenage armoury. Nonchalant sarcasm.

"What fire alarm? We haven't had a fire alarm..."

"You know exactly what I'm talking about. Two weeks ago..."

"Two weeks? I've slept since then!"

Giggles from a group of girls who were doing their very best impression of not looking at the thing that everybody couldn't help but look at. Connoly's comic delivery was good and enough to put yet more fuel onto the already raging Tovey fire, to the point where voices began to be raised. In the post-match commentary, this would be recognised as the moment that Jim well and truly lost.

"Don't get sarcastic with me, Ethan! I know full well you walked out of P.E because you didn't have any kit. Again!"

"Don't shout at me!"

"I'll do what I please, young man! Do you know how many people's exam pieces you screwed up? Twenty-two. Twenty-two year 11s who are probably going to fail their exam because of YOUR actions!"

"You can't prove anything."

"Well, we'll see what your Grandma has to say, shall we?"

Nice move, Tovey. Make it personal. Hit him where you know it hurts.

The decibel levels were already raised beyond 'acceptable for a grown man and a teenage boy'. The doors to the assembly hall were swung open by Janet, who was now exiting the hall accompanied by a fully beefed-up Police Officer and two slightly intimidated Year 9 members of the school council who were being placed on door duty. With the entrance to the hall behind him, there was no way that Ethan could have known who was to his rear as he tried to land his sucker punches.

"You can't prove shit, Tovey. Fuck off."

As the crowd behind him jeered, Ethan turned to walk away, thinking he had managed a notorious victory... only to be confronted by a bigger and significantly more heavily armed foe. Holy crap! The police moved fast nowadays. How the hell did he get there? Ethan panicked, picked up his bag, and tried to shove his way through the crowd of Year 9s who were rapidly streaming out of the hall. They knew that some sort of incident was taking place outside.

"Who is he, Jim? I don't teach him. What's his name?"

Janet desperately jumped on the case now, trying to quickly save face in front of her visitor.

"Ethan Connoly. He's in Year..."

"Ethan, come back here please..."

"Fuck off."

Ethan had nothing to lose and no longer cared. He just wanted out of this hall where people were lining up to have a go at him, bringing policemen in, laughing loudly, then bringing up in front of his mates that he lived with his Grandma. He wanted out and he wanted out now. He pushed into the crowd as they streamed out of the hall, knocking one of the smaller Year 9 girls to the floor in the process. She was doomed. Within seconds, members of the crowd were toppling over her and the dining room had become a mosh pit of flailing children and staff. By the time Ethan had got to the door and begun to run, the real damage had been done.

Janet was on the floor, clutching the back of her head that she'd caught on the edge of the dining room bench as she fell.
Ethan would be transferred to the Pupil Referral Unit before the week was out.

As he turned his key in the front door that evening, Jim couldn't help but feel hollow. He should be feeling happy at the outcome - over the moon, even. Janet, who'd received only a minor injury in the incident but whose her authority had been well and truly shot-down in front of half the school, had taken Jim's side. She had been pleased with Jim's pro-activeness at getting the evidence about Ethan's involvement in the fire alarm debacle. Her pride had been hit publicly and, for once, she stood shoulder-to-shoulder with the man who, until that very morning, had been a major thorn in her side. She had acted swiftly in dealing with Ethan, and had even spoken about applying to the exam board for special consideration regarding the deliberate attempt (as she now saw) it to sabotage Jim's exam.

Try as he might, however, he couldn't get the image out of his head of the panicking Ethan, tears in his eyes, looking, in every way that he could, for a way to escape from the jeering crowds who had poured out of the assembly hall. A boy of just thirteen, behaving like a wounded animal, snarling and trying desperately to be in any other place than the one that Jim - the so-called professional in the situation - had cornered him into.

The problem hadn't gone away. Instead, Ethan would now be caged up somewhere else, hating the world just that little bit more.

SUMMER TERM

Chapter Twenty

Visiting Time

With Ofsted imminent and Ethan already on his third warning of the month, the decision was taken for him to spend some time at the Pupil Referral Unit that had recently been taken under the wing of the Academy Trust. Having a PRU as part of the Trust made transitions between the mainstream site and the unit fairly simple, and the time from the straw breaking the camel's back through to Ethan checking in to misdemeanour central had been less than thirty-six hours. To give Janet credit, when she and SLT decided to put the boot in, she made sure it happened quickly.

The altercation with Janet had happened the week before they broke up for Easter, so everyone had had plenty of time to reflect on events while they enjoyed the holiest of holy holidays. Janet recuperated on the slopes in Switzerland from her agonising blow, telling tales to all who would listen of how she'd been brutally attacked by a young thug in her care. Jim returned to his retrospective lesson planning (he was behind on his paperwork, yet again) while trying to get Danny to understand that solid food was something you should really put in your mouth and not throw at the window. Ethan got a three-pack of Kinder eggs from his Grandma, with a promise that next month they'd get the coach up to see his mum who, thanks to her own altercation with one of the prison officers on her wing, had booked herself in for a further three months at her majesty's pleasure.

Getting Ethan so swiftly down to the PRU at the end of last term had been simple and when they all returned for the final phase of the school year in early April, there should really have been no reason for the situation to be reviewed. Ethan, despite still being on roll with the Academy, would be out of their hair and they would be left to educate the best of the best and turn all those annoying ambers to greens.

The problem with segregating Ethan from the rest of the school population, however, was that it immediately put everything but his core education on hold, including any chance he had of attending extra-curricular activities. He wouldn't have much in the way of Arts studies on his temporary timetable at the PRU, and certainly wouldn't have anything that would engage the boy's frenetic mind enough to warrant a swift return to mainstream schooling. This was how Jim found himself pulling up at the PRU, during one of his precious double-frees, to try and organise the latest in a long line of fool's errands carried out in the name of Tovey.

Why Jim should stick his neck out for Ethan, he really had no idea. After all, the kid had almost single-handedly wrecked any chance the GCSE group had of passing the practical exam, alongside being a constant thorn in Jim's side during his timetabled lessons. The sensible thing would be to leave the little bugger to stew in his own juices down at the PRU and make him realise what a grade one knob he had been. Let the little sod suffer. The problem was that, in his entire life, Jim had never really done the sensible thing.

Leaving Ethan at the PRU also left a huge hole in Jim's plans for the upcoming Shakespeare Festival, for which Ethan had been lined up for a juicy part. But this wasn't the only reason why Jim was now going out of his way to do the unthinkable. Seeing the panic in the boy's eyes on that fateful morning had reminded Jim a little of a slightly younger Tovey. A boy who, less than two decades earlier, had been given more than just a little care and support by the system as he himself came to terms with dealing with losing a parent in his teens. Alright, Ethan's mum was alive and well. But her absenteeism due to her own detention was more than enough for Jim to offer the boy at least the chance of redemption.

As he pulled into the car park of the PRU, he saw a young ginger-haired man, frantically waving his arms and pointing towards the far side of the visitors' car park.

"Brilliant. Not even out of the car yet and there's a drama."

Jim mumbled to himself like a tired old grandfather. He didn't know what it was about being near Ethan Connoly, but it seemed to age him by forty years.

As he stopped the car, the ginger arm-waver jogged up to the window, making motions for him to wind the screen down.

"You Jim from the Academy?"

"Yes, that's right, I'm here to see Eth..."

"Yeah, Ethan. Yeah, I know. Do you want to put your car on the road near the houses up there? Up at the top of the road?"

Jim looked at his welcoming committee. He was being given a look that was stating clearly, 'You're on our turf now. You'd best listen to the advice'. He also took a quick look at the backdrop -

a shabby-looking Victorian building, windows adorned with a mixture of bars and metal covers, a deserted yard and a flowerbed long since overrun with Britain's hardiest and ugliest wild flowers. He didn't need telling twice. He put the car into reverse and drove to the next street, as instructed. As he got out, he got a taste of the school's local neighbourhood - all too often a signature for what might be found inside the school. If, indeed, that was what he was going into.

At least three houses had boards on the windows, with many others sporting a look of post-modern junkyard chic - worn tyres, half-repaired dirt bikes, and shopping trolleys aplenty. Household waste from overflowing bins littered the sides of the street as if it had been sprinkled like the antidote to fairy dust, giving the place more than a faint of whiff of squalor. Jim thought about the poor souls who lived in the un-boarded houses and how they tried to sleep at night, clutching their Suns and Daily Mails tight to their chest, remembering a time when it didn't look like this. All but three sported 'For Sale' signs. "Good luck with that one", Jim thought as he made his way back to the PRU's main entrance.

Flappy-arm guy was waiting at the gates (the sign, full of graffiti, that Jim had passed on his first attempt claimed that this shell of a building was, after all, a seat of learning) and seemed pleased to see that someone from the outside had made the effort to visit.

"Hi. It is Jim, isn't it?"

"Yeah, that's me. Sorry, you are....?"

He had spoken to a woman on the phone. Apparently, Trudi had been given the delightful task of having Ethan under her wing.

"I'm Greg, Head of Key Stage 3. You spoke to Trudi yesterday on the phone?"

Jim nodded.

"Sorry about making you shift your car. Best you don't let them associate you with something they might be able to slash or smash, eh?"

Welcome to the Pleasuredome, Jimbo.

"So, you're Trudi's line manager?" Jim figured that getting down to brass tacks and getting out of here ASAP was the best way to proceed.

"Yeah, she's not going to make it today. She's having a rest day after getting stuck in the middle of a bit of do yesterday afternoon."

OK, the member of staff he was here to see had been injured in the line of duty. This was getting so much better.

"Oh. I hope she's okay...?"

Jim may have only spoken to her briefly over the phone but that officially made her a colleague. He had a strong sense of comradeship with anyone foolish enough to publicly call themselves a teacher. Plus, Jim had had more than his fair share of near misses in his time, particularly when one very small but very aggrieved Year 7 had tried to throw some plastic seating at him during his NQT year. There but for the grace of chair-controlling deities, and all that. Greg attempted to put his mind at rest.

"It actually wasn't the kid in question's fault this time. One of our mouthy Year 9s lost it with a Year 11 on a corridor at lunchtime, then hit the 'retreat at speed' button when he knew he was about to get jumped by the Year 11 and a couple of his mates. He was trying to get himself out of the building before he got lamped but got stuck at the double doors and hid in a classroom. The other mob thought he'd already gone through them. As a member of staff has to buzz you through, being Year 11s, they just kicked it in."

"They just kicked it in?"

Jim was loving the way that sentence rolled off Greg's tongue as if it were an everyday occurrence.

"It was just one of those things. Basically, they stormed through and didn't know Trudi was standing on duty on the other side. She's only short and they didn't see her through the glass at the top. She got a thump on the back of the head. It didn't do her any damage. Just shook her up a bit. Certainly nothing malicious in it. The Year 11 lad was just taking out his frustration on the nearest thing to him and, being six foot two, the door was always going to come off second best. He was really sorry. Even wanted to go to the hospital when we got her head checked out."

Jim was trying not to let his jaw drop, but the everyday manner in which Greg was relaying this tale of innocent sorrow was taking him aback more than just a tiny bit.

"Were the police not involved?" Jim was playing catch up in this new realm. Greg almost scoffed at the prospect.

"No, Trudi's been here a long time. Longer than most of us, actually. She knows that adding another offence to his long list isn't going to achieve anything. Plus, she takes him for English Lit and if he's not around for the exam it'll screw her results. She's not stupid."

Wow. And then some.

"Trudi just needs a day to get her head together and chill out. Darren's spending a day at home to cool off. His granddad came up last night and said he's going to pay for the damage. No harm done. But it does mean I'm on Ethan duty today instead of Trudi, who usually deals with anything to do with English stuff."

"Well, it's Drama but..."

Jim didn't get the chance to go into his long speech about why Drama and English were completely different subjects, as Greg was in full flow.

"We don't have Drama here as a subject. English is as close as you're gonna get."

They were now at Reception and Greg buzzed them both in. Jim signed himself in to the visitors' book and made a point of putting his car registration down, even though he had parked off-site. If anything did happen to his car, he wanted the paper trail to show that he was here on business, rather than parking on the edge of a war zone just for fun.

"So, what's your plan for Ethan?"

A plan? Jim wasn't sure that the thinking had made it as far as a plan. There had been ideas, some pondering and certainly a fair bit of mulling it over, but trying to describe it as a plan was pushing it a bit. He was going to see the kind of reaction he got first, then take it from there. Winging it was, after all, Jim's speciality.

"It's extra-curricular. I want him to see if I can get him back on site after school for a show we're doing. Need to see what kind of mood he's in first, though."

That sounded OK in his head. It sounded almost like it was a lark and that he wasn't sneaking a kid back on site to take a part in a play. A kid who, just a few weeks ago, had been sent down to what was essentially a young offenders' institute. It sounded fine. There was a precedent for this, after all. Other staff had come down to the PRU and worked with kids who had been excluded. Last year, Elizabeta in Music had come in her frees to give extra singing lessons to get Rhiannon Murphy through her GCSE practical. Janet herself had done the same when she'd had kids who needed prepping for their Spanish oral exam, as they didn't have a Spanish specialist at the PRU.

Jim had heard both members of staff trumpeting for many years in morning briefings about their respective 'educational triumphs', so why should things be any different here? Other than the fact that this time it wasn't for a GCSE exam. And this kid was only in Year 8. And all the work would be done after school. And he would be bringing Ethan back on site only three weeks after being suspended. And the offender in question would be back in circulation with at least five other kids, no matter how much Jim tried to plan the rehearsals. Other than that, this was exactly the same.

Greg showed Jim into the English office then shuffled off to locate Ethan. It took Greg all of two minutes. Ethan was still a relative newbie to this environment and hadn't yet had time to tag himself on to a group. Like a cat that had just moved home, Ethan was found trying to mark out new territory, skulking up and down one of the joyless corridors. Jim had briefly spotted him hanging about at the other side of the dank atrium as he was shown into the building but, in a bid to be vaguely professional, he chose not to shout "Cooee!" and wave like an embarrassing auntie at a nativity play.

Greg hadn't yet informed Ethan why he'd been brought into the English office so, when he did come in, his head was down. He wasn't expecting to be greeted by Jim's familiar face. As he lifted his gaze, something unexpected happened.

Ethan smiled.

Jim had known Ethan 'don't fuck with me' Connoly for around about six months and had met with him and his classmates for an hour a week, regular as clockwork. Yet this was the first time he'd ever seen anything like relief, happiness or youth in this boy's face. In an instant, all the vitriol and bitterness melted away, replaced by the look of what Jim understood to be a normal twelve-year-old-boy. In that brief instant, at least, Ethan looked happy to see him. Then he remembered who he was. And where he was.

"What are you doing here?"

243

"Nice to see you, too. I need to talk to you about something to do with Drama Club."

Jim explained the predicament. He needed someone to play Leontes in *Much Ado about Nothing* for the Shakespeare Festival. He had to use everyone from lower school who went to Drama Club as he wasn't allowed to take Year 10 or 11 out of class this year. Everyone in lower years would suck at doing this part, as it needs someone who could get away with acting considerate at the start of the play but would go mental and completely lose it in the middle.

As far as Jim could see, only Ethan could carry it off.

"So I get to shout at people?"

"In the middle of the play, yes. But you have to do a 'caring old man' bit at the beginning. It's a good part. Much better than Claudio, who's supposed to be the hero. That part's rubbish. You get one of the best speeches in the whole play."

Ethan looked quizzically at Jim, who had clearly gone well out of his way to try and square this circle. He had no idea why Jim was making all this effort.

"But I thought I'd mucked up your precious exam? Why go to all this hassle?"

That was a big question and Jim took some time before he spoke. After all, this was the going to be the key part of the sales pitch. Was there any point in trying to pull the wool over the kid's eyes and tell him it's because he believed everyone had a second chance? That we all had special talents and needed the chance to shine whenever we could? Yes, Jim firmly believed all that life-affirming, educationally noble gubbins (he was a Drama teacher, after all). But that wasn't the real reason he was sitting in the command bunker of teen crime central. He was going to have to level totally with this kid to get him to play ball.

"Don't get me wrong, Ethan. Don't think I haven't thought long and hard about all this. I wouldn't be here if I didn't think it was the best option. I had to get special permission from Mr Owen to even come and talk to you. Luckily, he seems to like Drama and wants to let me give this a go. The truth is, this is possibly the last production I'll get to do at school. My department hasn't had great results for the last couple of years, and there are some people at the top of the school who want to stop me doing things like Drama Club and all the shows. Mr Owen has to make a decision on it in the next couple of months, and it's not looking good. I want the last one to go off with a bit of a bang and, well… that's what you're good at."

There was a short moment as Ethan readjusted to being spoken to by an adult as if he were on the same level. It hadn't happened much before and he needed to make sure he wasn't being sucked into one of those double bluff 'make them think it's their idea' things that teachers do so well.

"Stuff what the others say. Just do them, anyway. They can't stop you from running shows if you really want to. It's your time."

Oh, for the rational mind of a teenager. How he would love to explain fully to this still-growing mind the way things actually were. Jim longed to start a discussion about the pedagogical opinions of the current chain of command at school, the blistering attacks that Arts teaching had suffered in the last ten years from the right-wing press, or the insidious, results-driven ethos from central government. Instead, the boy got a shrug of the shoulders.

"They won't let me. This is probably going to be the last one, at least while you'll be in the school. Don't ask why. It's just too complicated."

Jim surprised even himself at the candid nature of his approach, and realised at that moment why making the journey to bust the kid out of this state-sponsored prison had been so important to him. Despite all the hassle, the alarms, the swearing, the form-filling and the petulant abuse, Ethan Connoly represented something that was all too lacking in his work life.

He was honest. Ok, sometimes it was honest to the point of brutality. But it was refreshingly truthful, nonetheless.

"I'd tell them to go fuck themselves, but that's just me."

Jim wondered if there was a way that he could make Ethan an honorary member of SLT.

"That's why I'm the Drama teacher and you're stuck in here, hanging about on a corridor like a Billy no-mates. Now, do you want to do the play or not?"

Jim looked directly at Ethan. They had the measure of each other now.

"Do I have to see that old cow Murphy who got me excluded?"

"Mrs Murphy will be away from school on a training course for two out of the three evenings I need you to rehearse, and the chances of her coming over to the Drama studio on the other day are pretty slim. Anyway, the head has said its OK with him as long as you do your lessons down here without hassle and you don't interfere with anything else that's running at school."

By-passing Janet, and timing Ethan's rehearsals for when she would be out of school, had been the cornerstone of getting this to work. It was foolproof. Easy peasy. Surely?

"Alright I'll do it. Sounds like a laugh. You got a script I have to learn?"

"Right here. Your bits are highlighted in orange."

"It's not very long."

"It's only a half-hour version of the play. Did you think I'd try and put you in a full-length Shakespeare show with only three rehearsals?"

"I don't know. You do some weird shit sometimes. I wouldn't put it past you."

Touché, young Padawan. Touché.

Chapter Twenty-One

Much Ado

Being squeezed into the staff room for morning briefing was never the most fun way to spend a Wednesday morning and, as usual, Jim found himself only just making it into the room on time. He had never once managed to nab himself any of the posh new seats that had been installed, and took up his usual position - perched on the work table next to the photocopier, armed with a box full with theatre props. It was a precarious position; it gave him only a half-decent of what view of Mick was saying to the troops and it meant that he had half a ream of copier paper sticking into his bum, but beggars couldn't be choosers. There was no way in the world he was going to miss briefing this morning.

Mick rattled through his daily briefing notes pretty quickly. Maths revision classes at lunchtime were being rolled out to Year 10 as well as 11 from next week. The gym would be used alongside the assembly hall for exams in the summer. Please don't park in the verges at front of the school as yet another of the young trees had been ripped up by a staff member's car. Everyday run-of-the-mill stuff.

The staff, as usual, had the opportunity to chip in with their own last-minute requests. Could the senior choir please make their way down to the music room at break for a quick rehearsal with Elizabeta? Would whoever had taken the pile of English textbooks from E12 please return them ASAP? If you're going to make yourself a cup of coffee at break time, would you please only use the milk in the left-hand fridge as the other stuff is for the Support Assistants? Like every school in the country, the daily communication in morning briefing at Lancashire Academy was a mixture of information that would keep the school running like clockwork, and the more pressing issues of where you should store your dairy products.

It appeared that everything had finished for the morning, until Mick decided that this would be an opportune moment to bring a Columbo-style 'Just one more thing' to the proceedings. He drew everyone's attention to the front page of this morning's *Preston Herald* which, as everyone knew, was a news publication of the highest note. Forget *La Monde* or the *New York Times*. The PH was clearly where the next Pulitzer prize was heading, especially now they had covered the artistic event of the century.

MUCH ADO ABOUT SHAKESPEARE
Lancashire Academy students steal the show at Charter Theatre

The headline itself took up only about a quarter of the page, which was dominated by a story about yet another local library facing closure, but there it was alongside a striking picture of Ethan Connoly in full flow as a raging Leonato. If you wanted more information you should turn to page seventeen. Or you could go and ask the man who was now standing ten feet tall next to the photocopier.

"Massive congratulations to Jim Tovey and Steph Govin who took the Drama Club up to the theatre earlier in the week for the Shakespeare Festival. Seems you've made us all famous! Fantastic work on the show. I only managed to catch the end of the dress rehearsal but, from what I've read, you certainly

249

managed to capture everyone's attention on the night. Brilliant. Just brilliant."

Steph was blushing next to her Support Assistant colleagues, who were very proud that one of their own had been singled out for praise during Head Teacher's briefing. It was very rare that one of them got the credit that, actually, they deserved just as much as their teacher colleagues. And here was Steph, clearly being thanked as much as Jim had been. Maybe this new head WAS different from the previous ones. Maybe they would finally start to get a bit of respect.

The bell rang to signal form time and the staff dispersed, leaving Mick to pin the front page and the article to the staff notice board; this, however, took him a fair amount of time as, despite the board being replenished with extra pins on three separate occasions this year, none were immediately available. In the digital age, where any piece of data could be simultaneously transferred across seven continents at the touch of a button, it seemed that a pinned scrap of paper was still the medium of choice for teachers wanting to know who had nicked all the spoons from the kitchen.

Alan wandered over to Jim, offering his hand. Their relationship, although tested by the whole 'I failed to report the kid who was obviously guilty as hell and buggered up your exam', had made it to the other side and was possibly now stronger for it. Nothing helps a friendship more than the acknowledgement that you made a right royal cock-up but you can be forgiven anyway. Jim now had one in the bank with Alan, and he was certain that he'd repay him by being a complete arse at some, as yet unspecified, point in the future.

"Good work, mate. Classy job. I'll do the register this morning if you want. Let you revel in the glory a bit more now you're all over the papers."

This was true. As well as Ethan's cover photo, the reporter from the Herald had caught an excellent backstage shot of Jim's pre-show speech to the kids from up on a stage block, looking just a tiny bit like Henry the Fifth prepping everyone to go into battle at Agincourt. The picture was huge and really did make him look rather professional. He'd have to make sure he picked up a copy before he got home so that Sandra would have one for her keepsake box.

Jim's Mum had always been proud of his achievements and still kept clippings from even his earliest of shows. Looking back through them was always a cringe-worthy affair, especially any that were taken during his 'long hair' era at Uni (what WAS he thinking?) but he liked the fact that someone was at least keeping a track of things for him. It was all too easy to forget what you've achieved when you're on a downward curve, and a quick flick through his mum's collection showed that sometimes, occasionally, there was something to celebrate.

"Cheers, Alan. If you could take the register, I can get this box of props back to the hall and store them ready for when we do next week's show for parents."

Jim shifted the box of capes, masks and plastic glasses towards the door (their version of *Much Ado* had relied heavily on party scenes) and decided to quickly read the full article from the board before heading off to the hall.

Alan, in his haste to get to 10JT on time, nearly tripped over the box of props, swearing under his breath as he did so. He moved the box to the door to wedge it open so that no one else would make the same mistake, before heading off. As he turned to make his way up the stairs, he spotted some of Jim's form making their way lazily down the corridor.

"Come on Adeela! You've got just me for form this morning and you know I'll mark you late if I get there before you!"

Alan skipped off. Jim's success really had put him in a chipper mood.

The crowds in the staff room dispersed, leaving the room empty except for a handful of senior teachers without form groups; they were checking their in-trays for any new government diktats that had been dreamt up during the night. Micromanaging the curriculum from the top down inevitably meant that the demands placed on senior teachers were high, and it was their daily job to dutifully cascade that information down to those in their department. Today, we're teaching the times table up to twelve. Today, exclamation marks are taboo. Today, you must only use one sheet at a time when wiping your backside. The list of instructions from Westminster about how you'd been doing it wrong never ceased.

For heads of department who had reached the lofty heights of SLT, like Janet, this cascading of information was a simple affair. She had three other members of staff in her department who she could pass this on to. She was also blessed with a greatly reduced teaching timetable, which allowed her time during the working day to amend all her schemes of work, plan her lessons effectively and enjoy the nice view she had of the rolling hills out of her office window. As the only member of his department with a full timetable and no office at all, Jim rarely got the chance to implement any of the latest changes that Ofsted or the DFE imposed and mostly found himself doing what he did best. Winging it.

As they both removed the latest addition of Gareth's *Numeracy News* from their trays, Janet and Jim said nothing. She was clearly annoyed at him for going behind her back to work with that Connoly boy at the PRU. Luckily, she still knew nothing of the on-site rehearsals as they had been thoroughly sneaky in getting Ethan in and out of the building. To anyone who cared to be paying attention, the whole operation had been a direct contravention of the school's Child Protection policies, with Ethan being let in through the service entrance at 3:45 on the days in question, having made his way up from the PRU with bus fare paid entirely out of the Drama department's petty cash. The sight of a man dressed not unlike an international spy, lurking shiftily by the bins at the end of the school day, should have raised some serious alarm bells. But, luckily, everyone who might remotely care was too shattered by that time of day to even notice.

The rehearsals themselves went without a hitch, Ethan having learned all of his lines before even arriving at the first rehearsal. He took direction well and offered a refreshing amount of non-sugar-coated advice to those who hadn't quite hit the mark themselves. Sally (who, to give her credit, was only in Year 7) and Nasser from Year 9 were playing Beatrice and Benedick, and they didn't get the chance to be flat in their performances when Ethan came into the room. His confidence and ability to project his voice onstage naturally lifted their own previously nervous duologues. He also told them in no uncertain terms to 'get over it' about telling each other they were in love. Jim would have taken five rehearsals to carefully edge them towards a declaration of affection. It took Ethan about ten minutes to get them out of their shell.

By the time they arrived at the theatre for the technical rehearsal on the afternoon of show day (Jim had arranged a special dispensation for Ethan to be away from his lessons at the PRU for the performance day) everyone was buzzing. The kids were buzzing after Mr Owen had dropped in on their dress rehearsal at school the night before and had told them how well they had done in telling a really complicated story in such a simple way. Steph was buzzing as she realised that the compère for the show that night was that actor from Coronation Street who her Mum quite liked, and she managed she get a selfie with him backstage to share all over Instagram. Even Ethan was buzzing, but that may have had something to do with the five cans of Red Bull he'd downed since leaving the PRU. Jim was almost certain that, in later years, young Master Connoly would move onto something harder as his drug of choice but, for now, he would be content with getting his on-stage energy from a large dose of glucose.

Being backstage amongst the hustle and bustle of a theatre crew prepping for a show was always going to be an amazing experience for the kids from Dramarama, over half of whom had never even set foot in a professional theatre, let alone performed in one. The added excitement of being there with three other schools, sharing some of the greatest stories ever told at an evening entirely devoted to the Bard himself, was just the icing on the cake.

Lancashire Academy's half-hour version of *Much Ado About Nothing* was third on, so the kids got to see two other schools do their stuff before their turn after the interval. The first, a powerful version of *Macbeth* by a GCSE group from a school in Bolton, was thoroughly entertaining but got all the kids worried as the standard of performance was so unbelievably high. Jim knew that it was a simple case of physical maturity and the fact that they had the freedom to rehearse during lessons that was making the piece so polished, neither of which they were able to do back at their own school, but explaining that to a group of eleven- to thirteen-year-olds can be quite tricky.

Luckily, the second group on, who had travelled all the way down from Lancaster, put his kids' minds at rest. These were sixth-formers, young men and women who had chosen a BTEC in Performing Arts as their vocation and who were, on the face of it, aiming to be the next generation of theatrical artists to rock the world with a new brand of physical theatre. Inspired by their studies of Brecht, they would bring a new meaning to the long-established text that our William penned when he set *Romeo and Juliet* on paper. It was billed as dynamic, modern and completely in-yer-face. What it was, was rubbish.

Lines were fluffed, entrances slow and the actors were so intent on interweaving contemporary dance moves into the show that they completely forgot the golden rule of speaking in a way that your audience can understand you. When it got to Tybalt's death scene, fifteen children in row F turned simultaneously and looked at their Drama teacher. They were greeted by Jim's beaming face. Almost every single one of the pupils he was sitting with (bar the three Year 7s in the cast) had been through his lesson on how to approach this scene, and every single one of them knew that the over-acted, sometimes gurgling death that was being shown before them just wasn't going to cut the mustard. When their turn came to perform, they wouldn't be this pants. When it came to doing their version of *Much Ado About Nothing*, they were going to rock.

And rock they did. The opening party sequence, complete with disco-light chase sequence set to *The Boys are Back in Town*, was jam-packed with energy. Little Jason from Year 7, who was playing Don John, schemed appropriately. Gabriella swooned on command and played Hero (the most one-dimensional character in all of Shakespeare's work) in a way that suited her perfectly, in that she was overjoyed to be there but entirely incidental to proceedings. Sally and Nasser got some real belly laughs from the audience as Beatrice and Benedick. But there was no doubting the star of the show.

Cometh the moment, cometh the not-quite-entirely-grown man. Ethan Connoly, the boy who'd been labelled on a transfer form just six weeks previously as 'entirely dysfunctional within an education environment', had a theatre full of parents and pupils from across the region sitting on the edge of their seats, marvelling at how someone so small could create a performance so entrancing. To say that he had found his forte was a huge understatement. He kept in role throughout the show, clearly guiding the action and the audience's attention, but it was during his big speech at Hero and Claudio's aborted wedding that the real take-home memory came.

"Hath no man's dagger here a point for me?"

The boy was twelve. How on earth had life delivered him so much rubbish that, in such a short space of time, he would be able to not only understand that kind of desperate rage, but channel it through his voice and movement to convincingly play a man in his fifties who felt he'd been betrayed by his daughter, humiliating her publicly at her wedding? It takes some doing to deliver that kind of theatricality. The reporter from the Herald who was sitting in the front row captured it perfectly.

CLICK.

Even as the cast took their bows, wheels were being put in motion backstage for a smooth transition to a school from Bury who were putting on *The Comedy of Errors.* Steph guided the pupils from Lancashire Academy into the wings, where they would giggle at a tale of twins constantly mistaken in way that only a man who had twins himself could ever have written. Jim pondered in years to come if he would ever pen his own tales of parenthood, and decided very much against it. A tale of Danny's insomnia and projectile vomiting was unlikely to gain him worldwide acclaim as a playwright.

Ethan was the last one to come off stage, soaking up the atmosphere. As he reached the wings, Jim offered him a hand to shake - possibly as a sign that, from now on, they would be very much on the same side.

"I'm really proud of you, Ethan. That was some performance."

"It went alright, didn't it? Thanks for bringing us up here."

"That's ok. My pleasure. We were better than that lot of sixth-formers from Lancaster, weren't we?"

Ethan gave Jim the 'stern teacher' look. The look of 'I'm not angry… I'm just disappointed'. Jim pondered whether he had said something to upset Lancashire's rising star.

"Sir, it's not a competition. It's about everybody sharing really positive work with each other."

A further pause. Then a wink. The little bastard still knew how to keep Jim on his toes.

Now, two days later, the moment of Ethan's triumph was all over the front page and Jim was, once again, riding on the crest of a wave of positivity. This was Janet's cue. She knew full well that this had to be stopped in its tracks; if Jim were concentrating on extra-curricular work, he clearly couldn't be focusing on getting the Drama results that she needed. It was style over substance, yet again, and he needed to be told.

"Is your play completely finished with now? You don't need to do anything else with it?"

"We're doing another one after school next week in the hall for the kids who couldn't get down to the theatre. We're only charging £1 a ticket. Steph's trying to raise a bit of cash for Cancer Research. Thought it might be good way to kill two birds with one stone."

Janet had her face on.

"Don't you think you ought to be concentrating on the GCSE exam? It's less than four weeks away and Year 11 go on their study leave next week. Are they prepared?"

"It's one show. We're doing it so the kids can be proud of what they've done and show it off to the people in school who can't afford £8 a ticket to go a theatre show."

She was like a broken record these days, and there was no hiding her disdain. Everything Jim did seemed to wind her up. He refused to play ball the way she wanted him to. He insisted (despite her telling him in countless weekly meetings that none of these little Drama projects he kept running outside of class mattered) that he should carry on with his 'Drama 'Club'. He just didn't get it. This was a job, not a game. He was to be judged on his results and nothing else.

"Well, I can't help you if you're not willing to help yourself."

She turned to walk away, managing to avoid the box of props and almost getting out of the door. She thought she'd made her position pretty clear and obviously wasn't expecting a comeback.

"Excuse me? What exactly is that supposed to mean?"

"You know exactly what it means. You are already skating on very thin ice this year and you insist on taking further risks. I'm not going to be held responsible for that when the results come round. I don't think you take your job at all seriously."

This wasn't just 'gloves off to look mean' anymore. We were well into the third round of a bare-knuckle fight where there was only going to be one victor. Jim was buoyant this morning. How dare she come in here now and try to drag him down?

"In what way don't I take my job seriously? I'd love to know."

Come on. Come out and say it.

"I don't think you really understand what being a teacher is, Jim. Playing make-believe at the theatre isn't going to help move your percentages up. You can't turn around to Ofsted and tell them that you're sorry everyone got an F but wasn't it great when we took everyone to see a show?"

Really, Janet? REALLY?

"They aren't percentages, Janet, they're children. What's the point of teaching them if they hate what they're supposed to be learning?!"
Voices were becoming raised, and with the staff room empty neither of them felt the need to hold back. They were both in the mood for an altercation that was at least a term overdue.

"God, you are so naive! You've been in this job for five years now and you are still talking as if you were some sort of guidance counsellor to these little toe-rags. Getting that little shit Connoly in your show may have made you look fantastic in the paper, but will it make any actual difference in the long run? You'll still have terrible results and he'll still end up in a young offenders' institute. Doing a play with him doesn't stop him being from a family of criminals."

"But if we can make a difference...."

"You're not their parent, Jim. You don't have to be their friend, or make them enjoy what they're doing, or build up their character, or anything else. Your job is to squeeze every last mark you can out of them and send them on their way. Then next year you do the same with the next lot. And if you can't do that, then you may as well pack it all in and go home now. "

This was overly harsh, that was for certain, and was in direct contradiction to everything that had made Jim want to become a teacher in the first place. His response to Janet was petulant - childish, even - but it was more than apt for the situation.

"Well, at least I'm going down with a bit of charisma, Janet. I'd rather be deemed a failure by you than be hated by every kid on this site, which – newsflash - you are. Just leave me to do my job. You'll be shot of me in September."

He picked up his box of props and off he went. He knew exactly what he'd done, but at least now he'd done what Katie had been urging him to do for the last six months. No doubt about it, there would be consequences but they would be dealt with in another place at another time. Right now, he was going to put his box of props away in the hall, put some posters up for a show that Janet had told him not to do, and finalise the coach booking for a theatre trip that Janet had told him not to run. There was nothing to lose here. He was going out on his terms, doing the job the way he wanted it done.

For her part, Janet stormed away in the opposite direction, back to her office where she would go about trying to distance herself from Jim's actions by writing an immediate email to Mick. She would explain how she no longer had any confidence in Jim's ability to meet the teaching standards and suggest that he be recommended for a competence review as soon as possible. That was just stage one. She was determined to have him gone before the term was out.

261

H/W   Choices Evaluation   2nd February

We Watched the performance of 'Choices' by 'Youth on tour' theater company in our school hall. Their Was no lights or Sound effects used in it so I can't talk about What it Was they Would do With the lights or sound effects. They did put Some music on though Which Was claskal and made everything seem really slow at the end. The bit in the middle had Some rave music Which Was ~~pretty~~ really loud. That bit Was good and they probably Should have more of it So it Would be a bit more energetic as a play.

The acting in it Was ok but I think they should have spent less time talking to the audeince and more time getting on With story Which Was about a boy called Abdul and how he took drugs, and didn't lissen to his mates When they Said not to take drugs. Abdul dying at the end Was the best bit as he did that bit really realisthic and We all thought he had ~~prope~~ properley died When We Watched it.

To make it better I think they should have put Some sound efects and made it all Shorter.

David Hatherley 11 B

Chapter Twenty-Two

Showtime

They were in.

No more pointless pieces of writing about shabby productions in the school hall. Now they would see some PROPER theatre.

Jim looked across the auditorium and gave the thumbs up to Steph. She had positioned herself very cleverly behind Ethan, who had already started tucking into his insanely large tub of Haribo. The kids from the Shakespeare festival show had been brought to see *Wicked* as a reward this evening, but there was no worry about Ethan misbehaving tonight. He was clearly settled with his fructose infusion. There was actually more chance of him slipping into a diabetic coma, but they would cross that bridge if and when they came to it.

Jim began to relax. He went through his usual pre-show routine of looking at the ceiling, wondering at the magic of it all. On their way in, Robert had almost wet himself at the amount of kit hanging from the scaffolding bar beams in the roof. Lanterns of all shapes and sizes, Fresnels, pattern 23s, par cans of every shape and size set out in a myriad of angles facing the soon-to-be-illuminated stage area. Jim could just about follow what Robert was saying about the kit as he had been around plenty of techie people before, but wished he'd paid more attention in his lighting and sound module at uni.

Those on his course who weren't busy flouncing about on the stage had specialised in technical work, which had given them the ability to use all the magical plugs, switches, buttons and bells of theatre technology. Like any piece of kit, it looked complicated from a distance but once you get stuck in there and press a few buttons, you soon realise that the technology is actually about as advanced as using a *Speak and Spell*. It was just the lingo that made it complicated. Jim had developed a profound respect for techies, or at least he liked being able to follow what they were talking about while others around him drew blank faces. He didn't pretend to be an expert, though, and left the button-pushing to kids like Rob who clearly had a knack for this sort of thing.

They seemed to understand and were really inspired by the magic, and reveled in their ability to conjure effects using electrickery. They could harness the absolute power of light, dark and all that stood vibrantly in between, at the flick of a switch. Having the ability to execute a cross-fade between two contrasting stage washes created an illusion that Gandalf would have been proud of. Sure, the actors could entertain you with their funny voices and silly hats. But what the tech crew did was pure witchcraft. If Shakespeare had written Prospero today, he would most likely have dressed him all in black, hung a mini Maglite torch from a Caribena on his belt, and had him punching chase sequences into a 96-channel DMX board. Now that was magic.

"You want a Jelly Baby?"

His admiration of the pre-show state was temporarily interrupted by the emergence of Alan in the row behind him. Alan's entrance made him jump a little - not because he had an inherent fear of squishy, baby-shaped confectionary (although if you think about it, that IS weird) but because Alan was supposed to be stationed on the other side of the theatre. Traversing some eighty seats to offer him a sweet seemed rather excessive.

"How come you're over here? I though you were over there with Steph and the Year 10 girls?" Jim was not going through this again. There would no repeat of the textile museum incident. No child would be lost today.

"They're fine. They needed five minutes without their ancient Aussie P.E teacher. While I was there they were almost silent. I was clearly cramping their style. As soon as I left, they started chatting about what they were expecting to see, and giggling with Steph about girly stuff. Plus, I think Steph could do with an Alan-free ten minutes."

Jim's suspicions about the two of them getting together after the Christmas do had been proved right when it emerged that they had 'been out for a few drinks' over the break. Like all teacher relationships, they had kept it low profile to avoid them being gossip fodder for the kids, but outside of school they had been inseparable. Tonight was an excuse for them to have a night out together at work, on a strictly legit basis. That, alongside Jim's paranoia about something going wrong, was what led him to be so jittery about Alan having strayed from his post.

"You have got them all, haven't you? You know I'm for the high jump if this gets cocked up again, like when I went on that history trip…"

"Relax! They're okay. I counted them off the bus, I counted them into their seats, and I can see every one of those seats filled with excited teenagers. Now, do you want one of these Jelly Babies or not?"

Jim smiled and took a handful. Two greens and a yellow. Could've been worse.

"Are you sure you should be peddling these to the kids? I'm pretty sure this isn't on the recommended healthy eating list. You're supposed to be a P.E Teacher."

Jim wasn't usually so assured of himself when venturing into other people's subject areas, but he certain he was on safe ground here. A large dollop of colouring-enriched gelatine seemed to be pretty much the antithesis of what he considered to be balanced nutrition.

Alan smiled.

"You're wrong on both fronts, my Pommie friend. Jelly Babies are perfect for me at the moment. Running a marathon needs slow carb burn, which these little fellas are perfect for. Plus, right now it's after school. I'm not a P.E teacher. I'm a Designated Adult Supervisor."

He did that thing where you throw the sweet into your mouth - without it bouncing off and hitting you on the nose (which, in a life time of trying, Jim would never be able to do) then gave Jim the most cocksure wink he'd ever witnessed. It was the very essence of cheeky little boy. Despite the fact that this was one of the reasons Jim and Alan had become firm friends, there was nothing so smug and unappealing as sitting for a prolonged period of time next to an Aussie who was right about something. Jim had to put him back in his Antipodean place.

"Well, get your Designated Adult Supervisor backside over to Ethan and those Year 10s. You didn't get a free ticket to this thing so you could swan about all over the theatre!"

"No trouble, boss. Am I still on for that beer at half time?"

"Interval!"

"Gotcha..."

And off he went, bouncing his way across the empty back row. The epitome of every female Year 10's dream.

Perfect timing. The curtain rose to signal the beginning of the first act. Jim had seen *Wicked* before with Katie and her Mum in London last year, but seeing it at The Palace seemed to give it a different feel. Admittedly, last time they'd paid full price and seen it in the West End whereas now they were in Manchester's finest playhouse on bargain basement schools' night. Still, it really did feel like he was experiencing the show from a whole new angle. Being a punter and being a critic was very different, and he needed to keep his eyes peeled tonight for anything that might help the Year 11 kids eke out a mark or two on the review question in their exam.

After the awful essays he'd been given about the *Choices* show that Janet had organised, it was clear they needed something more meaty to inspire them for the exam. If they wanted A* essays, they'd have to watch some A* theatre. Jim would make sure he wrote up his own notes on the coach on the way back while they were fresh in his mind but, for now, he'd have to be content with watching a jolly musical romp about misunderstood witches while munching on over-priced confectionary. Life, as ever, could be worse.

He was almost immediately lost in the action, completely forgetting his role as Supervisor In General to Lancashire Academy's finest. The score, the atmosphere, the nervous anticipation of whether or not good would fail to triumph over evil, sent the outside world spiralling away into oblivion. It also helped that he quite fancied the woman playing Glinda. In any other social situation, he'd have been carted off for gormlessly staring at a woman in a giant meringue dress. But this was theatre, darling. Anything goes.

"No matter what, Jim", he said happily inside his head, which was already skipping happily down a yellow brick road. "You've got to love being a Drama teacher. By day, you're paid to put on strange hats and do silly voices to entertain a group of kids. By night, you get to watch women who are way out of your league singing beautifully in kinky attire. Forget the stresses. Forget the fact that it's pretty much coming to an end in the summer. You're not going to find a better job than this. Enjoy it while it lasts."

He sat back in his seat and took a deep breath.

And smelt chicken. Greasy chicken, with a magnificent secret blend of eleven herbs and spices. In a bucket, provided by a Colonel who most definitely did not work in this theatre.

He sat bolt upright and turned to find Sadie & Robert tucking happily into chicken legs, watching the show as if they were in front of *Corrie* with a cheeky Friday night take-away. All they were missing was a cat, a TV Times and sofa with a remote on the arm. Butter wouldn't melt. Jim's patience, however, was starting to wobble.

"What the hell are you doing?"

Sadie responded in the best way she could while chewing a mouthful of southern fried deliciousness.

"Watching the show."

Dumbass. What a stupid question.

"Where the hell did you get that?"

The young couple looked at each other. He really is being a dumbass. Sadie pointed to the military man on the bucket.

"I mean, when did you get it? You're supposed to stay in your seats!"

In hindsight (and we're talking a good ten to fifteen years of hindsight) Jim would chuckle at the ferocity that his younger self managed to generate in those few hushed sentences amongst Manchester's theatre-going public, and the way in which his arms flailed about like an octopus on heat. In fact, should anyone wishing to solve the energy crisis choose to do a study on how to produce low-cost, non-fossil-burning power, they could do no better than approach a panicking Drama teacher in a mid-show crisis. The Physics department would be exceptionally proud as he managed to capture both potential and kinetic energy in one short series of exasperated poses. He was that angry. To the rest of the world, though, it just looked hilarious.

"What were you thinking, going out in Manchester on your own? Anything could have happened!"

It was at this point that Sir Robert Drumstick of Lancashire waded into the debate at the defence of his fair maiden, whose honour he felt the need to defend in the face of the terrible limb-wobbling monster that confronted him.

"Nothing was going to happen. We stayed together the whole time. It's only on the corner where the coach dropped us off."

"It's completely irresponsible!"

Sadie wasn't one for chivalry and jumped straight back in.

"No, it's not. I've bought chicken loads of times. Do you want one a chip? I've gone off 'em."

"If we can't see you, then you're not safe! I'm in loco parentis for you on this trip and you can't just be trusted to look after yourselves!"

It was a good job this wasn't being recorded; Jim would squirm if it were ever played back to him. Sadie, though, had had enough of being told what to do. She was starving and needed chicken. End of story. She didn't give a monkey's backside what Sir considered safe. She needed chicken, she got chicken. She didn't need a chaperone to buy a bargain bucket.

"Will you just chill out and let me eat my tea in peace? Just watch the show, will you?"

"You are not to leave my sight from now on!"

Really, Tovey. You're trying that one?

"I'm going to go and take a dump in the interval. You planning on joining me?"

It was a perfectly timed retort. Hilarious, in fact. Certainly hilarious enough to make Robert smirk, exacerbating an already overly tense situation and giving Jim no option but go nuclear. In silence. Which actually turned the respected figure of Mr Tovey - confident and well-organised group leader - into yet another petulant teenager. Facing the front, arms sullenly folded across his chest, he began to sulk and fume simultaneously. He began plotting how to get her removed from his course on the basis that she had put them all in danger by casually walking off.

In return, Sadie shrugged her shoulders and tucked into another drumstick.

When the interval arrived, Jim located Alan and proceeded to vent his frustration in the best way he knew how, by turning the minor drama into a full-blown international crisis. If there were ever to be a forewarning of Jim's on-going descent into a major bout of depression, it was these few moments of ridiculous proclamations at the edge of the dress circle. Sadie was 'dangerous', 'crazy' and 'uncontrollable'. He was going to 'refuse' to teach her. He was going to resign and didn't care that he had a wife and child to support. SLT 'had to' suspend her immediately. They 'had to'. And if they didn't, he'd make them. It was exactly as it sounds. A futile attempt to relieve himself of the built-up stresses of his life, focussing on the minor issue of someone not quite getting lost on a school trip. And eating some chicken.

The punishments suggested in comparison to the crime were almost laughable but, at that moment, he didn't care. He'd had enough of it all. Dancing around Janet, perpetually trying to do the right thing, balancing the needs of a group of GCSE kids that life seemed determined to screw over on a weekly basis, constantly telling Katie that things were going to be alright and that this job was safe when he knew full well that his career was hanging by a thread.

Alan's suggestion that they swap seats and that Jim stay as far away from Sadie for the rest of the night became the only viable option, short of standing between the two of them and pleading with Jim to 'walk away - she ain't worth it mate'. When the play resumed, Alan found himself alongside the Year 10s who were disappointed to find that, unlike their previous care provider, Mr Tovey did not have any Jelly Babies to share. And he looked totally miserable.

Alan, however, relaxed on the other side of the theatre, enjoying the play in relative calm and tucking quietly into the remainder of Sadie's unwanted chips.

When they got back on the coach (this time EVERYONE was double counted) Sadie was the one who made the first move. Alan had clearly worked some magic and played peacemaker during the second half.

"I'm sorry I wandered off. I know I should have asked. Mr Cook said I was causing you to stress out so I should probably come and say I was sorry."

Jim hadn't known Sadie to apologise before, and this was quite a change in mood from her obstinate 'I'll eat my chicken when I want and you can't stop me' just an hour earlier. It always amazed Jim how the moods of teenagers could swing so violently, so quickly. But the second half had, as predicted, given Jim himself time to calm down and reflect and the conciliation was reciprocated.

"Don't worry about it. I flew off the handle a bit and the important thing, I suppose, is that you were safe. It's just that taking a trip out of school is always a really stressful thing. You know about what happened on the history trip don't you?"

Sadie smiled.

"Sir, EVERYONE knows about what happened on the history trip. Just chill out. We've had a good time. The show was brill. And it was a thousand times better than that rubbish you made us all watch at school. Writing those essays in the exam should be easy now."

Easy. That's what she said. Easy peasy.

He'd believe it when he saw it.

Chapter Twenty-Three

Heads down

Seven months earlier, Jim had found himself pacing outside a delivery suite waiting for a midwife to buzz him in, and for Danny to spring himself joyfully into their lives. That sense of anticipation, combined with the adrenaline of adventure, had been a moment that would stay with Jim forever.

Now, once again, he was pacing outside a room that he wasn't allowed to enter. But this time the overwhelming feeling was trepidation. There was no excitement. Just powerlessness, naked fear. There was absolutely nothing he could do. No matter what happened in the next... check... forty-eight minutes, he would have no part in it. All he could do was wait.

The written exam was in full swing.

Gareth hadn't even allowed him to see the paper, which he wouldn't get to look at until after the exam had finished. Apparently it was now 'recommended procedure'. With Drama being one of the many GCSE exams taken all over the world, the risk of information being shared over the internet was quite high. There would be students in international schools in the Far East who wouldn't be getting this paper for a good few hours, so keeping the questions under wraps was probably a very good idea. Understanding why he was being kept in the dark was one thing; living with it was another.

He knew that worrying was a pointless task. Worrying never had any affect on the events of the world, and he knew in his heart of hearts that there really wasn't anything more that he could have done. They all had pens. They'd all attended the breakfast cramming session, eaten all the pastries he'd provided, and had discussed in detail what they needed to write about when they got in there - section by section, question by question. Revision cards had been designed, printed, laminated and given to them on the morning they left for study leave. The online forum Jim had asked Imran to set up on the school website had been buzzing with questions for three solid days, and every single one of his students had logged into the system to have a look at the materials in advance of the exam. They were ready. They had to be. If they'd been a horse, you'd have been silly not to back them.

On the other side of the double doors, the mood was tense but OK. Jenna Asquith and Karen Gosforth were breezing their way through the paper, almost enjoying the chance to share their process of creating their exam pieces in written form. As top set pupils, they had years of experience in exams; structuring answers that informed the reader in a clear and concise way had become second nature to them. Both had breezed through the first section of the paper (which focused on their own pieces of practical drama) in less than half an hour, leaving them a full hour to devote to the questions on the live review.

Having seen *Wicked* less than a month ago - everyone being in agreement that it was absolutely the best piece of drama that anyone, anywhere had ever seen - both knew that this exam was going to go well for them. Their performance pieces may not have been the strongest and, because of their practical marks, they may not get the grade that the school said they needed but it would be enough to get them into college. And that was all both of them really cared about. The sooner Jenna and Karen were free of this dreary building, the better. It had gone right downhill since they changed it from being plain old Deepdale High, and both longed for somewhere that was a bit more... well, fun. They ploughed on. Karen was smiling. Jenna needed extra paper. Things were going well.

Elsewhere in the room, the mood wasn't quite so buoyant. David Hatherley was struggling with words again, or at least struggling to write them down. It had always puzzled him how words seemed to tumble out of his mouth in everyday life, yet when he wanted them to appear in front of him on paper, they were strangely absent. 'Talk less, write more' had been the mantra of all his teachers since Year 2 but at this particular moment, when oral communication wasn't even on the agenda, the words he wanted to say just couldn't find their way onto the page. How could he describe the costume of the good witch Glinda in *Wicked*? Pretty? Hmm... Hold on. What was that word Tovey had said to use instead of pretty? It was on the revision cards. What was it? It was spelt the same as that place in Belgium they'd all been to on that weekend trip in Year 7. Ostend!

Glinda's dress was Ostendatious.

David was trying hard and his reward would surely be in the D-F category on this section of the course. As long as it was above G that was fine by Jim, but David would forever come away thinking he was just a bit rubbish. Jim just hoped David didn't end up losing any marks on his practical, because that was going really well until the fire alarm went off.

Robert seemed fine and enjoyed the knowledge that he was answering slightly different questions from everyone else. The written paper allowed for candidates to discuss technical contributions with the same weighting as performance skills, and he was having a great time listing all the various pieces of expensive tech that the Palace Theatre had used in *Wicked*. From smoke machines to lasers to pyrotechnics, his essay about the show was bursting with examples of how to put on a sparkling professional performance. This would definitely make up for him getting all those cues wrong in the practical.

Sadie had her head down on the desk. The room was swirling and she couldn't make it stop. She'd answered the first question about the contribution she'd made to her practical piece, but had written little about evaluating it. It wasn't that she didn't know what to write. She had every intention of putting on paper a very honest account of how she'd turned up late for most of her rehearsals, been far too disorganised in learning the structure of the piece, and missed the actual performance due to tripping over a stupid first aid dummy that some loon had left lying around in the hall. In the revision session, Tovey had told her very clearly what to write.

"Listen, Sadie. You and I know that the last twelve months have lurched from chaos to disaster and back again. Your practical piece would have been alright but life transpired to make it all pants. When you go in there, don't try to dress it up. Just tell them how it was. They're looking for an evaluation of what actually happened, not a description of what the perfect piece of drama looks like. It's not like a normal exam. The person marking it will be interested in your opinion, and as long as you back it up with some evidence, you'll get the grade you need."

It wasn't often anyone told Sadie to be honest in an exam. She'd hated reading (or at least pretending to read) *Wuthering Heights* and then having to pretend to be enthusiastic by writing that she

277

thought it was some terrifying ghost story that had the reader recoiling in fear at the turn of every page. She'd seen *Saw 3*. There was no way some ancient book written half in Yorkshire dialect and the rest in flouncy posh speak was going to put the wind up her. And making her write otherwise just made her hate it all the more.

Right now, though, she couldn't even lift her pen. This bug had been getting worse all week and she wanted to chuck up again. Robert had been brilliant, coming round to look after her, bringing her cups of tea and helping her revise, and she wondered what it would have been like not having him there. She'd been out with and plenty of lads in the last couple of years, but this time it felt a bit different. Robert actually seemed to want to be with her when she wasn't at her best, something that boys of his age rarely cared about. It was no surprise that, at two and a half months, this had easily become her longest relationship. Actually, she didn't see it ending anytime soon.

How much would she give for Robert to be able get up from the other side of the room and bring her a brew. Something had to settle in her stomach soon. It felt like she was on The Big One at Blackpool, lurching about all over the place. She...

No. She had to get out of there. Now.

As she pushed her chair back and ran for the door, clutching her mouth to stop the inevitable from making an appearance in the exam room, she knocked over the box of spare stationery that was perched on a desk next to the door. This caused the whole room to turn in unison - first towards the invigilator who was trying to pick up a selection of pens, pencils and rulers from the floor and then to Robert, who had turned pale at his desk. This was the second time in a week Sadie had left the exam room to be sick… and everyone knew what that meant.

Being slow on the uptake as ever, Jim didn't know what that meant. All Jim knew was that he'd almost been hit by a door that had opened at breakneck speed, and that a flying Sadie hadn't even stopped to look back. He seemed to remember her saying something about being ill in the Physics paper they had on Monday morning as well, so she clearly had some sort of bug. It was odd, though, as she'd seemed fine in the revision session, happily munching down croissants with the rest of the kids. She'd certainly been fine the week before when he watched her devouring an entire bucket of chicken.

Jim had a quick look at his watch. Just over forty minutes left. Sadie was unlikely to be let back into the exam room if they thought she'd had contact with her Drama teacher, so he retreated to a safe distance to continue his worrying. There really was nothing he could do here other than be a bystander. A few moments later, one of the female invigilators followed Sadie out of the hall and tracked her down to the girls' toilet. Her job now was to ensure that there was no attempt at cheating that would put the integrity of the exam in jeopardy, while reassuring a teenage girl who felt like her entire innards were trying to evacuate for the second time this week.

When Sadie did return ten minutes later, she looked like she'd been to hell and back. Not only had she been crying; there was a look about her that Jim recognised in an instant. She was a shell of her bolshie, confident former self. She looked very fragile and, all of a sudden, very young. Jim's weekly contact with her over the last year and a half had shown her to be relentlessly self-assured, forthright and often downright rude. Today she looked more helpless than a baby panda in a YouTube video.

She didn't make any movement towards the hall and it was clear that she wouldn't be re-entering the exam room. Instead, she sat at one of long benches that had been set out for morning break. Jim motioned to the invigilator that he would take it from here, and went to sit opposite her. For the first time in ages, he looked at her for what she was - not the '4% of this year's cohort' that she had been for the last eighteen months. She was a kid. And a scared one, at that.

"I'm sorry. I can't do the exam. I was getting really dizzy in there. I've only answered the first question. I'm not going to..."

"It doesn't matter. Honestly."

Deep down, he knew that it did - she was C/D borderline, and one of half a dozen or so children who would be the difference between this year being a success or a failure – but, at this moment, there was no way he could tell her that. She looked hollow, staring into the middle distance in the same way that Jim had when he'd considered ending it all at the top of a water slide just last year. When a young girl who has her whole life ahead of her is looking like she might want the world to stop turning, it's usually advisable to refrain from discussing 'things that didn't go according to plan'. As it transpired, the non-completion of her Drama exam was very quickly jettisoned into the distant past. Something that would become a complete irrelevance. Five short words followed that would bring things quickly into very sharp focus.

"Sir, I've missed my period."

Nothing more needed to be said. Jim knew what this meant and, whatever transpired, Sadie and (he assumed) Robert's lives would be accelerated into the world of 'proper adult' decisions much sooner than they'd ever planned. Advice would have to wait until later, and would come from people who were much better qualified to deal with such a traumatic event. Jim just gave her a friendly smile that told her she had nothing to worry about right at this moment. Somehow, they'd all help her to deal with it.

"Does Robert know any of this yet?"

"Not yet. I was going to wait until after the exams to tell him. I don't think I can now. He's bound to put two and two together. Am I going to get into trouble?"

"I don't know, Sadie. For once, you've pretty much got me stumped. It's not everyday one of your students announces news like this."

As it happened, even if Jim wished to make some noble proclamation to Sadie about her future and how he was going to be able to fix it, he didn't get the chance. A second cataclysmic event that would rock the very foundations of the school happened at precisely the same time. Unlike most life-changing events, it started fairly innocuously but it soon snowballed into something much bigger.

Janet walked in with a box. It was a fairly heavy box, and one that seemed to contain an awful lot of items. She appeared to be struggling under the weight of it but her face was fighting hard not to show it in public. She crossed the dining room and walked past Jim without saying a word. That shouldn't have seemed odd in itself. After all, the mutual disrespect they had for each other had been quite open since she'd begun the procedure of reviewing his teaching competency two weeks earlier. He hadn't spoken to her. She hadn't spoken to him. If he needed to communicate with her in any way, he had to have Elaine, his union rep present.

The strange thing about Janet walking past them that morning was not the box. Or the silence. It was the presence of Mick, just ten feet behind. He followed her to the front door where they both stopped.

"I'll need your pass and your keys, please."

She took off her lanyard and handed it to him, then dug around in her box for the keys. She handed them over and was beeped through the automatic doors by Mick with his own staff pass.

Sadie was wide-eyed. Jim had a dropped jaw. Between them, they had 'shock' covered. Mick wandered over.

"Jim, I'm going to need a word with you straightaway."

Talk about poor timing. It was, however, abundantly clear that something needed to be spoken about. And it needed to be spoken about now. But Jim wasn't about to leave Sadie in her current state without any kind of support.

"I'm just dealing with Sadie, Mr Owen. She's..."

"I'll be fine. Robert will be out in a minute. I'll come over to the studio and tell you how the exam went after that, Sir. Don't worry. I'm alright."

Jim gave her one last look to ascertain if she was sure about this. For a young girl who had looked so vulnerable just minutes ago, she now seemed to holding herself in a way that most adults could only dream of. Teenagers. Utterly unfathomable. Sadie gave him a reassuring nod that gave him permission to excuse himself from their conversation, before he followed Mick across the hall to the staff room. An explanation of what the hell was happening was very much overdue.

Chapter Twenty-Four

A Sporting Chance

"Run! Come on! Run!!"

Jim loved Sports Days. It was one of those abiding memories from his own time at school that made him, just for a second, actually miss the time when he was growing up.

There were, inevitably, a lot of school memories tarnished by sad times. Dad's funeral, Mum's inevitable breakdowns, and the days he would come home to find her passed out on the sofa, were his overriding recollections of being eleven to sixteen, but punctuating those times were some real moments of fun at school. Being involved in school shows were obviously some of the best, bringing him the experience that would put him on his career path, but Sports Days had to come a close second. Ironic, really, that it was his Year 8 silver, not gold, medal triumph in the 800m that was engraved on his brain as his greatest sporting achievement.

All these years later, he could still remember the sound of his classmates cheering him on down the home straight, battling it out with Kevin Elliot as to who would get the spoils on a boiling hot July afternoon. Kev may have been the one to come out on top that day but it was, by a long way, Jim's greatest sporting triumph. Kev ran for the county and (Jim had heard) got pretty close to getting on the British team years later, before picking up a knee injury. Facebook told him that Kevin Elliot was now working as a store manager for Tesco in Carlisle, but in running someone with so much athletic potential to the line, Jim knew in his heart of hearts that he had done something worth remembering that day.

Now he had no part to play, outside of being a spectator, but was still enjoying sitting on the grass on a similarly sunny day, chilling with his form and shouting loudly for them to stuff the opposition as much as they could. He gave a "Well done!" to Azeem as he came and sat back with them. It was yet another valiant fourth place, but he had tried his hardest and was now recovering in the best way that he could - lying flat on his back, wheezing like an old man who was on forty a day. Azeem was, in fact, only on five a day but the tar was already working its dark magic on his lungs. Maybe he should listen to Tovey after all and pack in the fags.

For this auspicious occasion, 10JT had made a huge banner from thirty pieces of taped-together A4 paper. It had been jabbed into the ground and was flapping about loudly in the breeze. Jim sat proudly in front of it:

10JT - TOVEY'S TEAM - TAKING CENTRE STAGE

Complete with a depiction of Jim standing on the top of a podium, it was amateurish at best. It was nowhere near as eye-catching as some of the other forms' efforts, and was unlikely to be sturdy enough to make it through the day, but Jim didn't care. They'd put a bit of effort in to it and, for a change, his form actually seemed to be enthused by the prospect of being outside and doing something physical. Maybe it was because it was the last day of term and there were no lessons, or perhaps they were reveling in their new roles as 'most senior year group'. Either way, they were most definitely out to have a good time.

A voice came from behind him. A blast from the past.

"Hi, Sir."

It was Kayleigh.

Jim had managed to avoid her since the previous summer, never being able to work out what he would actually say to her if they ever came face-to-face again. He'd let her down and couldn't handle it. He was away for results day, then feigned illness on presentation evening when the former Year 11s had come to collect their certificates. Yes, it was cowardly. But what choice did he have? There was no way he could face this conversation.

Now she was making him face this conversation.

"Kayleigh! What are you doing here?"

It was a fairly sensible question. For very good reasons, you don't just get to wander into schools anymore. Being an ex-pupil was no exception.

"I'm doing some work experience for my college course. I'm doing Leisure and Tourism and I'm working with P.E to help with Sports Day."

"Leisure & Tourism? I thought you hated Sports."

It was true. He remembered that, during his first year, she'd had a full-on meltdown in the middle of the playground about getting changed for PE. She was only in Year 8 at the time and he hadn't really had much contact with her. But what was clear from that early memory was that when Kayleigh said she didn't want to do something, it usually meant it wasn't going to get done. Hearing that she'd done a complete U-turn and was now heading for a career in the leisure industry was quite a turn-up.

"I used to. I'm still not that keen on running about. I want to do Sports Administration. My college tutor says it might be the sort of thing I'll be good at. Since the Paralympics, there's a whole lot more jobs in disability sport. And if I can get a bit of experience, I could maybe do a university course. I'm not sure yet."

Jim was more than a little taken aback. For almost a year he'd had an image of Kayleigh as she would have been on results day last August. Crying at her disappointment, confused at how she got an E, resenting Jim for giving her false hope. In his mind's eye, Kayleigh was a victim of the system, embittered by the fact that those with the power to know better had let her down. It turns out that while Jim was carrying around an exaggerated sense of guilt, Kayleigh had dusted herself down and got on with things. Here she stood, a young woman. Still with that infectious child-like smile, but now confident in her ability to be... well... Kayleigh Clarke.

"From what I've seen, you've had quite an interesting time, too."

She'd seen it.

Who was he trying to kid? EVERYONE had seen it. The many forms of social media were a relative mystery to Jim and he was staggered by the way that he'd become a national – no, scratch that - international phenomenon. Twenty-seven-and-a-half-thousand retweets, eight-and-a-half-thousand shares on Facebook, radio phone-ins, debates, newspaper articles, the lot. There was even five minutes devoted to it on *Question*

Time. You'd have had to been hiding in a cave for the last six weeks not to have heard, seen, or taken part in a debate about it over a glass of red.

The key ingredients for Jim going viral? A box, a door and a senior teacher who, despite her many years of experience in the job, had not yet figured out that the world was watching.

"Did she not know someone was filming?"

Jim tried to explain to Kayleigh what had been previously been explained to Mick, the school governors, the head of the Trust, Katie, his mum, Jeremy Vine, and everybody else who had made him relive those brief moments in the last six weeks.

Neither of them had a clue anyone was filming.

Jim had simply been standing up for himself when placed under attack from Janet - something he had instinctively learned to do over the previous eight months. She attacked, he defended. This time, though, she had completely lost it with him and gone full-throttle into a tirade that she'd clearly been storing up for quite some time.

With Alan moving Jim's box of props (labelled clearly with the school's name and logo) to the staff room doorway, the shot had been framed perfectly. Janet had been made to look like she was a pedagogical spokeswoman for the school, the Trust and, indeed, the whole education system. With Jim hemmed into the corner by the photocopier, the camera didn't lie. The altercation looked exactly as it was. A work-place bullying incident that showed Janet's true feelings about the children who were placed in her care. Jim was doing his best to stand up for the little guy,

288

the common man, the million and one people watching through their screen at home. That guy in black? He's this week's YouTube hero.

"They aren't percentages, Janet. They're children. What's the point of teaching them if they hate what they're supposed to be learning?!"

The camerawork was amateurish and clunky, but the director was clever enough to zoom in for the reaction of the aggressor, who was snarling and looked like she wanted blood. Which, of course, she did.

"God, you are so naive! You've been in this job for five years now and you're still talking as if you were some sort of guidance counsellor to these little toerags...."

Toerags. Let's pause the video and add an on-screen caption to highlight what she said. 'Toerags'. On we go...

"...Getting that little shit Connoly in your show may have made you look fantastic in the paper, but will it make any actual difference in the long run? You'll still have terrible results and he'll still end up in a young offenders' institute. Doing a play with him doesn't stop him being from a family of criminals."

Cut to the image of Ethan in the newspaper, looking confident, fulfilled and bathed in theatrical limelight. Cut back to the action.

"But if we can make a difference...."

"You're not their parent, Jim. You don't have to be their friend, or make them enjoy what they are doing, or build up their character, or anything else. Your job is to squeeze every last mark you can out of them and send them on their way. Then next year you do the same with the next lot. And if you can't do that, then you may as well pack it all in and go home now."

Comedy rewind, with appropriate sound effect.

"Your job is to squeeze every last mark you can out of them and send them on their way."

Freeze. The money shot. One final caption.

IS THIS WHAT WE GO TO SCHOOL FOR? ARE WE PUPILS OR SLAVES TO THE SYSTEM?
#slaveschool

The video was uploaded a good two weeks after Janet and Jim had their argument in the staff room and, after later investigation, it transpired that initial take-up of the film was pretty slow. Posted by an anonymous whistleblower, known only as @prestonspy (whoever had caught these Oscar-winning moments on their phone wasn't stupid), the video was 'liked' by a handful of Year 10 pupils on Twitter, where it sat for twelve hours overnight... waiting quietly for the tornado to commence...

That was when Gemma shared it. Gemma was social media queen of the school and gossipmeister of the North West. At the tender age of fifteen, she had amassed over seven-hundred

Twitter followers, with her sharp wit and ability to abbreviate her thoughts into a mere 140 characters. With a simple smile, a LOL and a retweet, the viral process began. The net grew wider, moving from a handful of Year 10s to a significant proportion of the rest of the school. This is what led to Jenna Asquith sharing it, and her older brother (nineteen, Lancaster University, studying politics, closet militant) passing it on to the wider uni crowd. Soon, it was being retweeted by politics students, lecturers and professors up and down the country, with campaign groups seizing on the captured moments to make Jim their very own crusader for the kind of education they really wanted to see. By the time secondary teachers were coming home from work that day, the video was officially trending and had moved from Twitter to other social media platforms. It was everywhere.

Overnight, Janet became the devil incarnate, vilified online for her cruel behaviour towards the children in her care. Katie Hopkins tweeted to say how much she admired Janet. Esther Rantzen was asked for her opinion. Producers of radio phone-ins cleared the decks. Everyone was debating education and what it was really like behind closed doors. Things were very quickly spiraling out of control.

As the leader of the glorious institution now known worldwide as 'Slave School', Mick was given the nod early on the morning of the Drama exam. Phone calls from various media organisations were fielded by Reception, with the response of 'We're conducting a full investigation' being rolled out. Governors were contacted. Knee-jerk decisions were made over the phone. Janet would be placed on gardening leave until at least the end of academic year, with a strong recommendation that she should take early retirement. Bizarrely, when she was shown the video on Mick's phone (in what would, it turned out, become her exit interview), she hadn't seen it - despite half the world now knowing who she was. Not 'doing' technology had caught her unawares, and now she was at the centre of a furore that she would never fully comprehend.

No doubt about it, she had been humiliated both personally and professionally. Much of her pension would, in later years, be put towards counseling services to help her deal with the consequences of her unwanted fifteen minutes of fame. She didn't try to defend herself when journalists eventually got her number, deciding wisely that silence was probably the best option. Three weeks in Antigua, away from the media, away from the firestorm, and as far away as possible from Jim Tovey would be how she would start her journey of recovery.

"What's she doing now?"

Kayleigh wanted some gossip to tell everyone at college. After all, she now knew someone semi-famous, and seeing Mr Tovey today was one of the reasons she was so keen to take the volunteering job at the Academy.

"I haven't got a clue, Kayleigh. She got what she wanted, though. We're not running GCSE Drama next year, even if the results are brilliant. I guess it was her parting shot."

They wouldn't be running the course. That had now been confirmed. Even if a miracle did happen, and all the appeals they had lodged with the board in advance did come through, it was a non-starter. Mick was under pressure from the trust to drop Drama completely, what with it 'adding no significant value' to the overall results of the school. After all the positive feedback

292

he'd received over the year about how Drama had done, however, Mick found it hard to jettison it entirely. Couple that with the firestorm that Janet created in the media and Jim's job would, for this year at least, be safe.

Jim would be shifted back into the English department, where he would get one lesson a week with each of the Key Stage 3 classes. There, he would be given free reign to enter them for qualifications such as the *Trinity* exams or *Arts Award* and, if he needed to, he could use them for some small-scale performances. Dramarama would continue, and there was even a little bit of money put aside for a trip to London next year. (On the proviso that a senior member of staff assisted with the organisation)

To all intents and purposes, Jim would still be running his own department, just without his previous lofty title. Thanks to Elaine and the Union, he wouldn't take a hit on his salary - after threats to make Jim a martyr in the papers all over again if the Trust dared to try and knock him down the pay scale. The Trust had the power to do so if they wanted, but when looking down the barrel of a fully-loaded gun, risks don't tend to be taken.

"And is Sadie Masterson really pregnant?"

"You really have turned into a right old gossip, Kayleigh Clarke! What happened to the shy girl who wouldn't say boo to a goose?"

"Don't know. Maybe I got some confidence from somewhere..."

She gave him the look that told him that, despite his earlier fears, Kayleigh hadn't 'failed' at Drama. And he certainly hadn't

293

failed at teaching her. This was a girl who was ready for the world, who had carved herself the role at college of 'lovable gossip'. Going to college had been a real boost, but she'd have never felt solid enough to take it on without knowing that some of her friends from the Drama group were going as well. The Dramarama alumni, it seems, were still going strong.

Jim confirmed to Kayleigh what was already public knowledge round the rest of school. Sadie was, indeed, pregnant. But, luckily for her, one of her teachers had been the big school story of the week and had sheltered her from the ridicule, pointing and laughing during the remainder of her exams. Gareth arranged for her to take the rest of her papers in a separate space, with special dispensation to leave the room if she needed to. Robert, meanwhile, was very mature about the whole thing. Plans were made about how two relatively small people were going to be able bring an even smaller person into the world. Both kids had fairly supportive families and would muddle through the next twelve months, juggling childcare, money, college and a host of other issues that nobody had yet dreamt of. It wasn't perfect for any of them but, for now at least, they appeared to be supporting one another and not running away from their new-found responsibilities.

Now that she had grilled him for information, Kayleigh went back to do the job that she had been assigned for the day, namely helping with the high jump competition on the far side of the school field. As he looked over to where she had been posted, he spotted that the Year 10 girls were now attempting to get over that damned bar. It was the same group of girls that Jim had briefly observed in Alan's lesson. He had to say, there were some definite signs of improvement. Granted, nobody from this bunch was going to become the next Jessica Ennis-Hill but they were definitely getting better. The bar seemed to clang only sporadically now. Alan must be doing a good job.

It was true that Alan had done pretty well for his first year, although right now he was concentrating on enjoying the first proper British sunshine he'd experienced in well over twelve months on this dreary island. And he was opposite the woman who, as of the drive in this morning, he was officially considering as 'the one'. He hadn't told her yet, nor had he any intention of doing so for a while (he was both male AND Australian, after all) but it was clear that he and Steph would, in time, develop into something much more than an item. There was no rush. They had all the time in the world. From the other side of the crash mat, Steph gave her Aussie boyfriend the smile that confirmed exactly what he was thinking. Dreary weather or not, he was definitely here to stay.

In just a few short weeks, the happy-go-lucky feel of the school would be interrupted again by the stress, worry and head-scratching of results day. But, for now, all was tranquil. Jim lay back on his elbows and tried to take it all in. As usual, when teenagers are around, the peace was disturbed by the beep of a mobile phone as a pupil in his vicinity received a notification. Without even turning round to look, he gave the standard response.

"Phones away, please. It may be Sports Day and the last day of term, but the rules haven't changed."

Behind Jim, a screen was surreptitiously checked and @prestonspy saw that yet another four people had 'liked' the Tovey film. They also had another ten followers. They'd check the Facebook shares later, but it was sure to have gone up again.

For thirty seconds of filming, it was pretty clear that it had been worth the risk of getting the phone out during school time.

Adeela smiled to herself, did as she was told by her form tutor, and popped her phone into her bag.